Ferdinand's Gold

Based on Actual Events

A Novel By
Sheldon Charles

Ferdinand's Gold by Sheldon Charles, Published by Valkyrie Spirit Publishing, PO Box 4357, Battle Creek, MI 49016-4357. http://www.valkyriespirit.com

© 2020 Sheldon Charles, 1st Edition, 2nd Printing
Cover Art/Design © 2020 Sheldon Charles

ISBN (Paperback) 978-1-7339588-5-1
ISBN (ePub) 978-1-7339588-6-8

Available in ePub, Audiobook, Paperback & Hardback
Printed in the United States of America

Dedication

This book is dedicated to the soldiers of Company C, 1st Battalion, 8th Cavalry Regiment, 1st Air Cavalry Division, who served in Viet Nam March 1968 to February 1969.

They have my sincerest appreciation for ensuring my Dad made it back.

Table of Contents

Dedication 2

Acknowledgments..5

Prologue 6

Chapter 1...24

Chapter 2 49

Chapter 3 71

Chapter 4 93

Chapter 5 118

Chapter 6 141

Chapter 7 157

Chapter 8 183

Chapter 9 208

Chapter 10 231

Chapter 11 245

Epilogue...259

Glossary...263

From the Author 265

Acknowledgments

I may be the storyteller, but there are a lot of people I rely on to help me bring what is in my mind, to the page, and then eventually to you. Aside from things like editing and publishing, hundreds of elements need to flow in perfect concert and harmony from the moment they are identified as needed until the release of the book. At times it seems like chaos and other times chaos is too light a term. These folks lent their talent in one way, shape, or form to contribute to what you are reading today. I am grateful to them.

Thanks to Mike Novak for providing information I lacked about the front end of the C-141.

A Continuity Editor is essential to a thriller and Rebecca Schell made sure things were smoother, more in line and asked questions that identified where clarification might be needed.

My Editor Marni MacRae. Her input and support turned my story into the polished book you are now reading. A great partnership.

Akira, the brilliant artist who turns my concept into the picture you eventually see on the cover.

Many thanks to my puppy MacBeth for being there when I needed to find my own *Satori*.

Finally, thank you, Constance, for your love, support, words of encouragement, advice, and putting up with me during this journey.

Prologue

LZ Stallion – A Shau Valley, Vietnam

Kevan knew the percussive pounding that was torturing him was too rhythmic to be from an external source. It was the throbbing of a hangover so extreme, First Lieutenant Randall Dexter Kevan dared not open his eyes lest they explode and burst into flames. Last night, he'd been celebrating the departure of the man he was replacing, which, naturally, included a massive amount of *Ba mui ba* beer. He had been in country long enough to know the rumor about the beer containing formaldehyde was false, but at the moment, that bit of logic escaped him as he felt his brain had been extracted and placed inside a steel drum which was being beaten upon by sledgehammers.

He maneuvered his right foot to the edge of the cot then lowered it until it was firmly resting on the ground. *Please, just let the Earth stop spinning.* Before he began this maneuver, he knew putting his foot on the floor was at best a weak placebo, but he was willing to try anything that might help. He kept his eyes slammed shut while mentally reviewing yesterday's events.

There was his change of command ceremony. This was the Army's formal acknowledgment of a process which had started three months earlier. When Kevan had arrived in country, he was assigned to Kilo Company, 1st Battalion, 8th Cavalry as the Deputy Company Commander. After his first month in country, he'd been told he was part of a program that would eventually make him a Company Commander, even though he was just a lieutenant.

Due to a shortage of captains, the Army had decided if a first lieutenant was paired with an experienced captain for a few months, the younger officer would gain enough experience and knowledge to take over as a Company Commander. If the right first lieutenants were selected, at some point during their tour of duty, they would be promoted to captain and could train the next rotation of lieutenants.

Kevan's mouth was incredibly dry, so he reached out to the footlocker beside his bed which served as a nightstand. Eventually, he located what felt like a beer bottle and shook it side to side. Upon hearing the liquid slosh in the bottle, he brought it to his lips without raising his head and tilted it. His tongue immediately felt solid objects flowing into his mouth with the warm beer. He or someone else had used the bottle as an ashtray, so in addition to the beer, he was treated to a mixture of muddy ash and cigarette butts. As soon as he realized it, he immediately sat up, attempting to spit the foul mixture from his mouth back into the bottle.

The sudden physical movement drastically increased the spinning of the room, causing the contents of his stomach to desperately seek an exit from his body. He found himself puking into a helmet he managed to grab from under his cot. When his body stopped convulsing, he realized his stomach felt somewhat better, but his head still throbbed. "Welcome to my first full day of command," he said in a hoarse voice. He then slowly looked around the room to confirm he was alone in the hooch. One of the few benefits of being a company commander in a combat zone.

He leaned to one side and picked up another bottle from the top of his footlocker. After holding it up to the light to ensure the bottle contained nothing but beer, he put it to his lips and drained it. His stomach immediately objected, but somehow managed to keep it down at the urging of his dehydrated body. Kevan allowed himself a minute or so to become steady, then he stood up and grabbed a towel before stumbling toward the door of his hooch.

Next to the door was the tear-off day calendar he'd been given as a farewell gift by the man he'd replaced. Each page displayed the current date and the hand-printed number of days Kevan had remaining on his tour. He pulled off the top sheet, revealing the new page. 27 July 1969 - 272 days. *I wonder if the calendar includes R&R time?* On his way to the shower, he decided it must include those fourteen days or else the 272-day figure would be too high.

The water pouring down on him from the shower was almost unbearably hot. *Just like every damn thing else in this country.* As he washed off the sweat, dirt, beer, and puke from the last twenty-four hours, he began to feel more human. Now that stability was not his prime concern, he wondered if perhaps he should add a separate countdown on the calendar tracking the days until his planed R&R in Hawaii with Renée. By the time he shut the water off, his headache was down to a dull roar, and his stomach was now urging him to find something to eat. Even though today was his first full day of command, tomorrow would be his first day of command in the field, probably under fire. Given the way this day had started, he wasn't ready to contemplate what was going to happen tomorrow.

Flightline – Andersen Air Force Base, Guam

Airman First Class Socha from Fleet Service slowed his pickup and turned so he was parked at the aft end of the B-52D. Picking up the clipboard from the seat beside him, he verified the paperwork matched the aircraft tail #0630. Throwing the clipboard onto the dashboard and up against the windshield, he peered through the glass, trying to determine what part of the launch procedure the ground crew was currently performing.

"Shit," he said through clenched teeth as he saw the flight engineer and crew chief, both with checklists in hand, performing their initial examination of engine covers. Based on where they were in the process, he knew it would be at least twenty minutes more. Socha lowered the driver's side window and was immediately greeted by the loud sound of the auxiliary power unit currently providing electrical power to the aircraft. In the battle of cooler air versus noise, the desire for cooler air won. Slouching into the seat, he closed his eyes, trying to block out the APUs noise.

The sun was rising on July 27, 1969. He knew his departure date from Guam and separation from the service would occur on 1 September. Socha had begun counting the exact number of days left the week after he'd arrived. *Thirty-five and a wake-up.* As the sun started to break across the horizon, the temperature rose. Guam's weather could always be counted upon to be warm and extremely humid. Today would be no different, the temperature was already 75° with ninety percent humidity.

As Socha sat in the truck, he began to feel his sweat soaking into his T-shirt. A new squadron commander, Major Hassolt, had let them immediately know that one of his pet peeves was *his* Airmen running around with rolled-up sleeves or no uniform shirt on at all. Therefore, his first unit-wide order had been that all personnel were to wear the sleeves of their uniform down with the shirt completely buttoned up. This only served to increase the level of hatred from his troops. It was easy to hate a superior officer who never left his air-conditioned office during daylight hours. The major even had his meals delivered by Fleet Service, despite regulations against such personal deliveries.

"It's okay, thirty-five and a wake-up," he said aloud as he drummed his fingers on the steering wheel.

His countdown had become a mantra to help Socha get through the days since the arrival of the new commander, who, within a day, was referred to as Major Asshole.

Could be far worse. I could be on day shift, or it would be far hotter if I were in the 'Nam.

Like many, Socha's decision to be part of the Air Force had been driven not by any interest in the aeronautic science but the result of receiving a letter from his local draft board. Even though he had not opened the letter, he'd known it was an order for him to report for a physical, after which, Socha would be assigned to either the Marines or the Army. He'd also assumed either of those branches meant he'd had a hundred percent chance of going to Vietnam. He would learn after enlisting, only about fifty percent of draftees ever received orders to the combat zone.

The only thing that could've saved Socha at that point was an open secret among his peers—if he did not open the induction notice but instead took it to his local Air Force recruiter, his destiny could be changed. Any jailhouse lawyer would state opening the envelope meant the receiver was bound by the induction notice inside. However, if he did not open it and instead took it to an Air Force recruiter, or to a lesser degree, the Navy or Coast Guard recruiters, the recruiter might be able to get him enlisted in one of those services quick enough to avoid a future in the Army or Marines. Unlike many urban legends, Socha found this one to be absolutely true—as verified when his Air Force recruiter showed him a bottom desk drawer full of unopened induction notices.

Every day when Socha awoke on Guam as part of the Air Force, the young Airman was thankful he'd made the decision to be proactive about his induction. At least until Major Asshole had arrived, now it was a question of the days counting down quickly enough to avoid becoming too visible.

Socha's eyes flew open as he was alerted by a nearby motion. A Security Forces vehicle approached his truck then slowly drove by with the two sky cops inside looking toward him. He gave them a weak wave as they cruised past, *at least they didn't see me with my eyes closed, or they'd report me as sleeping.*

Reaching into the glove box of the truck, he withdrew a small AM transistor radio and turned it on. Using the dial, he gradually raised the volume until he could hear it above the APU. One of the transmitter antennas for the Armed Forces Network (AFN) was close enough to the flightline for his radio to pick up a clear signal, and he was greeted by the sound of *Crimson and Clover* by Tommy James and the Shondells.

Distracted by the music, he physically jumped when one of the fueling technicians slammed his fist on the hood of the truck.

"Fleet. They're ready for you."

It took a few seconds for the meaning of what the fueler said to sink in, but when it did, he nodded. Turning off the radio, he exited the truck and reached into the cargo bed to retrieve a cardboard box filled with in-flight lunches before heading toward the aircraft.

In the days when B-52s were flying exclusively nuclear missions, Fleet Service was not allowed to walk over the red line to enter the security zone surrounding the aircraft. Now, four years into Operation Arc Light with B-52s only carrying loads of conventional munitions, the rules were relaxed. After arriving at the bottom of the crew ladder, Socha paused. Unlike cargo aircraft, he was still not allowed to enter a B-52, so he would wait outside near the door. He was waiting on one of two things to happen—someone from inside the aircraft would notice him and come down to retrieve the meals, or an approved individual who was outside the aircraft would take the meals from Fleet Service and carry them inside. Today, the latter occurred.

"Don't forget, you've got two sets of meals. One for right after takeoff, and the other for the flight back. Eat the chicken first, the peanut butter and jelly on the return flight. Don't want you guys getting food poisoning."

The crew chief was wearing his headset, and Socha knew he couldn't hear a word he was saying, but he nodded anyway, then, holding the box under his arm, climbed the ladder into the aircraft.

With the first aircraft done, A1C Socha turned his truck toward the other two aircraft waiting for meals. He had been working Arc Light long enough to know this would be a typical three-ship cell of aircraft and, based on its parking position, #0630 would be the lead aircraft.

Operation Arc Light had started in 1965. Initially, it had been an experiment to determine if B-52 crews and ground personnel could be retrained from a mission of carrying strategic nuclear weapons to dropping conventional bombs in a close air support (CAS) role. Until Arc Light, no heavy bombers had been used in the Vietnam War, but the new operation gave commanders on the ground a powerful new capability.

Currently, all of the B-52s were stationed at Andersen Air Force Base, Guam, and from there would fly missions over Vietnam, Laos, and Cambodia. Because the B-52 could drop bombs from stratospheric altitudes, they were at a lower risk of being targeted by ground antiaircraft fire. Occasionally, an enemy fighter would try to engage a B-52 but quickly found each of the aircraft was equipped with a tail gunner. The bombers could also reach out and bring in air to air fighters if the situation called for it.

Pentagon brass benefited because none of the manpower used in this operation was considered to be boots on the ground in Vietnam. All of the personnel involved were officially stationed in the United States and sent to Andersen Air Force Base on temporary tours of duty lasting 179 days. Therefore, none of the troops engaged in the operation counted against warzone manpower limitations. Even when Arc Light was expanded to include bases in Thailand and Okinawa, the manpower utilized never counted against Vietnam forces.

Not all Arc Light Airmen were lucky enough to be at these rear bases outside of the combat zone. Combat controllers with the 1st Combat Evaluation Group (1CEVG) had a mission which required them to be on the ground in Vietnam as they were directing the operations of the B-52s. Nineteen of these controllers were lost during Operation Arc Light.

As Socha exited the flightline through the checkpoint, he glanced in his rearview mirror at the three B-52s sitting on the flightline behind him. Even though he was ready to be done with this assignment and get back to life as he wanted it to be, Socha took a moment to send good and hopeful vibes to the crews who were about to take off. *May they all return home safe.*

He turned left onto the perimeter road, circling the base, which would eventually return him to the in-flight kitchen.

Technical Sergeant McGovern's butt hurt. In fact, his butt had been hurting for the past hour and half. The only reason he did not reposition himself was his desire to allow his partner, who was sitting directly behind him with his back pressed against his own, to get some rest. The four-man 1CEVG team he was leading had been dropped into the jungle at a clearing about twenty km from where he now sat. While he and his partner rested, the other two members of the team were on close patrol, keeping an eye out for danger. It was almost time for them to swap position and purpose.

McGovern slowly raised his eyes skyward without moving his head. Even though they were under the triple jungle canopy, occasionally the light of a star would peer through the leaves. *Maybe tomorrow if the clouds clear.* A few weeks ago, his wife had written that some nights she would go outside and find a star in the sky, hoping he might be looking at the same one. When he first read her words, they made him smile, even though they were sappy. Her next letter had arrived two days before he'd departed for the field, and it announced her intent to file for divorce. *I guess she was looking at the stars from underneath someone else.* McGovern had suddenly been left dangling on his own, her love ripped from him, leaving raw and bleeding edges inside.

He closed his eyes and leaned his head forward. This time of night, the jungle settled down, and the constant noise which usually filled the air became quieter but never entirely silent. The occasional tapping sound of the sergeant's tears hitting the leaves between his legs as they fell from his face would go unnoticed.

Kevan spent the remainder of his day checking in with his troops and ensuring their gear was properly prepared to move out when required. He noticed the attitude of the men toward him was more formal than the day before. He knew it was a result of his assumption of command. The change in his position required the troops to rethink how they were going to interact with him.

As he moved from man to man, he considered how he was now the one fully responsible for the mission when assigned. Kevan also knew as he spoke to each man, it was likely at least one of them would come back injured, or worse—not at all. Whatever happened, good or bad, it was on him.

Almost every evening at 2000, the Battalion Commander and the Ops Division Chief would hold a meeting at the Command tent. During these meetings, assignments were made for missions occurring the following day, along with any available intelligence.

"Kevan, you and your men will be heading to a drop point here." As the Major spoke, he used a stick to point to a spot near the Laotian border on the wall map. "You'll meet up with some folks already there and remain in place until Arc Light BUFFs complete their runs along the border here." As he moved his stick from one point to another, he turned to look at Kevan and waited for acknowledgment.

"Rog. We're teaming up with Sneaky Pete's?"

"Nope, FACs. Forward air controllers for the flyboys. The bombers will be targeting an NVA force of about 500 traveling down the trail bringing logistical support to their boys in the south."

"You've got me going up against a force of 500?"

"10-4," the major nodded, looking directly at Kevan, "Don't worry about it, the BUFFS will take care of everything on the ground before you even get there. You're not there to engage but to observe.

MACV wants to know how well the bombers are doing on these close air support missions."

As Kevan stood there listening, he could feel the sweat rolling down his body. The size of the NVA force was almost ten times greater than his current company strength.

"In fact," the Battalion Commander said as he rose from his seat in the back of the room, "We have a shortage of slicks tomorrow morning, so you'll only be taking twenty-five or so of your troops. Hell, you could put a senior NCO in charge and skip the mission yourself." While speaking, he moved to a position in front of Kevan, making direct eye contact. This Colonel was known for using options like this to test his junior officers. The right answer could ensure his support for the rest of his tour, the wrong one could find him being given the shittiest missions available.

"No, sir. My mission, my men. I lead."

The Battalion CO nodded. Kevan had heard the boss liked to see junior officers step up without hesitation. The CO reached into the side pocket of his jungle pants and pulled out a metal cylinder. Everyone in the tent knew it contained a single Cuban cigar. It was something the old man had started when he'd arrived and was now a tradition. He would present one of these from time to time to a Company Commander who was heading into the field. It was meant to be a good luck charm to be smoked after the mission was complete and all the troops returned to base safely.

Kevan took the cigar, and while thanking the Colonel, he slipped it into his breast pocket.

"Just a simple walk in the woods, have a quick look around, and you'll be home by dinnertime," the Major said, trying to take back control of his meeting, "Next up, some S&D fun for Charlie Company."

Before returning to his hooch, Kevan went to the tent housing his senior NCOs and informed them he would need twenty-five soldiers for a mission in the morning. They would need to be ready to move out at 0300. He was letting the senior NCOs do their jobs instead of him going to the men directly. Before he went to bed that night, he wrote a

15

letter to Renée and enclosed the tear off page for 28 July from his calendar to let her know he was counting the days. Many troops considered it bad luck to mark off a day in country before it was completed.

At 0300, Kevan watched as his men boarded the four helicopters taking them to the rendezvous point. He was the last one to board, and as soon as his foot was off the ground, the slicks lifted off and headed into the darkness. His stomach felt queasy as the Huey banked and turned. Once it achieved level flight, he closed his eyes and tried to relax.

Flightline, Andersen AFB, Guam

The crew chief climbed down the ladder of tail #0630. When he reached the bottom, he removed the portable ladder from the open portal on the aircraft and watched as the navigator inside the plane first gave him a thumbs up then closed the hatch. The sun was now up and scorching the flightline, quickly rising to what would be the high temperature of the day. In his mind, the crew chief was already looking forward to his first cold beer and two days off since his aircraft would be downrange.

If viewed from a vantage point above the flightline, the preparation for the three-ship cell's departure might look like a bastardized form of ballet. Specialty vehicles moved around the aircraft as they relocated various pieces of equipment which were used to prepare the aircraft for flight. Security forces were rolling up the ropes which had marked the secure area around the plane. When all of this was done, the finale consisted of a sole crew chief standing at the nose of the aircraft.

As the crew chief stood there, his headset was still connected to the B-52 via a long cable. He listened as the pilot called off various items on the checklist, and the crew chief verified those items which could only be observed from outside the aircraft. Once the list was complete, he walked up to the side of the airplane and unplugged the final physical connection of the aircraft to anyone on the ground. As he walked back out in front of the plane, he coiled up the cable and fastened it to a loop on his belt.

Turning toward the aircraft, the crew chief raised his arms and began to guide the bomber out of its parking spot and onto the apron which led to the runway. As the aircraft made the turn onto the apron and just before the pilot was out of sight, the crew chief stood at attention and saluted. Both the pilot and co-pilot inside the aircraft returned the salute then turned their attention to their huge aircraft now in motion toward the runway.

When aircraft #0630 reached the final turn for the runway, they contacted the tower to get clearance for takeoff. Each of the following aircraft would wait for the one in front to be three-quarters of the way down the runway before they throttled their engines up for takeoff. Once all of them were in flight, the three aircraft would assemble in a loose formation for the trip to Vietnam.

A1C Socha had just completed his duty day and was exiting the flight kitchen when he saw the bombers on the runway. With nowhere to be, he walked out to one of the parked pickups and dropped the tailgate so he could have a seat to watch them take off.

The B-52 was given clearance for takeoff, and the pilot and copilot moved the thrust levers forward in unison as the aircraft started to roll down the runway. When they were three-quarters of the way down the runway, the next plane started its roll.

The B52 had just lifted off the ground and began to clear the end of the runway when the entire right wing of the aircraft separated from the fuselage and fell off.

Socha was slack jawed as the aircraft continued to fly after the wing fell. For a few moments, he thought what he saw falling was an accidental bomb release or something similar. But when gravity took hold of the aircraft and pulled it down, Socha realized the disaster taking place as he watched.

The aircraft, already on a roll behind #0630 had no option but to continue their takeoff. By the time the second aircraft was able to circle around and come back, the only thing visible in the ocean below was the Russian trawler that maintained vigil, reporting on Arc Light takeoffs. None of the aircrew members saw any survivors.

Because #0630 had cleared the cliff at Pati Point, there was no land which might have given the crew some chance of survival. The aircraft commander was thought to have pulled his ejection seat because his body was found separate from the aircraft and tangled in a parachute. Eventually, four other bodies were recovered. The plane was declared a loss and remained on the ocean bottom below the cliff. It was rumored when the weather conditions were right, and the water is still, aircrews can see its silhouette beneath the sea as they take off.

Because of the loss of the lead aircraft, the Arc Light missions for the day were scrubbed.

Triple Canopy Jungle Near Laotian Border

As they approached the drop point, each of the slicks descended far enough for the troops inside to jump out, before quickly returning to a safer altitude. Kevan and his men scrambled into the jungle to avoid being caught out in the open. He then radioed the lead chopper to let them know all was well, and they were released to return to base. Return pick up was scheduled for three days later.

The sun was now fully up, and steam was visibly rising off the dense jungle. Even though they were under enough jungle growth to block out most sunlight, the air was still uncomfortably hot and humid with heavy rains expected later in the day. As soon as location and directions were verified and the men leading point were identified, the troops began their trek toward the assigned rendezvous spot. After a few hours, they came upon a clearing, and Kevan had a perimeter set up so the men could take a break. While drinking from his canteen, Kevan heard a rhythmic clicking noise over the radio. The signal was to notify them the FACs were about to make contact. This was done to prevent friendly fire as Kevan's men might have thought they were enemy troops and started shooting.

A few minutes later, the four FACs with the 1CEVG stepped out of the jungle and into the clearing. As in any war zone, no salutes were given or returned as McGovern simply shook hands with the lieutenant.

"We're a couple hours away from our radio check-in. When we call in, they'll verify the arrival time for the Buffs, then, based on that, we'll march in to see what's what."

"I didn't realize you were going with us."

"Ten-Rog. We'll be there in case anything happens and you need close air support to mop up whatever is left. With the tonnage being dropped, it shouldn't be much."

"Sounds like. I've never seen the aftermath of a B-52 run."

"They're pretty good at putting bombs on target, don't leave a whole lot once it's all said and done."

Kevan told his senior NCO to have the men relax but remain vigilant, then ordered him to check on the men manning the perimeter to make sure they were alert.

When the coded transmission came in to the 1CEVG, it was not good. For an unknown reason, the Arc Light mission was scrubbed. This left them with no mission and dangerously close to 500 fully supplied and combat ready NVA regulars. Upon hearing the news, Kevan turned around for a moment and stared off into the jungle to consider the words he had just heard. *Shit, shit, shit—some damn walk in the woods.* Turning around again, Kevan said, "I don't suppose in addition to close air support you could get us a ride home?"

McGovern remained expressionless, "No, sir, in-country it's all up to the Army. But if you can get a cab, we'd appreciate a ride out too."

Kevan nodded and waved for his radioman.

"Contact home base, let them know our mission was scrubbed and tell them we need four slicks to get us out ASAP as we have beaucoup hostiles nearby. Recommend they pick us up here," Kevan looked around at the clearing and then added, "They should be able to get at least two on the ground at a time."

A few minutes later, the radioman returned to let Kevan know the slicks could not be there until the following morning as the area was due for heavy rain starting just after sunset. They were also ordered to return to their original drop off point. Kevan knew this meant they would be walking most of the night. In some ways, it might be safer because of the cover of darkness and the rain. After a discussion with McGovern, it was agreed the 1CEVG would lead the way back, and Kevan would provide two additional troops to assist with point duties. They would depart at sunset.

With several hours before departure, McGovern yawned then stretched out on the ground, closing his eyes. The man needed sleep. It'd been two days since he'd slept, but instead of sleeping now, he lay there with his eyes closed, mulling over the situation with his wife.

When it came time for them to depart, McGovern stood while pulling his backpack on, having gone without sleep for over fifty hours. As he began to dig in his pocket for the map Kevan had given him, the rain began. Then, in his grogginess, McGovern made the decision not to bother with the map or compass. *After all, I just need to backtrack the trail Kevan's troops established on their walk in.* Wadding the map down in his pocket, he started through the jungle. Instead of following their path, he mistakenly took one established by the VC. The trail he chose led them directly to the enemy camp. Nothing stopped them until McGovern became the first fatality as they crossed the VC's perimeter.

The firefight which followed should have been recorded as

historic. Unfortunately, because it occurred in Laos and not Vietnam, it was also an unapproved incursion outside of the approved war zone. The acts of bravery deserving of medals went unrecorded and unrecognized. In the end, fourteen of Kevan's men and two of the FACs were able to escape back into Vietnam and eventual pickup.

At the zenith of the battle, with almost half of Kevan's men dead and ammunition running low, the enemy continued to come at them unabated. It was apparent to Kevan, unless he did something unexpected, none of them were going to survive. He then made the hardest decision of his short command—he would be the diversion drawing the enemy's attention while his men escaped. As Kevan led the NVA north, his troops fled south. To prevent being followed once the diversion was discovered, Kevan had one of the FAC's call in an airstrike at the edge of the Laotian border.

The following morning, a two-line report was entered into the official record for 28 July. "Overnight, a sub-element of Company K was assaulted by NVA regulars from across the Laotian border. They were able to drive back the attack with the help of airstrikes. Company Commander MIA, presumed dead."

Junior Officer Housing – Fort Ord, California

Even though Dex Kevan was only seven years old when he saw the Army staff car pull up to his house on base, it was the moment he would always remember as the end of his childhood and the end of his family. He was playing across the street, and as soon as the chaplain and other officer exited the staff car, his friend's mother ran outside and shuffled the boys into her house. Once inside, they were promptly sat down in front of the black and white television to watch cartoons.

Dex heard his friend's mom on the phone, calling other

neighborhood moms to inform them of what was going on. Something catastrophic had happened to Dex's father, and support was needed for Renée while she kept her son occupied so his mother could process the devastating news.

Renee had heard that the chaplain and accompanying officer would typically spend about an hour with the spouse upon death notification. However, because her husband was designated missing in action (MIA) and not confirmed dead, everything was handled differently. She would be required to vacate base housing within sixty days as if he were a casualty, but because he was MIA, she was told she would not receive an immediate death gratuity to financially assist with the transition. Also, she would not receive the life insurance proceeds for the same reason. However, because he was MIA, his military pay would continue, at least that was how it should have worked.

Because the after-action report on how Lieutenant Kevan became MIA did not definitively state he was involved in combat against the enemy, a low-ranking bureaucrat jumped into action. A second lieutenant from Albany, Georgia apparently saw this as a chance to flex his newly found administrator muscles, and he put a hold on all payments until a full investigation was completed into the manner of Kevan's disappearance. Though Renee argued there must be some mistake, that she had no funds and her husband served his country, the second lieutenant stood firm in the decision she would not receive any governmental funds until the issue was resolved.

By the time the investigation was started, eight months later, most of the troops who survived the mission had moved on to other assignments or back into civilian life. When information from them was finally gathered, compiled, and completely adjudicated, three full years had passed. The report unquestionably showed Kevan did not desert but acted heroically at self-sacrifice to save the remaining men in his company by creating a diversion. Unfortunately, this conclusion was drawn at the same time Congress began investigating unauthorized incursions into Laos which caused Kevan's file to be quickly buried rather than processed.

While the Army took its time to determine how to handle Lieutenant Kevan's status, his wife and son were devastated by its aftermath. Initially, after relocating off base, they lived in a small efficiency apartment. Like many junior officers, a majority of the furniture in their base housing was supplied by the Army and therefore returned when they moved off base. Likewise, the forced relocation took them away from all the support systems provided to assist a family losing a soldier in the war zone. The resulting psychological damage of having to cope on their own would affect both for the rest of their lives.

Within a year, Renée had moved them in with a man she was sleeping with. He was not an ideal choice but kept a roof over their head and food on the table. The psychological toll of the arrangement began to weigh on her as she saw her position as equivalent to an indentured servant. The situation also found her needing someone tangible to blame. Rather than allowing that to be the Army, she chose to blame her missing husband, openly criticizing him in front of Dex and referring to him as a deserter and traitor. Renée began to drink. Heavily. Her next relationship lasted less than a year, and each relationship that followed continued the downward economic and status spiral that started the day the Army evicted them from the base.

Dex, in addition to losing his father and the security he knew, became witness to the slow mental and physical disintegration of his mother. The father he had known for his first few years was now having his stature destroyed by the only parent he had left. He began to withdraw and lash out against all authority since he saw authority as the cause of his problems. With no one to assist him in working through his grief and confusion, Dex developed a belief he was entitled to much more than he was getting. By the time he was twelve, he was regularly shoplifting as well as stealing money from any vulnerable source. After all, his father was taken, he was owed. This caused Dex to amass a lengthy juvenile record.

Chapter 1

Dex lay on his back in bed, staring at the acoustic tile ceiling, and smoking a cigarette. The dormitory room he was in was like all the others in the newly renovated dormitories on the base. It contained three distinct areas, with each resident having their own sleeping space and a shared common area for socializing. The bathrooms and showers were both down the hall, but the room did have a shared sink and mirror.

Like most of the Airmen assigned to Guam, Dex began counting down to his DEROS on the day he arrived. As the assignment started to sour, he started counting days until the current month would be over. Now, he found himself staring at the calendar hanging on the wall and, with some relief, saw his next weekend was only two days from today, 25 February 1986.

Senior Airman Jessica Anders had arrived a couple hours ago, wrapping her naked body around his after silently creeping into the room. He knew they were going to get caught. The only protection against unannounced intrusion was a sign on the door stating "Day-Sleeper." Until recently, day-sleepers in the dorms received no deference. It was only after a sleep-deprived airman had written his Congressman. *I give it a month, then that little sign won't matter, and surprise daytime inspections will be back.*

He stubbed his cigarette out in the ashtray on his bedside table and began to gently stroke Jessi's hair. If he turned his head slightly, there was enough light in the room to see the golden blonde strands as they moved under his fingertips. Between his self-destructive tendencies and general bad attitude, he had no idea why this beautiful woman was with him. He'd asked her once, and her only reply had been, "There is so much more to you under the surface."

With almost seven years in the Air Force, he should have been at least a staff sergeant. But along the way, he picked up an Article 15 for insubordination, which cost him a stripe and pushed his promotion trajectory downward. As things stood now, he was probably not going to be recommended for reenlistment. Dex wasn't sure how he felt about it since his entry into the Air Force had been mandatory.

In 1979, Dex had found himself standing before a judge who'd been about to sentence him to at least five years in jail for grand theft auto. To him, he hadn't stolen the car per se but borrowed it from a neighbor without asking. When he'd been pulled over, rather than trying to explain the situation, Dex had become belligerent. His attitude had led to his being placed in handcuffs and taken into the police station versus the officer simply checking out his story. Once things had gone that far, neither the police nor the county prosecutor would allow his neighbor to drop the charges. Dex had then been awaiting sentencing.

The judge flipped through the folder regarding the case while Dex sat fidgeting at the defendant's table. After a few minutes, the judge asked both lawyers to step up to the bench, where there was a brief conversation that ended with everyone nodding in agreement before returning to their original positions.

"Randall Dexter Kevan Junior, because you have no prior criminal record," the judge said as he peered over the top of his glasses toward the prosecutor who nodded, "and this entire matter seems to be a misunderstanding, I am inclined to give you a customized sentence."

Dex winced, "Customized, your Honor?"

"Yes, as a judge, I have some latitude, and I'm going to use it. I'll give you a simple choice between two options, but once you've made a choice, you're stuck with it. Agreed?"

"Yeah."

The judge took off his glasses and dropped them on the folder in front of him, then narrowed his eyes, staring at Dex for a moment before proceeding.

"You can choose to have me pass a standard sentence and incarcerate you for up to five years, or, by close of business today, you can enlist in any branch of the Armed Forces. Also, you must depart for initial training in your chosen branch by noon tomorrow. Once your training is done, you'll report to me in uniform along with proof of successful completion. At that time," as he spoke, he picked up the case folder, "I'll drop this in a shredder, leaving no record this ever happened. Your choice."

Dex was perplexed. He was trying to figure out the ups and downs of each option. In no way did jail seem like the right option.

"I like the second option better."

The judge dropped the folder while hitting it with his fist, producing a loud bang when it hit the desk in front of him, "Your Honor."

"Your Honor," Dex repeated in a soft voice.

"Fine, you do this with the understanding if you fail any part of this, to include the deadlines today, and tomorrow, I'll issue a warrant and have you brought back in here. Then I'll send you to prison for every single day of the full five years."

"Yes, your Honor."

Dex was returned to Courthouse Processing, then released into the custody of his lawyer, who took him to the military induction center in town that had representatives from all military branches. When he completed his ASVAB test, he found out he scored high enough to have his choice of any branch of the military. His choice of the Air Force was arbitrary. Dex liked their shade of blue uniform better than the Coast Guard's. Walking into the recruiter's office, he handed him his test results and explained the situation.

Even though his test scores were high enough for every Air Force specialty, there were only two jobs guaranteeing departure for basic training by noon the following day. Air Cargo or Culinary Arts Technician. Having no desire to be a cook, Dex chose the air cargo path.

After completion of basic training, and the required trip back to the judge, Dex proceeded to technical training, then his first assignment in Europe. Upon arrival, he proved himself on the job. He was a quick study of the skills required. Soon, he was licensed on all necessary equipment and familiar with all of the aircraft models transiting the base. He was feeling something he had never felt before—pride.

He felt free of the demons of his past, but it didn't last long. At the start of his second year there, Dex found himself heading into his commander's office for counseling after being disrespectful to a senior NCO. The Commander had made up his mind before Dex entered his office, and short of proving the NCO had insulted his mother, there was no way Dex was going to escape losing a stripe over the incident. He never mentioned the conflict started after he had been on shift for a straight twenty hours and the senior NCO had just arrived after a full night's sleep. Or that the senior NCO had informed Dex his duty day had just been extended another eight hours so the NCO could spend the day on the golf course. With no option to fight, Dex accepted the disciplinary action as another unfairness in life. His love for his job and ability to do it well kept him on the borderline of discharge rather than finding himself on the street. He knew determination on allowing him to reenlist was about to be made.

Now, lying on the cot in the lingering cigarette smoke, Dex felt Jessi's body shift against him as she pulled him closer and repositioned her leg over his. At the moment, Jessi was a compelling reason for staying in. Even though she never said it out loud, he knew if he did get out, their relationship was over.

Presidential Palace – Manila, Philippines

Colonel Talan Madulás had stopped watching the televised news a week ago. Even though Philippine President Ferdinand Marcos could claim loyalty from the people in the countryside, the middle class in the city and the church had turned against him. It was just a matter of time before he was deposed, especially since Marcos had been egotistical enough to declare victory in the national election two weeks ago. Instead of it being a way to continue in power, it was the last straw for a majority of the population and Aquino's charisma only served to accelerate his ouster.

Madulás knew he needed to ensure any exit plan being worked out by Marcos included him. He read too many reports of coup d'états, which ended with all allies of the deposed leader being jailed or killed without trial or question. After years of faithful service, he had no desire to end up in an unmarked grave.

Colonel Madulás had been with Marcos since the beginning of his rise to power. During World War II, Marcos had been inspecting the aftermath of a raid on a small village in the country. His attention was drawn to the brutality with which the Japanese fighters had been questioned and executed. Inquiries into who was responsible for such viciousness eventually led to Madulás. The men were contemporaries and after a brief discussion found much in common. Marcos had asked for Madulás to be reassigned to his unit, beginning a lifetime together.

Both men were from small villages in the country, and even though Marcos possessed a broad formal education in the law, he admired Madulás' multilayered way of thinking and planning operations. The only thing Marcos did not like about Madulás was a habit drawn from his country life—*betel* nut. Chewing the nut brought the user a mild sense of euphoria. But, with constant use, the *betel* nut permanently stained the user's teeth dark purple and black. Eventually, the nut would eat away at the protective enzymes on the teeth and gums, leading to tooth loss and gum disease.

Madulás, aware of Marcos' sentiment, had eventually stopped using the substance, replacing it with chain-smoking. As his boss had risen in power, he'd been able to have dental work accomplished, including capping seven of his teeth with gold crowns, but the stains on his other teeth remained. Three of the gold teeth were in the front of his mouth, one covering a canine tooth and the other two covering bottom incisors. As a result, when he pulled his lips back, it would give him the appearance of a wild animal. He was aware of this and used the threatening visual when needed. Ordinarily, he tried his best to hide his teeth by keeping his lips tight over them. His bad breath from diseased gums and smoking was whispered about among his subordinates.

As Marcos rose in power through the political structure, it was Madulás who took care of problems requiring a certain level of absolute obedience instead of moral self-examination. His level of loyalty saw him consistently rewarded throughout his life. Now, with his boss' fall from grace, his concern was hanging on to those rewards, and his life.

As he sat at his desk, he was thumbing through the small notebook he always carried with him. Each page listed various bits of financial security he'd managed to acquire throughout his career. Madulás was trying to identify an exit plan for each class of goods. The notebook listed artwork, jewelry, raw diamonds, bearer bonds, and stacks of Philippine currency.

Among the treasures was a large, fairly nondescript, unpainted, wooden crate, like those used for machine parts, but this crate was different. Unlike the rest, it was built out of *mangkono*, the hardest wood in the P.I. Inside of it was 137 bars of the most fluid of all assets—gold. The twenty-five-pound gold bars each bore the seal of the Philippine National Bank and assayed to be 99.9% pure. Calculating the total weight in his head, he knew the 137 bars would be over 3,400 pounds. He ran his finger from the tip of his nose, up to his forehead, then tapped himself several times as if to signal his brain he needed a solution. After repeating this for the third time, an idea began to foment. The president's alliance with the United States would cause them to facilitate his departure. Knowing Marcos would also want to take certain assets with him might lead the U.S. to provide him with cargo as well as passenger transport.

"Santos!" Madulás yelled while he took a cigarette from the pack on his desk and lit it.

A large uniformed man stuck his head through the door and entered after being motioned in. He came to attention in front of Madulás' desk and saluted while the Colonel tucked his notebook back in his shirt pocket.

"I need you to take care of something for me," Madulás said, launching into a series of instructions for Santos. As he took deep puffs from the cigarette, the office began to fill with smoke rapidly. The most important task given to Santos was to pick up a collection of wooden crates from the secure warehouse, then transport them to Clark Air Base. Once there, he was to request the item's preparation for air shipment. When the containers were ready, Santos was to stand by at Clark to guard the inventory.

"You got it. What if the Americans ask what is inside the boxes?"

"Tell them it is the property of President Marcos. They won't ask again. And change out of your uniform before going out there. It is getting dangerous."

As Santos left, Madulás used the cigarette in his hand to light another. He considered Santos for a moment. The man knew when to be personable and when to be tough. At twenty-six years old, he had maturity, was loyal and duty-driven, with an excellent command of English. All qualities worth having around in an uncertain future to come. Regardless of where he ended up, Madulás knew he would need at least one loyal soldier.

Within an hour, the colonel found himself called into a meeting with Marcos. Unlike meetings of the past where Marcos insisted upon a large crowd of yes-men to feed his ego, this meeting consisted of just five people. People who were known to provide him with honest assessments. Details of a conversation between Marcos and U.S. Senator Paul Laxalt were shared.

As Marcos stood, he looked at each of them before speaking, "I told the senator I needed assistance, and he talks about cutting and running. Bah! If I'm abandoned by my allies, I may have no other choice. Do any of you see another way forward?"

Glances were shot around the table from person to person, but no one spoke as Marcos took his seat. At last, Madulás broke the silence, "Perhaps it's time to remember—a departure from one place does not preclude a return to the same place later."

No one said a word, but all eyes turned to Marcos. The man was known for sudden and irrational violent outbursts. Every man at the table knew Marcos was cornered and likely to become even more unpredictable. At a time like this, out of favor advice could lead to an immediate death sentence. Marcos was silent as he leaned back into his chair and folded his hands in front of him.

"The senator's advice might not be the wanted option," Madulás continued in a calm voice, "but it allows you to survive. Because you survive, you can reclaim what is yours at a time when you're in a better position."

Madulás was not sure how his leader might take any of this, but he knew the only distasteful advice Marcos ever accepted was that which gave him a path to strength.

Before Marcos responded, Defense Minister Ponce entered the room, and they were all dismissed.

As he walked from the conference room back to his office, Madulás now knew for sure the end was coming soon. Marcos probably summoned Ponce to arrange for transportation out for his family. *It is up to me to make sure he doesn't forget the rest of us.*

Madulás waited a long ten minutes before returning to Marcos' office. The door was standing open, and Marcos was alone, seated behind his desk, reading papers. As soon as he walked in, Marcos told him to close the door and have a seat. As Madulás waited on the expected revelation, the president's departure was imminent. He stared at Marcos. The man looked tired and drawn. He knew there were health issues further exacerbated by exhaustion. Rather than immediately speaking to him, Marcos leaned back in his chair and closing his eyes, gently rubbed them with his fingers.

"You talked about a future return even if I'm forced to leave now."

Rather than answering, Madulás remained quiet. He knew

Marcos wanted to say more. He needed to know what the man was thinking, and the lingering silence would urge the man to speak. Without opening his eyes, Marcos said in a flat voice, "The time has come. I will have Ponce arrange for the Americans to supply me with two helicopters to transport my family and me to Clark Air Base. From there. the Americans will supply airlift to Hawaii. Imelda is packing now."

Madulás waited for Marcos to continue, giving him a chance to explain his plan for the rest of the staff. But the man sat in silence—*time to drag the reticent dog by his leash.*

"You know, if you plan ever to return, you'll need more than whatever you're putting into a few valises."

Marcos opened his eyes and looked directly at Madulás. He was not sure what the look meant, even though he'd worked for the man for decades. Rather than letting stillness fill the room, he continued.

"You have some assets on hand here at Malacanang Palace, and elsewhere. You should ask the Americans to supply you with one or two cargo aircraft in addition to passenger aircraft. Tell them you will need your records and some personal belongings to transition into exile. In truth, they'll be transporting the means of your return out of harm's way," again, Marcos just stared at Madulás silently. Madulás' decision to continue speaking was more about nothing left to lose rather than anything to gain.

"If you can get two cargo aircraft, they could easily accommodate not only your assets for the future but also some additional people. The personnel you will need to assist with your eventual return, like General Ver and other allies who have been loyal you." *Like me.*

His words were again met with Marcos' silence. Marcos eventually broke his stare and lay his head back against his chair before slowly closing his eyes and gently rocking.

Madulás' mind was tumbling backward and forward. He was looking for something to grab onto which might cause a positive reaction. He was coming up empty. He knew if he spoke again, it might only be seen as more babble. So, instead, he sat silently. Two minutes passed then another with the only sound in the room being a gentle squeak as Marcos' chair rocked.

"Agreed. Call Ponce to work out the airlift details. Your skills and loyalty will be needed for my future plans, so you'll need to pack as well. Bring your best man to assist you in planning my return. I'll call the Americans about my departure and needing airlift to Hawaii. They will have to be quick about it. Truck transport of the cargo from the Malacanang to Clark Air Base will take almost two hours."

Madulás was almost giddy as he rose to exit Marcos' office.

"Wait," Marcos stood up from his chair. He pointed at Madulás, "If I am going to return later to resume my position, then before I leave, I must be sworn in as the true and legitimate president. This way, when I return, it is liberation, not some sort of outside invasion."

Madulás watched as Marcos turned from where he was standing to look out the window behind him.

"Yes, I must do it before I call the American ambassador about my departure."

The man has lost it, Madulás thought as he nodded in agreement with Marcos' latest desperate attempt to hold on to some semblance of power. He then turned and returned to his office. When he sat down at his desk, he first lit a cigarette, then withdrew a familiar talisman from his pocket—a gold Spanish doubloon dated 1720. The coin was one of ten he'd taken from the first man he'd killed in service to Marcos. The man had owed money to Marcos for protection, and his keeping ten percent established what Madulás considered to be his share of anything of value recovered from then forward.

As he sat at his desk, he finger-rolled the coin back-and-forth in his hand while puffing on the cigarette he held between his teeth, considering what needed doing next. Looking down at his desk calendar, he noted it was 24 February. By the twenty-fifth, all of this would be over.

Truck Gate - Clark Air Base, Philippines

It was sunset when Santos passed his identification card to the truck's driver, who, in turn, handed it to the gate guard at the entry point to the American base. The current unrest had led to the gate being closed to most Filipinos. The only exception was those in a select group of Filipino leadership. As a prime member of Madulás' team, Santos carried a variety of identity cards to handle situations like this one. After calling for confirmation, the guard agreed to let Santos and the truck through, but not the driver. Santos instructed the driver to get out but to remain near the gatehouse. As he spoke to the driver, he worked his hand behind him and removed the Colt 1911 pistol from his waistband, sliding it across the seat to the driver who took the gun with him when he got out of the truck. Even with his position, Santos didn't want to get caught having an unauthorized weapon on the base. He then moved behind the wheel to drive the truck onto the base.

Most Filipino men were smaller in stature and thin. Being almost six feet tall and a muscled, toned 270 pounds, Santos was an anomaly. As family legend had it, at some point, a Samoan became part of the bloodline, which led the men in the family to be larger than average. His size and strength had made him stand out in his army unit. It was there Madulás first spotted him and selected him for a special assignment.

Madulás was a student of military history and knew Genghis Khan had seized more territory through perceived threat than in actual battle. Khan's army was in a constant state of readiness. If fear did not bring them victory, they were prepared to wage war. Madulás realized this the first time he saw Santos. The man possessed a similar quality. He could send Santos into a situation, and he would usually win just by the threat of his size. If fear was not sufficient, then Santos was more than capable of winning the altercation through violence.

After testing his perception in the field, Madulás had

permanently reassigned Santos to his team. Even though he was no longer in a formal military unit, he kept the bearing and discipline of a soldier. Santos obeyed orders completely, and if the situation became confused, he was intelligent enough to figure out a way through it while maintaining loyalty to his commander. As a result, he'd become Madulás' prime functionary being called upon to handle all manner of tasks with total success.

Santos had grown up in Angeles City, which resulted in his intimate familiarity with Clark, having worked a variety of odd jobs on the base as he grew up. Once in the Army, and later in service to Madulás, Santos was on the base often as the Air Force provided the Philippines with logistical support. In a few minutes, he pulled up to the flightline gate, which connected to the cargo preparation area. After being admitted, he pulled the truck into an open space in the cargo yard and got out.

"Santos! How you doing, buddy? Looks like things outside the gate are getting kind of hairy."

Santos smiled as he approached the Air Force sergeant. He was never sure why a smile so easily disarmed Americans, but it was a handy tool for times like these.

"*Que pasa*, Trey," he first shook the sergeant's hand then gave him a quick, firm hug, "I need a favor," he nodded toward the truck.

"You got it. I can hook you up. No problem," then Trey lowered the volume of his voice and said, "I know you'll hook me up later."

Santos continued to smile, considering the quid pro quo request, "You know it. For now, though, I need this stuff palletized for possible airlift later tonight."

The sergeant nodded. When he arrived on shift, he'd been briefed on the likelihood of needing to prepare cargo for special airlift if Marcos decided to leave the island. Without asking questions, he assumed this was the start of it, "I'll handle it for you personally."

"*Salamat*. I'll make sure *she* handles you just as personally—all night long," both men chuckled at the innuendo. "Given the importance, I've got to hang out with this stuff until it gets packed. That okay?"

"No problem," as he spoke, the sergeant pointed toward a door in the side of a nearby building, "you should be able to keep an eye on it even while you're sitting in the nice air-conditioned breakroom right over there."

"You got it," from where he stood, he could see into the windows of the breakroom and knew they would provide excellent visibility.

Trey started to walk away, then called over his shoulder for Santos to remain with the truck until they got the boxes offloaded. He wanted Santos to move the truck out of the preparation area as quickly as possible. Santos walked back to the truck and leaned against it with his arms crossed over his chest. Several minutes later, two young Airmen showed up and started to spread out pieces of dunnage near the truck. Santos pulled on a pair of gloves and offered to assist. Each 463L pallet would require three pieces of dunnage underneath, one on each side and another in the middle. After positioning the dunnage, a forklift placed a pallet on top of the lumber. The Airmen estimated the load would require four pallets.

A 463L pallet was a flat piece of aluminum used to facilitate the movement of cargo through the Air Force transportation system. It was 108 inches by 88 inches by 2 1/4 inches and weighed approximately 300 pounds when empty. On all four edges were tabs to allow the device to fit into rail systems onboard aircraft which held it in place. Between the tabs were loops used to attach tie-down straps and chains used to secure cargo onto the top of the pallet. One of these platforms could handle up to 10,000 pounds with a maximum height of 96 inches. Two or more of these could also be attached to form a train for moving longer pieces of cargo.

Once the four empties were in position, Santos moved off to one side and let the Airmen get to work building up the cargo. It reminded him of putting a puzzle together, as they positioned each box on top of the platform. The goal was to maximize space usage and, at the same time, keep the weight of the load spread evenly. They were using a forklift capable of lifting 4000 pounds to position and move the more massive cargo around on the pallets. But they encountered one box the forklift was having problems lifting. One of the Airmen looked over at Santos as if to ask for an explanation.

"Stainless steel machine parts. Heavy stuff maybe 5K or so," Santos explained.

The Airman nodded then swapped the smaller forklift for a larger model capable of lifting 10,000 pounds. In an attempt to maintain balance, the heavy crate was placed in the center of the pallet with other lighter boxes surrounding it. When the load was complete, the wooden crate was hidden in the center.

Soon, all four were complete, and the truck was empty. They covered each pallet with plastic sheeting, then began using cargo nets and straps to secure the load. Santos was surprised at how fast the two men worked but was grateful—he was ready to get out of the sun. While he was moving the truck out of the way, each of the pallets was weighed. A placard was created for each with dimension and weight data. Santos was examining each load when something curious struck him about the placards.

"Hey, what is this destination ZZZ?"

"Nobody told us where it's going. Do you know where the stuff is going?"

"Uh, no. Not for sure, anyway."

"So, without knowing more," the Airman shrugged with his open palms in the air, giving Santos a Gallic shrug before saying, "ZZZ. It'll keep the four of them together."

Their job complete, the two Airmen departed, leaving Santos standing alone in the cargo yard. After he finished looking over the four pallets, Santos headed for the breakroom. Before sitting down, he found a phone and called Madulás.

"Everything's palletized and ready to go. It took four pallets. No problems. I've got an eye on them."

"Good, it looks like we will be departing within twenty-four hours. Are the pallets in the secure yard?"

"Yes, and packed tight."

Madulás knew the base was secure, but he'd stolen things out of the cargo yard himself, and this was his entire financial security package. He didn't want to cause greater interest by having Santos hang around, but he needed a way to secure those pallets.

"Take a look around and tell me what kind of aircraft are on the tarmac."

"Hang on a sec," setting the phone down on the counter, Santos walked outside and took inventory of what was visible on the flightline. Because of his childhood near the base, he was familiar with all the airframes parked there. Returning to the phone, he recited the details of what he saw, "looks like a pair of C-5's, two or three C-9's, half a dozen C-130s, and two C-141s."

"Fine, I'll make a few phone calls and see if I can get those pallets loaded right now. As soon as they're onboard the aircraft, you can take off, but I need you to check in every few hours because I'm not sure when things may start to happen."

"You got it, Boss."

Madulás decided Santos was leaving the P.I. with him but had yet to tell the man.

"I'll need you to come along to handle details as needed. You might want to go by your place and pack a bag."

"Naw, I'm good. Anything I need, I can pick up on the other end. Just going to grab a *serbesa* at *Red Lips*."

"You realize it may be a while before we get back."

"I've got nothing holding me here."

"Good. Keep an eye on things there. I'll do what I can to get those pallets loaded quickly.

Once Santos hung up the telephone, he walked back to a chair sitting near the window so he could keep watch over the pallets.

Madulás knew the Americans would probably facilitate any request for cargo transport using the C-141s currently sitting on the flightline. The C-141 was the workhorse of logistics in the Pacific theater, with more missions being flown by them than any other aircraft. It also had a stellar record for on-time departures and minimal maintenance downtime.

Madulás picked up the phone and dialed a number from memory. The phone would be answered by a major who was in charge of Flight Operations, whom he had known for years. A man who owed him favors. After a few pleasantries, he learned two of the C-141's were already identified to handle a special mission in the evening. It took a few more minutes of cajoling before Madulás convinced the major the pallets currently sitting in the processing yard were part of the special mission.

"For security sake, they need to be loaded onboard the aircraft immediately."

"I just got the word, there are several trucks on the way to Clark right now with more stuff for those airplanes," the major reasoned.

"You know how fucked up traffic is right now, it could be hours before that one arrives. I need to take care of this one now."

Even though there was no hierarchy calling for it, the major perceived Madulás outranked him because he was a Colonel. Therefore, he gave him the same respect he would give an American Colonel.

"Fine, fine. You do know once the arriving cargo gets built up, they'll have to reload plan the aircraft for the additional weight. In all likelihood, these four will have to come off to get planned for onward transport."

The thought had already occurred to Madulás. He decided the risk of one of his pallets being stolen while the cargo was being repositioned to match a new load plan was minimal.

"It'll be no problem, my friend, right now, I'm concerned about the security of those items. Placing them inside one of your airplanes will help prevent pilferage."

"You know, I could just call over a few extra sky cops to keep an eye on them until the other trucks arrive."

"It'd also increase interest, which neither of us wants."

"Your call," the American was now wondering what was really

going on, "They'll be loaded in the next thirty minutes or so."

Madulás hung up the phone and leaned back in his chair once again, taking the doubloon from his pocket. He let his mind run through various possibilities as he considered the myriad of things that could happen in the next few hours. He looked at the coin in his hand and rubbed his nicotine-stained thumb over the raised portraits on it, Ferdinand and Isabella. The monarchs of Spain, who somehow always brought him at least a tiny sliver of luck when needed.

Santos was still staring out the window when a 40K loader pulled into the cargo yard accompanied by a forklift. The 40K looked like a forty-foot flatbed trailer with a box attached to the side housing the controls and driver. It was designed to ferry up to four pallets from the cargo yard to whatever aircraft needed to be loaded. Santos peered out the window like a child watching a parade as each of the pallets were picked up and placed onto the 40K. Once all four pallets were loaded, he watched as the vehicle drove past the window and headed toward the flightline.

Santos walked outside the building and looked in the direction the 40K was headed. He could see the vehicle pulling up to the back of the C-141, whose aft doors were now open. Even though he'd observed loading operations many times, it always fascinated him. After arriving at the back of the aircraft, the 40K could be raised or lowered as needed to align the bed of the loader with the floor of the plane. Once aligned, pallets would be pushed from the rollerized floor of the 40K onto the rollerized floor of the aircraft. Each pallet would be pushed into the forward most open pallet position inside the aircraft then locked in place. It took less than twenty minutes for the four pallets to be loaded on the aircraft and its doors closed and re-secured.

Even though Santos knew Madulás was probably aware the cargo was being loaded, he still took a moment to call him and confirm. Once he was back outside the gate of Clark Air Base, Santos climbed out of the truck, handed the keys to the driver, and took his sidearm back in exchange. He nodded toward the truck, dismissing his subordinate. Once the truck departed, Santos waved down a jeepney and told the driver to take him to the *Red Lips Bar. A few local beers and maybe a local girl before leaving the Philippines*. There was no telling when he might get back.

An hour or so after Santos departed from the gate of the Air Base, two tractor-trailers pulled in carrying large wooden crates from the Malacanang Palace. These crates were used by the U.S. military to transport household goods to and from overseas locations. The design allowed for two of them to fit back to back on a 463L pallet. Once the trucks arrived in the cargo yard, several teams of Airmen began to construct pallets from the thirteen large crates offloaded. Soon, two more vehicles came with smaller boxes, which was also assembled onto 463L pallets. Eventually, eight pallets were built and sitting in the cargo yard.

The C-141 was capable of carrying thirteen pallets. With only eight spaces used for cargo, the open spaces could be used for a comfort pallet, airline seats for passengers, and a pallet for passenger baggage. A comfort pallet supplied the aircraft, both a kitchen and multiple bathrooms. Using the load plan as guidance, the pallets were loaded in proper order on two 40Ks, which proceeded out to the C-141.

However, when they opened the aircraft, they discovered the plane already contained a four-pallet load. A terse conversation broke out on the radio between the loading crew and the Air Terminal Operations Center (ATOC). At the ATOCs direction, the load crew gathered the data from the placards on the four pallets and relayed it back for research.

Santos just received a plate of food to go with his fourth beer at the bar when ATOC called the load crew back. ATOC told them there was no record of the cargo on board the plane, and no "ZZZ" mission scheduled for at least another three days. For the time being, the cargo was to be offloaded on an empty 40K, which was on its way to the aircraft.

With the aircraft emptied, the load team completed the loadout and secured the aircraft. The 40K holding the four rogue pallets was to return to the cargo yard with the pallets left on the loader until resolved. The ATOC chief decided he was dealing with enough bullshit today. *The next crew can figure out where those fucking pallets came from.* Unbeknownst to anyone, a variety of valuables, including gold bars worth almost twenty million dollars, was now sitting in a cargo yard unlocked, unmonitored, and unguarded.

Airman Dormitories - Andersen AFB, Guam

Ernie carefully placed his thumbs on the two top edge corners of the computer circuit board. Slowly applying increasing pressure, he pushed downward until he heard it click securely into the motherboard. He then allowed himself to exhale. Picking up a small screwdriver, he replaced the Phillips head screw on the back of the computer case. He wasn't finished yet, but at least all the pieces were assembled.

A1C Ernest Crenshaw had been raised by a single parent. His father. When Ernie was two years old, his mother left home. She'd decided the rigors of being a mother and the economics of being married to a junior college professor were not what she wanted in life. They had not seen or heard from her since.

His father taught American literature at the University of Maryland. As a result, Ernie was well educated in American classics, and as he grew older, his father had introduced him to new authors with different perspectives. His father had stressed two things above all—family and education. Because of this, Ernie's life was full of educational opportunities meant to be accepted and successfully completed as well as family events to fill his calendar.

He spent much of his time when his dad was busy learning from his grandmother, who taught him not only how to cook and bake but other domestic skills. Ernie often reflected that the best times of his life had been spent in her kitchen, listening to her instructions as she taught him how to make various dishes. Once the preparation was complete, he would work on his homework at the kitchen table. At the same time, she sat with him, reading the newspaper. As they would sit there, the wonderful aroma of what they prepared began to rise in intensity until, at last, the reward of a meal he helped make.

When he'd decided to go into the Air Force instead of directly to college, his father, of course, was disappointed. But he'd explained he needed a break after the rigors of high school, and he wasn't planning on making it a career. After a year at a stateside base, he found himself facing an assignment in Guam. The furthest away from his family he'd ever been. Luckily, he had met Dex on his first day at work, and they'd become fast friends as they both seemed to understand each other, despite cultural differences. They also shared a strange and dark sense of humor, which made time when they were together enjoyable.

During last night's shift, he'd gotten notification of a package for pickup in the orderly room. He was excited to finally have all the pieces needed for the computer he was building on the island. It had been torture waiting for his shift to be over, then waiting for the orderly room to open for the day. With the package in hand, he'd ran back to his dorm and pulled all the other pieces out of his wall locker.

Putting it together would take several more hours, which meant he would be up most of the day. It was the equivalent of an average person pulling an all-nighter. Ernie was accustomed to a lack of sleep, but this time it served his purpose, not just because the asshole he shared a room with failed to understand he was a day-sleeper.

Ernie hated having a daytime person as a roommate and knew it would make a lot more sense for him to room with his best friend, Dex. They both worked the same shift and knew each other since they'd arrived on the island. But Dex was opposed for a reason most men of their age would understand—sex.

"Buddy, my current roommate is always on the road TDY. It

means I basically have the room to myself most of the time. Because he's gone, Jessi comes over when she gets off shift, and we're able to have some—time… You've got to understand that."

Ernie understood it, and he liked Jessi. On days off, the three of them would hang out together, but it left him stranded in his current roommate situation.

But now, he was currently in a state of euphoria because he was finally able to complete building his computer. It would've been easier just to buy an already assembled model, but it would have cost more, and Ernie was poor. He was not poor just because he was a two striper. He was poor because as a two striper, he was sending a third of Everything he made to his grandmother.

It was almost six months ago when a letter from his father mentioned a bit of family business about a cousin who was not known for stability. The cousin was having financial difficulties due to failed relationships and a penchant for spending before she earned. She'd convinced his grandmother to take her two small children so she could move away from the rest of the family in Pasadena, hoping for a fresh start. His grandmother was from a generation that placed family loyalty above all else, so she accepted the two children without realizing how much cost was involved.

Ernie knew his father's mention of this was not something said in passing. It was an unspoken directive for him to take action. Knowing his grandmother was on a fixed income, the action he took was to help her financially. On the next payday, he obtained a money order for one-third of the amount he was paid and sent it to his grandmother. From then on, every time he was paid, he did the same. Eventually, he got banking information from her so that he could set up an allotment. Now, the money was taken out of his check automatically and deposited directly into her account on payday. He was single, and the Air Force paid his rent and for his meals. Ernie did what he could to reduce spending on everything else. Like buying computer parts rather than a computer.

Ernie sighed, then plugged the cord from the computer into the newly acquired power strip. Worse than the reliability of electricity on Guam, managing about 99% uptime per week, was its instability. The electricity flowing from any outlet could range from 85 to 150 volts. Dangerous for most electronics, fatal for computers. To prevent an overload disaster, Ernie spent over $50 for the surge suppressing power strip he just plugged into the outlet. Sitting down in front of the freshly built P.C., he snaked his hand up the right side of the machine and exhaled before he flipped the power switch up.

The monitor in front of him flickered for a moment. Amber-colored letters began to appear on the screen as the computer performed its power-on self-test. When the scrolling letters paused, Ernie could see the light on the disk drive flicker as the computer began to read its operating system from the 5.25" disk drive.

"Yes!" Ernie yelled as he thrust a fist into the air.

He sat for a moment, looking at the screen, listening to the clunking and whirring sound of the computer reading the floppy disk before glancing over to the bookcase beside his bed. Stacked on its shelves were piles of computer disks filled with games and other mysteries waiting for exploration.

Weapons Armory - Andersen AFB, Guam

A1C Angelina Perez first handed her cleared M-16 to the Armory Chief behind the counter. He dutifully verified the weapon was clear and verified the serial number against his checklist. After her 9mm pistol was turned in, she set the ammo magazines for both weapons on the counter. The Armory Chief confirmed the number of bullets in each, before initialing it off on the checklist.

"It all checked out, thanks."

Angel nodded, then turned and exited the armory. She had been doing this long enough that the process no longer left her feeling anxious. The warnings about what could happen to you if you ever lost a weapon or showed up short on a bullet count were dire. The truth was, it had been years since anyone in the entire Air Force lost a weapon, and missing bullets were usually cleared up in a matter of hours.

She placed her wool security forces beret on her head then adjusted it with her hands. Like every other sky cop stationed in a tropical region, she hated the beret. By the time she walked from the armory back to her dorm room, her body heat would build up enough to cause her to sweat profusely. When she removed the beret and released the form-fitting leather rim, her face would be covered by the wave of sweat the beret managed to hold in.

Angel was raised to believe hardships were meant to be endured and eventually overcome rather than complained about openly. As a result, she didn't join in the bitch-fest taking place in the ready room before the shift. She also never complained about repetitive processes she saw as more time consuming than worthwhile. Angel was here to serve and serve was precisely what she would do. *Defensor Fortis*— Defenders of the Force.

Because of her non-complaining demeanor, few of the people on her shift, to include her supervisor, knew much about her or how she felt about… anything. To most, she was just known to be quiet but reliable. The only one who knew more about her was Dawne.

They had arrived within a few days of each other at Andersen AFB, which resulted in their meeting during the first day of in-processing courses and paperwork. Because of the many ice-breaking exercises they participated in, the women had spent the day exchanging personal histories. Dawne found out Angel was from a large Latino family who lived in Kiowa, Kansas, and Angel knew Dawne was an only child from Hastings, Michigan. Dawne's mother had died during childbirth, and her father never remarried, choosing to raise Dawne on his own. They were the only two SecFo in-processing that day, which drew them to each other on breaks. Even though most of the breaks were only ten minutes, they gradually got to know a bit more about each other. Dawne had been a bit of a wild child growing up, running away once and getting her first tattoo at twelve. Angel was heavily involved in the Church, with Sacred Heart Catholic Church in nearby Alva being the center social establishment for her and her family.

When they reported for dorm assignment at the end of the day, the dorm chief had asked if there was any objection to being assigned to a room together. It had been apparent to both they were going to be friends, so neither objected. At the end of a week of base-specific security training, each had been given their duty assignment. Angel was assigned to grave shift, but Dawne became a floater, and her shift changed every few days.

Security Forces Headquarters - Andersen AFB, Guam

"Well, Ramirez, I don't give a shit. It's bullshit. I'm being put on night shift just because I'm the only one capable of handling people." After he spoke, Technical Sergeant Warren Gubler glared across the desk at Master Sergeant David Ramirez, then clicked his tongue on the side of his cheek.

"Gube, it's not just that," even though the Gube was borderline disrespectful, Ramirez was trying to calm things down. "Do you realize how embarrassing the entire incident was? We had cops, who not only brought a foreign national on base, they were taking turns having sex together inside our security checkpoints."

"Again, not my fault. You're punishing me for something when I wasn't even involved."

"Well, it isn't like we can leave the old supervisor on grave shift. He failed. Before it's all said and done, he'll lose at least one stripe, if not two," the volume of Ramirez's voice began to rise, "He won't even be a supervisor when this is finished. The only reason he didn't get court-martialed too was he knew nothing at all about it. The chuckle-heads who got caught were stupid enough to brag to the OSI during questioning about how they did this all behind his back."

"Maybe if he were involved, he would've told them what they picked up in town and got a blow job from wasn't even a woman."

"Enough!" Ramirez shouted. He stared at Gube for a moment in silence. He hated having to do things like this. He knew Gube had a wife and kids, which multiplied the problems of putting him on a grave shift. He also knew if he didn't assign Gube to the shift, he would end up taking it himself. *Not going to happen. I didn't sew on Master Sergeant to be back on grave shift.*

Ramirez leaned forward in his chair and folded his hands on the center of his desk, interlocking his fingers. He shook his head to clear it and began to speak authoritatively.

"You're off tomorrow. Then, starting 26 February, you're the new grave shift supervisor. You will report at 2330 to the armory on the twenty-fifth to check out weapons before shift turnover. You are relieved of your current duty assignment as of now, so you can go home and get some sleep. You own the flightline, you make sure it is secure." He paused then added, "Defend the Force."

The two men were silent for a moment, and when it appeared Gube was about to say something else, Ramirez stuck his finger out at him,

"Don't. If you have anything more to say, take it up with the Old Man, this discussion is over."

Gube stood up and shook his head. As he turned to grab for the doorknob to leave Ramirez's office, he turned toward him and asked, "We still on for cards at the club in 1600?"

"Of course."

As Ramirez watched Gube leave his office, he felt sorry for the man. Not only was he going on the night shift, but before he reported for his first tour of duty, he was going to lose some money. Gube was no poker player.

Chapter 2

Red Lips Bar - Angeles City, Philippines

"Santos!" The bartender yelled, covering the mouthpiece of the phone with his hand as he looked around the bar for someone to react.

The pretty girl who was wearing a thick coat of the bar's signature scarlet lipstick was leading Santos by the hand. She was guiding him through the bar's exit door to somewhere more private inside the building when Santos froze. He leaned forward and told her to wait, giving her a quick kiss on the cheek before heading to the bar. As soon as he started to walk away, she returned to her stool near the bar and began to scan the room for someone else to take somewhere more private.

Santos knew the bar would be a noisy place to try and have a conversation. T.V.s were blaring a recorded football game, air conditioners were working overtime to keep the room a balmy seventy-five degrees, and a myriad of drunk conversations were all taking place at high volume. As soon as he took the phone from the bartender, he pointed toward the T.V. and motioned for him to turn down the volume. The bartender shook his head while shrugging his shoulders. Santos' response was to take the pistol from his waistband and set it on the bar directly in front of him. Immediately, the volume of the T.V. went down. As other people became aware of what just transpired, the volume of conversations dropped as well.

Santos put the phone against one ear while putting his finger in the opposite ear, "Hello?" It was Madulás, but he couldn't make out everything he was saying. The essential words did come through, 'Clark Air Base' and 'problem.' *I guess I'll wait till I get there to find out what's going on.*

"You got it, Boss."

As he picked his pistol up off the bar, he replaced it with a $100 bill. Waving his gun to get the bartender's attention, he tapped the bill with the gun's barrel then twirled a raised finger to let him know he was buying a round for the house. As soon as the information spread through the crowd, the noise returned, at an even higher level

It was dark before he made it back on base. Having nowhere to store it, he hid the pistol under his shirt before entering the base and heading to the cargo yard. Once there, he saw four pallets sitting in the cargo yard on dunnage. There was no way he could be sure without looking at the placards, but Santos' gut feeling was they were the ones he'd seen loaded earlier. Jumping out of the truck, he walked over to the pallets and verified they were indeed his. A staff sergeant drove into the yard and stopped near Santos.

"Can I help you?"

"Yeah, uh. Is Trey on duty?"

"Nope, gone for the day. I'm Cargo Control now, is there a problem?"

"Uh, yeah. This one," Santos waved his arms to indicate he was talking about all four pallets, "was loaded on a C-141 earlier, but for some reason is back in the yard."

The staff sergeant put the truck in park and got out. Walking over to the pallets, he called ATOC on the radio and read them the information from one of the placards. As the back-and-forth took place, Santos examined the tiedowns on each of the pallets to ensure everything was still intact and ready to go.

"Hey, these were taken off a T-tail when they reassigned the plane to a special mission departing at 0600 tomorrow. We had no record of these. Do you know the story?"

"Yeah, the cargo is part of the same special mission. It just got here earlier than the rest of the stuff."

Santos exhausted the facts. Now he started to blend in details about the second batch of cargo and what happened since he arrived at Clark, "This stuff came out of a warehouse that was closer than the Presidential Palace. Since it got here first, it was loaded on the plane to keep it safe. Things are a little unstable, you know?" to build rapport with the staff sergeant, he added, "but you know how it is. They never give details to us guys at the bottom."

The staff sergeant nodded, but as the man said, he was at the bottom and what happened next was way above his pay grade. He radioed the controller at ATOC and relayed the details Santos had provided to him. The added information brought about several reactions. The load planner who was sitting near the controller and overheard the conversation, immediately argued the plane which was now loaded could not be reconfigured to handle four more pallets. The controller relayed this back and said the four pallets would have to wait for opportune airlift headed for Hawaii later on.

Santos heard this news and firmly responded, "No."

"What are you going to do? We've got a total of twelve pallets and only ten positions open, once we take out what we need for passengers, baggage, and the comfort pallet. You might be able to get the load reconfigured, but at least two pallets get left behind. I have no idea which ones have a higher priority. Do you?"

Santos thought better than to argue with the man who held no power on getting these four pallets out of country. *Naw, this is way over our heads.*

"Okay, okay. I'll call my boss and see what he wants to do about it."

"Fine, I gotta make a run over to the Hazmat yard, but I'll come back when I'm done there," as the staff sergeant spoke, he got back into his air-conditioned pickup rather than standing on the hot concrete pad.

After watching him pull away, Santos walked back to the break room where he'd been ensconced before. Picking up the phone, he called Madulás and told him what was going on.

"You stand by there and guard the cargo until you hear back from me."

"You got it, boss."

Madulás dialed the number for the major at flight operations. Luckily, the man was still on shift.

"Major, I thought we were square on what was supposed to happen with those four pallets."

"Yes, sir, but I warned you they would probably have to come off if the airframe needed reconfiguration. Cargo came in from the Presidential Palace, and it was given priority, bumping yours. There is no space left for your stuff, but don't worry, we'll get those four pallets to Hickam in the next week or so."

"No," Madulás was doing his best to control his anger. At this point, yelling at this man was going to get nowhere, especially since the major was doing the right thing in this situation. "Don't you have another aircraft you could use to transport these last few pallets? It'd get this entire matter out of the Philippines and out of your hair," he paused to let those words sink in. Pulling a cigarette out of the pack in front of him, he lit it while holding it between his teeth.

"I've got two other C141s on deck, one is hard broke, and the other has no crew in country. The next C141 crew gets in at 0600. If they arrive on schedule, they can't take off until 0100 on the twenty-sixth due to crew rest. Will that work?"

Madulás considered this for only a moment. The Americans had moved Marcos to Clark Air Base a few hours ago, and he'd likely leave for Hawaii first thing in the morning. The new Philippine government would immediately prohibit the takeoff of any aircraft which might hold property of interest to the new regime. The Americans, wanting to start things off on the right foot, would comply after a delay to finish up anything in motion and wash their hands of any dirt. At most, he had until 2100 tomorrow to get his riches in the air.

"So, there is no way to utilize the inbound crew earlier? Not even in a national emergency?" He started to push the sternness more in his voice. He needed this major to comply.

"I'm sorry, them's the rules. The crew came in off a 16-hour mission, and I can't touch them for at least a day and a half."

"What time is the other C141 scheduled out?"

"Can't tell, it's paired with a C9 mission, which is TBA. Sometime before 1800 tomorrow night."

"But, Major, based on that, if you gave the crew a twelve-hour break, all three aircraft could depart together."

"You don't understand. The crew would need to be at the aircraft at least three hours before departure to load and prep the plane for takeoff. That would mean a 1500 alert, which would take them down to nine hours crew rest."

Madulás turned up the heat, "Major, you and I have worked together for a long time. Suffice it to say I have given you many favors over time and asked for little in return."

"Unless you have a way to fold thirty-six hours into nine, there is nothing I can do for you," the major knew there would be questions from higher up if he was to pull the crew in early.

"Not even to assist with the departure of a lifelong friend to the United States?"

"Sorry, no. We're already giving the friend a cargo aircraft, plus a Nightingale MEDEVAC out of here. There is a debate right now if we will need to provide a fighter escort."

He still thinks this is all for Marcos. "Suppose I tell you I have photos from a weekend you spent in *Leyte* while your wife was on leave back home. I could send her a few so she knows what you were up to all weekend. Would that assist in folding the hours we currently lack?"

The silence on the phone line was familiar to Madulás. It was the sound of a man making a decision which had already been made for him. Then, he heard the familiar large exhale and sigh of resignation.

"I could possibly see clear to alert the crew at 1700. It would give them eleven hours of crew rest. We'll Phase turn the bird and load it without a loadmaster, which will save a little time, and looking at the fuel levels they came in with. They should be able to make it to Guam before needing fuel."

"In the end, when would they take off?"

"I don't know exactly. No later than 2100 on the twenty-fifth."

Madulás thought about it for a moment, and he knew he was talking to the only game in town. Pushing any more would get him nowhere, it might even cause the major to realize if he did nothing, a mob with torches might take care of the problem.

"I think we can make it work. I appreciate your willingness to be cooperative about this. I'll make certain any photographs of you in my files end up in one of the burn barrels before I depart."

"Please do,"

Madulás stubbed out his cigarette and sat back in his chair after hanging up the phone. Reaching into his pocket, he withdrew the doubloon and flipped it between his thumb and forefinger. He knew he'd burned a bridge, but at this point, maintaining it would provide little benefit. Of course, there weren't any photos. Even if there were, Madulás was aware the major's wife seemed to spend many nights in the Airmen's dorms when her husband was gone TDY. As he slipped the coin back into his pocket, he wondered what those photos might look like.

Santos answered the phone on the first ring. Madulás relayed a new plane was arranged, but it was going to be several hours before the pallets would be loaded. He was to stand by to guard the cargo.

"When will I be told how I am departing?" Santos hadn't been concerned about his safety up to this point. But as soon as the cargo left, he was no longer needed, therefore easy to leave behind.

"Worst case, if you don't hear from me otherwise, go along with those pallets and tell them you're a courier. There will be plenty of room on the airplane for you."

"You got it, boss."

The beer was affecting him. He pulled one of the lounge chairs over close to the window and sat down, putting his feet up on the windowsill. Santos was regretful he didn't have time to finish what he planned at the *Red Lips Bar* and knew neither Guam nor Hawaii would have places with similar services. As he pondered if he could call the bar to get a girl delivered, he dozed off.

The sound which awakened Santos would have gone unnoticed by anyone who had not fought in the Philippine jungle. It was the shuffling of a large group of bare feet. His immediate reaction was to look out the window, it was still a few hours until sunrise, and the waxing moon was providing no light. He stumbled to his feet and walked out the door, marching directly to the spot where the four pallets were sitting. Because this section of the cargo yard was not used for permanent storage, it did not have surveillance cameras or guards and therefore was considered quick shopping by thieves.

While he'd slept, a half-dozen thieves had begun disassembling the pallets and positioning the boxes to be carried off. By the time he made it there, all of the thieves had disappeared into the night. Santos surveyed the situation as his eyes continued to adjust the darkness. He could see all four pallets were unnetted and unstrapped. Some of the wooden crates were now scattered across the concrete pad. The crates still sitting on the pallets were those too heavy to be lifted without equipment. The only thing fortunate about the situation was that none of the boxes appeared to have been opened.

"Oh shit. Shit. Shit," Santos said aloud as he punched one of the crates with his fist out of frustration.

Then, he looked for someone to blame, thinking, *The cargo guys always come out as soon as I walk in the yard, but they let these guys get away with this.* Once he mentally accepted what had happened, he realized there was only a limited amount of time to get these pallets put back together. First, he picked up most of the smaller boxes and grouped them around the bigger boxes on three of the pallets. He was mixing up the cargo, but it was dark, and he couldn't remember how they were assembled the first time. After he finished, he reattached the netting and tightened down the straps.

Looking around, he spotted a small forklift sitting next to a hanger and retrieved it. He used it to put the last of the larger boxes on the fourth pallet, surrounding the *mangkono* box. He then used straps to tighten down the load. It took him over an hour to complete the job, and when done, there was a complete set of nets and five straps left over. Unsure what to do with those, he left them sitting next to the forklift when he returned it.

He walked back to the break room to make use of the toilet he had seen there. Upon returning, he saw a team of Airmen were already loading the pallets he just built onto a 40K loader. Walking over to them, he was surprised to find the staff sergeant he'd met earlier directing the action.

"Hey, I see you got transport of these worked out," the sergeant said without turning to look at Santos as he approached him.

"Yeah, it just took someone above our level to make it all work," Santos patted the staff sergeant on the back, "by the way, I'll be going with the load as a courier."

The staff sergeant hadn't heard anything about this. Still, it wasn't unusual for the Philippine military to send a courier without bothering to tell them anything about it.

"Whatever, we'll be ready to go here in a minute. You can ride out with me in my pickup."

Airman Dormitories - Andersen AFB, Guam

When she got back to her room, Angel was surprised to find her roommate asleep. She couldn't recall if her roommate was on a swing or grave shift this week, but it didn't matter. She changed out of her uniform as quietly as possible.

After taking a hot shower in the floor's shared shower room

down the hall, she put on a pair of shorts and a camisole then took a seat in the room's common area to read for a bit before climbing into bed. From there, she could see the form of her roommate under the blankets. She allowed herself to be curious about what Dawne might be wearing under the blanket. Several months had passed since they'd become roommates, and she knew her roommate's preference was to sleep nude if she was alone or to wear just a T-shirt and panties if Angel was in the room. Of course, all that had stopped two weeks ago. Ever since then, she was wearing regular pajamas. Tops and bottoms.

The change in behavior had been brought about because of a specific event that happened between them. Neither had spoken about the incident since, even though both insisted on the need to talk about it sometime. There just never seemed to be the time. It started one night when Angel worked a double shift and had gone to bed early. Then Dawne had come in drunk.

The sound of a key sliding into the room's lock was usually enough to wake Angel up. Add a drunk's laughter and inability to find the right key and the situation was guaranteed to end restful sleep. She'd looked at her clock and saw it was only 2200—*not even three hours.*

Realizing if she wanted to try to bring this disturbance to an end quickly, it would be easier if she got up and unlocked the door. Upon opening the door, she saw her roommate standing there, bent over, about to attempt a different key. Angel immediately turned and walked back into the room as Dawne entered, attempting to drop her keys on the table near the door but missing it. Angel stood on the opposite side of the common room and watched her inebriated roommate attempt to function.

Dawne stumbled through the room then dropped into a chair and began taking off her shoes.

"After work, we went by the gym, then to the club. These new arrivals saw fit to buy, not one or two rounds—but six. That was after we'd already had a couple. I convinced one of them to try a Salty Dog— I thought he would puke," pausing, she looked wistfully off into space, "Poor boys, they all thought they were going to get laid," she next took off her socks and dropped them on the floor beside the chair. Angel was staring at the floor instead of directly at Dawne and shaking her head.

"Look how pretty," sitting back, she extended her feet and pointed them toward Angel to have her fresh pedicure admired. Dark purple.

Finally, noticing her roommate's sour look, "Something wrong, Ang?" after taking a glance at the clock, she added, "Sorry if I got you up a little early for your shift."

"I pulled a double. I'm not going in tonight. I just got into bed," Angel's stilted tone was intentional. She wanted to make her roommate feel bad and maybe get an apology.

"Oh my God, I am sooo bad," as she rose out of the chair, she stumbled toward Angel, throwing her arms around her, attempting an apologetic hug. Angel didn't move. Then, backing off, Dawne continued to undress while describing the events of earlier in the evening.

Angel was nonplussed, leaning against a wall locker with her arms crossed in front of her.

"Well, I guess it's time for bed," Dawne said when she had stripped down to a T-shirt and underwear. Then a strange look crossed her face. Her roommate knew what the expression meant, having seen it before, and managed to retrieve a trashcan to place in front of Dawne just before she threw up.

After the first round, Angel helped Dawne sit down in the chair and stroked her friend's back. At the same time, Dawne continued to deposit the rest of the evening's alcohol into the trashcan.

"Ugh, no more Salty Dogs for me."

After Dawne assured her the room was no longer spinning, Angel helped her over to the sink so Dawne could rinse her mouth out and brush her teeth. After administering several mouthfuls of Scope, Angel took a seat. She was hoping once this was done, she could go back to bed. Then, for some reason, Dawne became preoccupied with trying to take off her necklace. Angel finally walked over and, while standing behind her, batted her hands away so she could unfasten the troublesome chain. Once it was removed, Dawne unexpectedly spun around, and the two women found each other face-to-face, just an inch or so apart.

Angel was about to take a step back when she felt Dawne's hands on her shoulders, her fingers gently stroking the spaghetti straps of her camisole. Then, without warning, Dawne leaned forward and placed her mouth on Angel's. Dawne's soft, wet tongue immediately invaded Angel's mouth as she pressed her lips against the other woman's. Dawne's fingers became more urgent, pressing harder against the Angel's flesh.

Angel's first cognizant reaction was one of shock. As she felt Dawne's tongue exploring her mouth and Dawne's breath across her cheek, the reaction quickly moved from shock to one of arousal. She felt the need to close her eyes and knew her face was beginning to flush. She could feel her nipples getting hard. As she felt Dawne's fingertips move from her shoulders down her back, Angel felt a tornado of heat centered in her stomach spinning outward across her body. Even though she was standing there motionless, many things were going on within her and within her mind.

Then it ended.

"I—uh. Sorry, I didn't. Um," Dawne's expression was tortured as she tried to put together an intelligent phrase. Finally, stepping to the side, she walked around Angel toward her sleeping area. Turning, before she disappeared within it, she glanced back toward Angel, "I'm sorry, must've been the booze. Don't hate me."

Dawne looked at Angel for another minute, hoping she would say something. When she didn't, Dawne turned and disappeared. Seconds later, Angel heard the sound of her crawling into her bed. Angel remained standing exactly where she had been, mouth slightly agape. She was debating with herself, not entirely sure what had happened or if she'd imagined it. Either way, and most curious of all, was that she was more aroused than she'd ever experienced before.

Eventually, Angel went back to bed. She lay there for an hour feeling aroused, confused, and rejected as she listened to Dawne's steady breathing. Finally, she climbed out of bed and walked over to Dawne's section of the room. She was facing toward the wall.

"You awake?"

"Of course." She didn't move.

"Look, something happened here more than alcohol. I don't know what it was. But you're in no shape to talk about it, and I'm not in the mood right now either."

"Fine, we'll talk later."

As Angel stood there, she could feel the pain her friend was experiencing, possibly confusion or maybe even rejection. Either way, she wanted to reach out. She wanted to do something to ease the pain her friend was feeling.

In a soft voice bordering on a whisper, she finally said, "Can I sleep with you."

Dawne knew what Angel meant. Not sleep with you like sexual, but sleep with you like comforting and loving. Still facing the wall, she reached behind her and flipped the blankets down, "Please."

Angel walked toward the bed, then, looking down at Dawne's body she said, "You know this bed is so small, the only way we'll fit is if I'm spooning you."

She could almost hear her roommate smile as Dawne said, "Well, I've always heard I am best by the spoonful."

Angel climbed into bed behind Dawne, wrapping her body around hers. Soon, Dawne's breathing became deep and slow. Angel was glad of that, but she couldn't sleep. She found herself enjoying the feel of the other body against hers. Their bare legs were gently rubbing against each other, Dawne's ass pressed into her hips, and the smell of Dawne's soft hair was wonderful.

Angel wasn't a virgin, but the things she was feeling now were sensations unknown to her body before. Sensations that seemed worthy of exploration and enjoyment.

From that night on, the two slept together. Whoever came in second, would join the other, and they would hold each other throughout the night. What they hadn't done was speak about any of this, not even to explain why Dawne suddenly felt the need to wear full pajamas to bed every night. To ensure Dawne didn't take anything the wrong way, Angel continued to sleep in a camisole with satin shorts.

Shaking her head, she shook off her past timidity. Tonight, she would try something different. Moments later, Angel climbed into the bed, completely naked, throwing the camisole and shorts on the floor. She wanted to be sure her roommate would see them before she got in the bed and could make an informed choice.

Andy South Housing Area - Andersen AFB, Guam

As TSgt. Gubler pulled into the parking spot in front of his base quarters, he slipped the truck into Park and sat for a moment. Being thrown onto a grave shift was always a possibility in his career field. To some degree, it was complimentary to be assigned nights. After all, putting a screw up on nights was a surefire way for Command to end up sleepless. With him on shift, they wouldn't be called in at all hours.

Having to explain this change to his wife and children was one thing, but the stakes were much higher than just inconvenience. While he was known as an inept card player to his buddies on base, his debt to the Happy Luck Resort off base was less widely known but much more troublesome. Usually, an airman would fear a creditor going to his First Sergeant or Commander regarding a past-due debt. The kind of people Gubler was indebted to simply kidnapped and tortured family members or removed body parts.

Officially, casinos on Guam had been illegal since 1977. But where there is a hunger, someone will figure out a way to satisfy it. While there were many small poker rooms around the island, gaming at the Happy Luck Resort functioned as if it were a legal enterprise. Sufficient money was paid to politicians and law enforcement to allow what happened on the second floor of the hotel to exist without interruption.

It was widely rumored the Chinese or Filipino Mafia ran the casino. The rumor was reality.

Normally, the casino wouldn't allow a military man's debt to run beyond a few thousand dollars. Under pressure, most could produce that amount of money one way or another. Even if they needed to have it wired from the States, the debt was eventually paid. Occasionally, the casino found someone who could be leveraged for much more than just dollars owed because of access to information due to their position. Gubler was in control of something the casino had hoped to find for an exceptionally long time.

As a Security Forces shift supervisor, one of his duties on the flightline was to handle entry control for U.S. Customs agents needing access. Military cargo aircraft were still subject to standard clearance procedures. Since Guam was the first U.S. soil most flights from the Far East encountered, it was where aircraft and passengers were cleared.

Strategic military aircraft, like bombers and such, were cleared differently. Customs agents were not allowed on the plane until classified material was removed. Even then, some portions of an aircraft could be restricted. In most instances, this was done on the spot, and agents only rarely checked the plane physically. Instead, they only asked a few questions. However, at any point, an agent could seize an aircraft if they felt the need. Then the Wing Commander and people in Washington got involved. The most desired state of affairs was one where U.S. Customs and the Security Forces handling their access had an excellent working relationship and respect for one another. Even with Gubler's reputation for being contentious at times, the customs agents assigned to the base saw him as a trusted agent. He gave them quick access and little hassle. It was a positive relationship.

Gubler's memory of what happened in the casino a few weeks before during the most disastrous night of his life was blurred at best. He thought of it is the fastest night of his life, which, at the same time, had sent his life on a skewed trajectory. His first mistake was going to the casino by himself. This meant there was no one to drag him out when things started to turn bad. Before it was over, things turned terrifyingly bad.

He'd started the evening by sitting down at the blackjack table with a female dealer named Tala. He had promised himself if he got a few hundred dollars ahead, he would quit and go home, taking his winnings with him. Within an hour, he'd turned the $200 he walked in with into almost $5000. Ignoring his promise, he had remained in the seat until he lost the $5000 and signed casino promissory notes for another $10,000 in his second hour. Soon, all that had remained was the $145 in chips he was fingering as the dealer shuffled the five decks for the table. His mind was exhausted by the emotional rollercoaster he'd been on.

Above the table, concealed behind one-way mirrors, were two men watching what was happening below. They'd been aware of Gubler for several months. He was a consistent loser who regularly walked out owing the casino under $1500, which he would dutifully pay off in a month or so with thirty percent interest. Tonight, the two assumed the role of Greek gods playing with the destinies of men. The idea was to get Gubler heavily indebted to them. Once he was, they would be able to leverage the amount owed for services they needed based on Gubler's position.

The taller of the two men used a handheld radio to give instructions in *Tagalog* to the dealer below them, "*Hayaan siyang manalo. Malaki.*" The dealer gave a slight nod and began to deal the cards. She had been instructed to let Gubler win big and was now bottom dealing cards to ensure it.

Turning Gubler into a winner took longer than it should have due to Gubler's bad betting and hitting or miscounting the card totals. The dealer began to prompt and cajole him into proper bets and when to take a hit. Even with the dealer helping him, it took two hours for Gubler to dig out of his hole. He was still not ahead, but he saw this as an event worthy of celebration. Rather than paying off the promissory notes Gubler had already signed, he continued to play with the chips which would have erased the debt. He also began to drink more heavily.

After another intercession from the gods above, Gubler's luck turned, and he began to lose again. This time, it was harder and faster than before. Additional promissory notes were signed without the typical delays. With an unlimited credit line and immediate approval, all he needed to do was sign and continue playing. As other players left the table, new ones were not allowed to join. The gods wanted to ensure there were no interruptions. Gubler quickly lost track of what he signed, what he lost, and even the cards on the table—at one point, even attempting to hit twenty-one. Then, the gods put a halt to all of it.

Gubler sat there, numb, looking at the two remaining $25 chips. Looking across the table, he was searching for the receipts to total the amounts of money he'd signed for from the casino. However, Tala had disposed of them long ago so they wouldn't be a distraction. He wasn't sure what he was supposed to do, but Gubler had reached a point where he knew he didn't want to play anymore. He felt the presence of someone behind him and knew it was probably someone from the casino who wanted to discuss his debt. Standing up, he slid the two remaining chips toward the dealer, for the first time all evening noticing how extraordinarily attractive his Filipina dealer was.

He turned around and came face-to-face with the gods who had played with his fate all evening. Both were dressed in black suits and shorter than he was. The shorter of the two was balding and wore large black-framed glasses. The other was visibly muscular, with slicked-down, thick, black hair, combed straight back. Slick-hair moved to the side while the other man motioned for him to walk between them. Soon, they were off the casino floor and in a small office located somewhere in the bowels of the building. The shorter man took off his glasses and dropped them on the desk as he took a seat behind it. Slick hair motioned for Gubler to sit in the chair directly in front of the desk.

"Mr. Gubler, it would seem you had a rather difficult evening." His accent was thick but understandable.

"No, shit. I just couldn't catch a break. Now what? I owe you guys $20,000, maybe $30,000? I'm sure you know what I do and that I don't have that kind of money."

"My name is Jack Wu, and it is my job to manage money the Happy Luck Resort has advanced to his customers. So, just to ensure we are both in the same place, the amount owed, based on the promissory notes you signed, and that my friend Mr. Mendoza is holding, comes to a total of $148,000."

Gubler couldn't breathe. All air left his body when the amount due was spoken, and now he couldn't inhale. His tongue swelled, taking his ability to swallow away as well. He could hear his heart beating, and he thought it was getting slower and slower, then everything faded to nothing. The next thing he recalled was having his face slapped and the awful smell of ammonia from which he could not escape.

"Ah, you are back with us. Good. I'd hate for anything bad to happen to you. I know it must be overwhelming to find out you owe more than you recall requesting. Rest assured, all the paperwork is signed and legal. You currently owe the casino more than you earn in four years. Perhaps you should bring a friend when you're gambling to prevent things from getting out of hand."

"Yeah," Gubler finally managed to squeak out. He found he still could not swallow.

Looking up at Mendoza, Wu said, "Why don't you get Mr. Gubler, a glass of water." Once the standing man left, Wu began to paint his current situation in stark reality.

"Mr. Gubler, you'll never be able to pay off this debt, even if I was to allow it to be loaned out at zero percent interest. You have reached a point where payback is a financial impossibility. Therefore, we must look at other options. Other things of value you may have."

"What, like my truck?"

"No, other things have much greater value. Maybe your wife could spend her evenings working for a friend of mine who operates a whorehouse for a few years until the debt is paid," as he said this, he was sadistically enjoying the sick look on Gubler's face as he realized how hopeless his situation was, "or, maybe you, you could spend your nights there. I hear Japanese men sometimes like being submissive to large men from the West. Ah, and you have children, yes?"

Gubler looked directly at Wu, clenching and unclenching his fists. Finally, the anger passed—first to fear, then hopelessness.

Now, to present him with an alternative lacking a direct emotional sacrifice. "I understand your job at the base includes dealing with aircraft arriving from the Philippines and other places in Asia, yes?"

"Yes, everything transiting the flightline going either direction."

"Ah, but my interest would be those aircraft arriving from non-US ports. Those which have to complete customs in Guam."

"Yeah, but I don't really have anything to do with the way U.S. Customs works, Wu. I just get them to the planes then back off the flightline when needed."

"But let's say the aircraft has classified information on it. You hold Customs back until it is removed, do you not?"

"Yes, but it only takes a few minutes. It's no big deal. They still have to go through customs. The only difference between customs here in the states is we don't use drug dogs because of the insecticide used on the planes due to Ag requirements."

Gubler quickly ran everything he just said through his mind to ensure he had not divulged any classified information. It was all common knowledge, even *Stars & Stripes* had published an article about how customs worked in Guam.

"So, let's say a plane with a footlocker one of my friends loaded on it in the Philippines arrives. Then another friend of mine who works on the base here needs a few minutes to remove the footlocker from the aircraft. You could stop Customs from entering the airplane until after the footlocker is removed, could you not?"

Where is he going with this? "I suppose I could, but I really don't see what difference it makes. I already told you, we don't use drug dogs."

"True. True," while saying this, Wu picked up his glasses from the desk and used a handkerchief from his pocket to clean the lenses, "but, seeing the same kind of package arriving from the Philippines or somewhere else regularly might arouse suspicions we would rather not have aroused."

Gubler rolled his eyes and shook his head. He was blindsided by what came next.

"Mr. Gubler. Let's say I provide you with a list of planes once a week or so for which I would prefer customs not have immediate access. You simply hold them back while associates of mine remove things I want to be kept private. When they're done, you can release the customs agents to do their job."

"But it's not doing my job, you're making me an accomplice, Wu."

"I can see where you might see it that way, but it doesn't make you any part of any crime. You are merely slowing things down, and for your bit of traffic control, I reduce your balance owed by say $500 for each aircraft.

Gubler's mind attempted to work the math, "You mean, after I do this for 3000 planes, my debt is paid off?"

The man behind the desk smiled, *he can't do simple math, but he's playing blackjack?* "Actually, it would be just under 300 planes. To clarify, you'd only be paid for the aircraft arrivals I identify, so there might be one aircraft this week and four next week. The flow is determined by—how do you say it? Ah, mission needs."

"But this could take years."

"Not so many. Your current tour has a two-year automatic extension about to take effect. You might only need to extend by one year more to complete your obligation. Also, as a show of my generosity, as long as things are going well, I will not add interest to what you owe. Your obligation will not grow."

Gubler had been so quick to listen to the proposal he'd forgotten one vital question, "What is in the footlocker?"

"That's my business. It has nothing to do with you or our arrangement. This is simple enough, you either accept this opportunity, or we begin to make more *creative* arrangements.

Gubler shook his head, and somewhere inside him, he knew

what he was being offered was the least repugnant solution. There was a light knock upon the door, then Mendoza slid into the room without fully opening the door. In his hand, a glass of ice water, which he handed to Gubler. After taking it, he placed the glass to his lips and drained it.

"Well?"

"Fine. You just give me a list of flights, and I'll make sure there are delays before anyone from U.S. Customs boards them."

"Good, good. I will make arrangements to have someone deliver the necessary information to you," Wu then put his glasses on, rose from behind the desk, and offered his hand. Gubler reached out and took it, but as soon as he did, Wu gripped his hand and slammed it onto the desk, holding it in place. Mendoza then pressed a machete sized knife against Gubler's wrist, almost cutting the skin.

"If you ever appear in this casino or any of the casinos on this island ever again, win or lose, I'll remove this hand. You cannot afford to create more debt. Hopefully, you'll see the risk is not worth losing your hand," Mendoza raised the knife, and Wu released Gubler's hand.

Gubler was in shock as Mendoza turned him around and opened the door. Before exiting the room, Mendoza raised his eyebrows at Wu as if to ask an unspoken question. In response, Wu nodded his approval. Mendoza kept his hand on Gubler's shoulder, guiding him down an array of tunnels under the casino.

"You know, Mr. Wu must like you," Mendoza said as they walked.

"Oh yeah, he loves me."

"You'll see."

He didn't know if it was exhaustion, the alcohol still left in his system, or just his body being on the verge of panic for the last few hours. Gubler felt spaced out and was getting more unsteady by the moment. If he were a more logical man, he would have known something besides water was in the glass he'd downed so greedily.

Mendoza stopped him in front of an unmarked door, reached into his pocket, and withdrew a key. For a moment, Gubler started to panic, wondering what horrible thing was about to happen. After unlocking the door, Mendoza opened it and shoved Gubler into the room.

"I will let you out in a few hours so you can go home. You've been through an awful lot, and most men will immediately try to think their way out of it only to make some ridiculously bad choices. Right now, you need to calm down and accept what has happened. By the way, now is when you'll find out how much Mr. Wu really does like you," Mendoza departed, slamming the door behind him. Gubler could hear the lock click into place.

He turned around and found he was inside an ornately decorated bedroom. As he looked around, he noted there were mirrors on the ceiling and what appeared to be a full bar sitting to one side. He was exhausted. Sitting down on the edge of the bed, he allowed himself to fall backward on it and closed his eyes.

Gubler wasn't sure if he'd fallen asleep, and if so, for how long, but he felt the bed jostle. Suddenly, his mouth was being invaded by someone's tongue. He pushed away from the unknown kisser and tried to focus his eyes.

"What the hell?"

"It's okay, baby. I make you feel good now."

Even though he could not focus his eyes, the accent let him know the woman kissing him was Asian. She seemed to be scantily dressed and had long hair. The cloudiness of his vision obscured the details. Without any encouragement, she began to unbutton his shirt and slide her hand inside, running it across his chest. Gubler smiled and began to enjoy the feeling of her fingertips on his flesh. *But wait*, he pulled away and sat up. When he did this, she took it as an opportunity to remove his shirt. Then she began to run her nails across the bare flesh of his back.

He shook his head several times, then looked directly at her. Her eyes were accented by heavy makeup with long lashes. For some reason, she seemed oddly familiar. With his eyes on her, she wanted to tempt him and stuck her tongue out, licking his lips, "Come on, let me make you feel good."

Gubler felt no will to resist and dropped back onto the bed. He could feel the bed jostling as she removed first his shoes then his pants. He then felt her moving again as she climbed on top of his now naked body and straddled him. Looking up at her, he suddenly had an epiphany, "Tala?" But it came out as a hoarse whisper. It was the last thing he remembered about the night. But many more things did happen.

For the next hour or so, video cameras recorded the action between Tala and Gubler. Great care was taken to make him look like a willing participant in numerous sex acts, which might have been considered fetishist. Many close-ups of his face and undeniable pictures of his tattoos and other body markings ensured there was no doubt who the male in the video was. The videotape created would serve as an insurance policy to ensure Gubler kept his word. As for Tala, she would only need to perform like this two or three more times for her debt to be fully paid.

Gubler's next recollection was driving home from the casino in his truck. The sun was up, and he knew his life had changed in ways he had not fully digested. His more immediate concern was an explanation to his wife as to where he'd been all night.

Sitting here now, he could see his children down the street playing kickball or something similar with their friends. Inside, he knew his wife was cooking dinner, and he was going to spoil the evening by telling her about the shift change. But his greatest dread was having to contact Wu to explain the change. His debt would no longer be decreasing since he was no longer there during the day to delay customs inspections. "So how do I pay it off now?" he said aloud before exiting his vehicle.

Chapter 3

On-Board Tail #0022, Flightline Clark AB, Philippines

As soon as the crew finished loading the plane, they departed. Santos was left inside the aircraft by the load crew. He managed to convince the team chief to secure him inside the aircraft rather than leaving it open or forcing him to leave. This, of course, was against regulations for safety reasons. The staff sergeant in charge of the load crew capitulated, after all, many things going on today were beyond regulations. This left the Filipino inside the airplane with no way to see what was happening on the flightline.

Santos thought the time was opportune for him to hide his Colt 1911 somewhere onboard. He hoped that by doing this, it would disconnect the weapon from him and prevent problems when he went through customs. He decided that if he put the weapon on one of the pallets, the Air Force would take care of getting it off the airplane for him, then he could casually retrieve it before the pallets were deconstructed at Hickam.

After loosening the nets and pulling back the plastic on the pallet, he found a space between two of the tall wooden crates surrounding the *mangkono* box and slipped the pistol into it. The two boxes were close enough to hold the weapon in place. As he reattached the straps and repositioned the plastic cover, he remembered when he'd first been given the weapon.

At the end of World War II, the United States had been trying to solidify its relationship with the Philippine government. As a result, much excess military equipment was handed over directly to the Philippine military instead of being returned to the United States. Since Madulás had been a rising star in the new Philippine military, he'd been able to abscond with some of what was donated for his personal use. Part of what he had obtained was a crate of U.S. military Colt M1911 pistols. The pistol had been the star handgun used during the war. The U.S. military continued to use the sidearm until 1986.

Even though the weapon was somewhat bulky, as a semiautomatic, it was desirable for soldiers who only carried one weapon. Also, the forty-five caliber rounds the pistol fired were capable of bringing down a target with a single shot. To make the 1911s more useful in guerrilla operations, Madulás had the barrels of each of the pistols threaded so they could accept a silencer.

Over the years, Madulás had presented Colt 1911's to the personnel on his team as a way of awarding specific valor or the successful accomplishment of a high-risk mission. It was such a mission that had earned Santos his weapon. As Marcos had risen in power, ghosts from his past would appear and disappear after making claims against him, going back to his service in World War II. When another of these arose, Marcos had wanted to send a firm signal he would stop these distractors from appearing through fear and intimidation. Marcos asked Madulás to take care of the situation. He, in turn, had passed it on to Santos.

Santos had never told Madulás how he'd taken care of the latest individual to make claims against Marcos, just that it was no longer a problem. The disappearance had quieted dissent amongst others who might have spoken against him. Marcos had been grateful and rewarded Madulás. He, in turn, had rewarded Santos by giving him the last of the pistols from the case he'd taken so long ago.

Santos' only regret as he sat on the aircraft was that he did not have the silencer for the weapon with him. When he'd started the day, he did not foresee a mission requiring the item, nor did he expect to be departing the Philippines this way.

The aircraft had been configured with a comfort pallet and two pallets of rear-facing airline seats. Santos surmised he would be the only passenger on the aircraft, so he flipped the armrests between the seats up across the front row and laid down. The sound of a taxing C-9 aircraft woke Santos an hour later. He knew it was likely the plane was being used to carry Marcos out of the Philippines. Using a screwdriver, he found he was able to pry the door of the cockpit open so he could climb into it and see what was going on.

Just as he got in position, he saw an Air Force C-9 with a red cross, and the number 22583 emblazoned on the tail pass in front of him. He knew he was watching the end of the Marcos era. Almost as soon as the C9 disappeared from view, Santos heard the C-141 aircraft to the right side of him powering up engines and preparing to taxi. Ten minutes later, he watched as C-141 tail number 8088 taxied past. He had no way of knowing Colonel Madulás was on board. After the plane had passed by, he watched the sun rising in the east and knew that the temperature inside the plane was going to rise quickly. He secured the door as he climbed out of the cockpit. Then, after returning to his seat, he lay down and fell asleep.

Airman Dormitories - Andersen AFB, Guam

Dex was roused by the sound of someone knocking on his door. After several rounds of knocking, he knew it wasn't going away.

"Hang on," he called out without moving. He was enjoying lying in bed with Jessica wrapped around him and had no desire to get up. When he heard a key slipping into the lock, he realized fast action was needed to avoid being caught in a compromising position. There was no written rule against having sex with a female Airman in his dorm room. But, given his current situation, he did not need additional attention. He quickly climbed over Jessi, and as he did, he pulled the blanket over the top of her. Even before he made it to the main section of his room, he heard the door open, and sunlight flooded the room.

"What the fuck! I'm a day sleeper," Dex shouted as he picked up a pair of shorts from the floor and pulled them on. He took a moment to kick Jessi's underwear under his bed before walking into his room's common area where he found his flight chief, Technical Sergeant Barr, standing.

"Dex, cool your ass down. I'm a day sleeper too, but you see they got me up, so something must be going on."

Dex quickly calmed down once he saw who the interloper was. *At least it wasn't the First Sergeant or some other asshole.*

"Well," Dex picked up a pack of cigarettes off the coffee table and lit one, "what's up, Jeff?"

"We have a pair of high-priority missions landing in a few hours. The entire night shift is being called in to handle them separately from regular ops. There's going to be a briefing in three hours which will explain everything."

"What are we supposed to be doing with them?"

"Did you hear what I said? You will get your explanations in three hours. I'm just here to tell you to be there, in uniform and ready to go."

It was unusual for Jeff to be this stilted, Dex looked at his watch and did some quick math in his head, "Do they realize we just got off duty?"

"Dammit, when are you going to stop being a pain in my ass and just do what you're told?"

Barr was one of the few NCOs who treated Dex well. He knew the kid knew the job, but, for some reason, just seemed out of sync with everything around him that might make him look good. Barr identified with Dex having gone through something of a bad spell when he was young, but he was getting tired of the constant whining and insubordination.

Dex took a deep drag of his cigarette and slowly nodded, "Shift briefing room?"

"No, for some reason they're holding it over in the Command Conference Room. 0830, be there."

"Got it."

TSgt Barr then took a step toward Dex and leaned forward, speaking softly and hoping only Dex to hear, "I know you've got a woman in here. I understand that part, but this room is a trash heap, and it smells like beer, cigarette butts, and pussy. I'm doing a lot of things to cover your ass, you could at least do a few things to help yourself. Fix it."

Dex squinted at the NCO for a moment, then nodded, "Gotcha."

Once Barr departed, Dex closed and locked the door before climbing back into bed with Jessi. He wrapped his body around hers, moving slowly and gently in an attempt not to wake her. As soon as Dex was in a comfortable position behind her, he exhaled and allowed his body to relax. Within a few moments, he felt her ass pressing him in a rotating motion.

"Since you've got to be up in a few hours, why don't we make sure this room smells like sex to drown out the cigarettes and beer," Jessi purred in her soft southern twang. She reached back and took Dex's hand, pulling his arm around her and pushing his hand between her legs.

Sleep? Who needs to sleep?

Before leaving the dormitory, TSgt Barr went by two other dorm rooms of people on his shift. Had he been in the United States, he could have done this by telephone, but because he was on Guam, few of his troops had private phones in their room. Aside from being notoriously unreliable, there was a limit to the number of phones which could be brought into operation due to the island's World War II phone system. Dorm rats were the lowest priority, which led to few having one.

He went by Ernie Crenshaw's room first and found the Airman not only awake but excitedly playing with his newest toy, a personal computer. Barr directed the young man to get some sleep because it was going to be a long afternoon and evening. He found the next room on

75

his list empty. He left a note with details of when and where the Airman needed to report. Finally, Barr returned the master key to the First Sergeant before going home and trying to get some rest before things got underway later.

Commander's Briefing Room - Andersen AFB, Guam

As Ernie walked into the crowded briefing room, his military I.D. card was requested for security clearance validation. While the technician worked, he looked from face to face at the people already in the room and realized he didn't know many of them. Once cleared, he walked over to Dex and took an empty seat.

"Who the hell are all these people?" he whispered.

"No telling. I'm guessing whatever we're doing is pretty high level. Too many bars and birds and too few stripes."

Once the doors were closed, the Colonel called the room to order, before proceeding directly into his briefing. As the Colonel began droning on about weather and safety, Dex looked around the room, studying the identification badges hanging around the necks of people he didn't know. Immigration, Customs, State Department, and PACAF HQ.

When the preliminaries were done, the Colonel provided a situation report, SITREP, about the situation in the Philippines and Ferdinand Marcos' departure.

"Once they have Marcos safely out of the P.I., Guam will be his first destination. A Nightingale medevac, tail number 22583, will arrive first with him, his wife, and a few others on board. The medical folks will handle those passengers. The C-141 trailing the C-9 will definitely have cargo but may have passengers as well. It is our part of this exodus mission."

"May have?"

The Colonel looked around the room to find the source of the question. Finding no acknowledgment, he answered it anyway.

"May have," motioning with his hand, he offered an alternative, "Possibly. Due to OPSEC and communication security, we only have general information about what is on each of the aircraft. This is all the information I have for you right now. Nothing on the aircraft terminates in Guam," question answered, he continued with his briefing.

"You folks will handle the C-141. If there are passengers, they'll be transported to the terminal and cleared through Immigration, at which point, we no longer have anything more to do with them. The cargo on board was supposed to be built and load planned by the folks at Clark. Not knowing what kind of rush they might've been in, I want every pallet inspected in place to ensure there aren't any problems. If anything is out of line, fix it without removing anything from the airplane. If we run into something in need of too much work, we need to be prepared to download the entire aircraft if necessary."

"Sir, this all sounds rather straightforward. How come dayshift couldn't handle it? There's not much on the schedule today," a sergeant on the far side of the room asked.

"Due to the nature of these evacuation flights, we want to keep them as low-key as possible. While the C-9 will need to be parked on the main ramp due to issues with loading and unloading, the C-141 can be a bit more versatile. We will establish a temporary restricted aircraft parking area on the backside of the flightline away from the public view for those operations. The area will be referred to as Slot Zulu. Because this is a more secure area, it'll take longer to travel to and from the aircraft, which necessitates it having a dedicated cargo handling operation. Each of you has sufficient clearance to be over there. No one outside of this room, other than Security Forces, will be allowed to enter or exit Zulu during this process. ATOC will control both sides of the flightline and coordinate anything nonorganic you might need."

During his entire time at Andersen, Dex had never been to the far side of the flightline. Aside from it being a long distance from the main ramp, it required clearing several entry points to get to the area shown on the Colonel's slide. It was an open rumor the base stored nuclear weapons somewhere over there. He was unaware of it ever being formally acknowledged.

For most in the room, attention levels faded from this point forward. Although selected by chance, everyone in the room knew how to do their job and do it well. What they wanted to know was why they were being disturbed on their time off and if it was worthwhile. They now had an explanation, and most determined it was worthwhile. The final item briefed was the arrival time of the aircraft, 1230 local. Which meant they were left with over two hours to prepare.

As the meeting broke up, TSgt Barr gathered the members of his team to one side and instructed them to take half an hour to take care of any personal business they needed to get done. Given the unexpected nature of this mission, he knew he had thrown a monkey wrench into their time off.

"So, get to the freight yard in about half an hour, and start pulling the needed equipment and vehicles to make this happen."

As he watched his people depart, the Colonel caught Barr's attention from the far side of the room and motioned for him to come over.

"I forgot to mention, all MILAIR in the theater to or from the P.I. or Hawaii has been suspended for the next forty-eight hours. Realistically, you shouldn't have anything coming through at all tonight unless it's an emergency."

"Got it, sir, things keep shifting and changing, don't they?"

"Roger. Nature of the beast. Also, I wanted to let you know in advance, Dex Kevan is going to be denied reenlistment. The First Sergeant will notify him sometime tomorrow. I just couldn't legitimately sign it, too many strikes against him for stuff at his last base. Just a heads up. Once he gets the word, he might not be as dedicated."

Damn, "Understood, sir."

"Well, have at it," as the Colonel said this, he turned his attention to other people in the room and walked away.

Well, shit. What's about to happen to Dex is really going to suck. With that thought bouncing around his brain, Barr headed for the freight yard. Upon arriving, Dispatch informed him the C-141, tail #8088, would be arriving in under an hour, two and a half hours early. "Well, this fucking day just keeps getting better and better."

As the members of his crew arrived one by one, he immediately sent them scrambling to prepare for the early arrival of the C-141. Eventually, a convoy was formed, which consisted of Barr's pickup as lead vehicle, two 40K's, a forklift, and a bread truck with all the extra personnel. They departed for Slot Zulu thirty minutes before the plane was scheduled to land.

As they approached the first security checkpoint, a C-9 passed just overhead as it landed. Rather than risking being any later getting into position, Barr instructed his folks over the radio to travel at double the normal speed limit. As they cleared the final checkpoint, fifteen minutes later, they could hear the engines of the C-141 preparing to land.

The aircraft took almost forty-five minutes to taxi from the main ramp over to the isolated section of the flightline, where the load crew was pre-positioned. This gave them time to get the location set up and ready for the arrival. Once the aircraft was parked and the doors opened, Barr climbed through the front door and spoke to the loadmaster. There were thirty-one passengers on board, including one high-ranking military, Col. Talan Madulás. While the passengers were deplaning to board a bus destined for the terminal, Barr and his team began inspecting the load, only to be told they would need to wait until U.S. Customs cleared the plane.

The team found itself waiting almost two hours until someone from Customs made their way out to the aircraft. After the Customs agent boarded the plane, he immediately began questioning the loadmaster.

"Any of this stuff staying here?"

"Not that I am aware of."

"Good. Cash or high-value items?"

The loadmaster shrugged his shoulders, "It's not a normal load.

I don't have an itemized list, hell I don't even have a manifest."

The Customs agent turned toward Barr, "You going to download this stuff, re-pack it, or anything?"

"Not if we can help it. Well, I mean, as far as the cargo goes. The baggage pallet on the back end has to go into the terminal."

"Fine, my guys will take care of clearing it once it gets offloaded. As for this cargo, I will sign off there is no agriculture then I'll send a twix to the folks in Hawaii letting them know they will need to fully clear the load there," as he was saying this, he was rapidly signing his name to a collection of forms which he handed to the loadmaster as he finished talking, "*Hafa Adai*. Welcome to Guam and the United States."

"How's the load look?" Barr asked the loadmaster as the Customs agent climbed out of the aircraft.

"Good. Cargo guys in the P.I. built it up and put it on. As I said, I got no itemized manifest. If the weights are right, the plane is load-balanced as she sits."

"Cool, my crew will give it a quick once over and get you out of here and into crew rest," Barr got on his radio and called in the rest of his team who spent twenty minutes looking over the eight cargo pallets. With no findings, he radioed back to ATOC. The plane was complete, and he released the loadmaster so he could catch the crew bus.

Barr started to relax as he led his convoy of equipment handling vehicles back to the freight yard from Zulu.

"Box-Kicker Three, this is ATOC," the sudden interruption of silence inside his pickup truck startled Barr.

"BK-Three, go."

"You need to go back to the aircraft. We've got a change to the load plan."

"Roger. Give me a second to get ready to take the changes," Barr began to pull off the road so he could write down the changes from ATOC.

"Negative. Go back to the aircraft and start downloading the whole A.C. We'll send someone out with the new load plan. I'll call you when they reach the security checkpoint, and you can send someone to pick it up."

"Full download, what's up?"

"Adding passengers to the aircraft, need to add a pallet of seats upfront and rebalance the load."

"Rog," *well, shit, there goes the rest of the day.*

Barr knew his crew was monitoring the radio, so he didn't bother to say a word as he made a three-point turn with his truck to go back to the aircraft. The 40Ks were too long to do the same. They would have to go to the next turnout point to get turned around.

On his way back, he waved down the crew bus and told the loadmaster he would need to return to the aircraft. Rather than dragging the entire crew back to the plane, the loadmaster opted to jump in the pickup truck with Barr and head back to tail #8088.

It took 30 minutes for everyone to return to the aircraft and begin downloading it, placing the pallets off to the side on dunnage. The new load plan was passed on, and shortly after 1400, the aircraft was reconfigured. They again closed the doors on it, and the load crew with the loadmaster began the trek from Zulu to the main base.

After dropping the loadmaster off, Barr returned to the cargo yard where his people had just parked the 40Ks and were stowing their gear. As soon as he got out of his truck, his radio crackled to life.

"Box-Kicker Three, this is ATOC," anyone standing near him could hear the groan.

Picking the radio up, he pushed the mic button and said, "Sorry, BK3's already left for the day."

ATOC was not going to allow itself to be brushed off, "Fine, call him back in. We need to download and reconfigure the plane again. Mixed Medevac/Pax load."

Shit. Shit. Shit, "Are you serious?"

"Yeah, sorry, we just got the word on it."

Barr knew there was no *next shift* to handle this. It would have to be done by him and his crew so the aircraft was ready to leave at a moment's notice. This reconfiguration would involve not only downloading the entire aircraft but installing stanchions on the sides for stretchers and adding floor secured airline seats for the passengers. It would take hours.

"BK3, this is Cargo Twelve."

He knew this was Dex and looked around for him. Not seeing him, he keyed his mic, "What?"

"How long?"

Barr paused. *Dammit, Dex, we don't have time for this.* Speaking through gritted teeth, he said, "How long what?"

"How long will this bullshit go on?"

Immediately, there was a cacophony of microphones clicking in approval. Barr inhaled and was about to speak again when another voice came on and commanded, "Enough. Radio discipline, people. Get the job done."

He would deal with Dex later, then Barr brought his team together and informed them of the change. He also let them decide whether they wanted to take a break now or go straight back to work and be done for the day when complete. The answer was the one Barr expected—do it now. He assigned tasks, and everyone launched into what needed to be done while he went and retrieved the new load plan from ATOC. Soon, the convoy was again headed to Zulu with an added 40' flatbed truck carrying the required airline seats, stanchions, and other parts to make the necessary adjustments.

When they arrived at the aircraft, they were met by a new loadmaster who had been called in to observe and approve the changes. He pulled a copy of the load plan out of one of his zippered pockets as he walked toward them, "So, what're we bumping?"

Barr stared at him quizzically for a moment, he pulled out his copy of the load plan and looked at it, "This calls for thirteen positions, we have thirteen."

"Yeah, but there's a mistake. A mixed load of fifty patients and pax requires two baggage pallets. They never planned for the second baggage pallet. I figured I would talk to you before we called ATOC to correct it."

Barr shook his head. Usually, he looked for such things before he ever went out to an aircraft. Today, he expected everyone else to be on their A game so he wouldn't need to do their job for them.

The loadmaster, noticing Barr was now crestfallen, continued, "For what it's worth, looking over the load, I think there are two pallets that could be combined into one and prevent anything being bumped."

Barr stopped shaking his head and began nodding. He'd missed that trick too. *The loadmaster craps in your Cornflakes tells you to fix it, and once you're upset over your soiled breakfast food, he presents the perfect solution he had in his back pocket the whole time.* It was a power trick to boost his own ego.

"Fine. We'll download it and see where we are."

Barr gathered his crew around them and explained what had just happened, which was met with groans and expletives, "But not to worry, Dex has volunteered to take charge of tearing down and rebuilding the two smallest pallets into one," he then looked directly at Dex, "you wanted to know how long—at least that much longer."

The team reacted with a mixture of laughs and more expletives. As the noise calmed down, Ernie's snorting could still be heard.

"Dex, once we get this crap downloaded, take Crenshaw and turn the two smallest pallets into one big one, then call the weights back to ATOC. Everyone else, once we get the load down, we start rebuilding the airplane." Barr immediately felt terrible for what he had just done. On any other day, he would have laughed at what Dex had said. This just wasn't the day. Adding Crenshaw into the mix didn't make him feel any better. *Shit happens.*

Dex wasn't upset about the reaction to what he'd done. He'd known it would come back on him at some point. At least this way, it was done and over. When the download was complete, he motioned for Ernie to follow him, and they walked over to the side of the flightline.

As they walked, Ernie remarked, "Ya know, being friends with you has a distinct downside."

Dex laughed then gently punched Ernie's shoulder, "And don't you forget it."

The eight pallets built at Clark Air Base were now in a neat row on the side of the flightline at Andersen Air Force Base. Dex and Ernie quickly identified the two shortest pallets. They began to remove the nets and other tiedown materials so the loads could be combined.

Once they removed all of the wooden and cardboard boxes from both pallets, they began to reconstruct the load on a single pallet. As they manually moved the boxes one at a time, Dex started to wonder what might be in these boxes, which were only marked with numbers and not words. "Marcos sacked the P.I. for decades, but what made the final cut to be taken into exile?" He allowed his mind to take it one step further, "I wonder if he would know if something came up missing?" As he was mulling this, Ernie lost his grip on a box, and it fell, breaking open one side.

As the two men righted the box, Dex took a moment to look into the split in an attempt to get a glimpse at the contents.

"Might be a painting," he told Ernie when he determined what he was looking at. The wooden box was four-foot square, so it could easily hold several paintings. After first looking around, Dex kneeled, slipped his hand into the crack, and pulled back a bit further so he could get a better view of what was inside, "Yep, a painting of him and Ismelda."

"Imelda."

"Huh?"

"His wife's name is Imelda."

Dex rolled his eyes, "Imedla, Ismelda, Izzymelda. Hell, doesn't he have a kid named Bongbong? Who gives a crap?" he squinted and again peered into the opening, "Well, it isn't a Van Gogh. Doesn't make sense he'd grab this with the limitations on what he could take."

Ernie shrugged as Dex released the board and stood up. Using his foot, he slowly pushed the broken board back into place. When he removed his foot, the fissure didn't reopen, "Fixed."

The two men completed building the contents into a fairly square pallet before netting and tying it down. Once they weighed the pallet and retrieved the dimension data, Ernie passed it to ATOC so a new load plan could be completed. The two then rejoined the rest of the team to help with the installation of the stretchers and airline seats at the front of the aircraft.

The new load plan arrived just as the team finished the internal redesign. Barr directed them to start arranging the load as needed on the two 40Ks. When this was done, he called the entire team into a huddle,

"I just got a call from ATOC. There's another C-141 coming in, Balls 22. Right now, it is scheduled to land around midnight," the groans from the team were loud and meant to be heard, "Calm your asses down, it's only four pallets and no pax. I think two guys can easily handle it. Clark built the load, so it should be good. I'm looking for volunteers. If you go on standby and come back to handle this tonight, you don't have to come in tomorrow night. Takers?"

No one's hand went up quicker than Dex's. He then grabbed Ernie's and lifted it into the air as well.

"Yours. Pick up the on-call beeper at the freight office on your way out," he directed, throwing his pickup keys to them, "Use my truck. I'll catch a ride when we're done here."

Barr and his team arrived back at the freight yard at 1900 and were immediately released. By then, Dex and Ernie were in the dorm sleeping. Marcos, along with his family and associates were all to depart on tail #8088 with their personal property just before midnight.

On Board C-141B Tail #0022, Flightline Clark AB

He had been asleep almost 12 hours when Santos awoke covered in sweat and with a throbbing headache. The temperature inside the sealed aircraft was easily over 110° with no air circulation. Santos sat up just as the forward door opened, and the loadmaster entered.

"Who the hell are you?" the loadmaster asked in a slight Southern accent as he soon as he noticed Santos.

Santos held both hands up to show he was no threat, "Courier for the cargo," as he spoke, he pointed to the pallets.

Giving them a quick look, the loadmaster calmed himself and said, "Sorry, man, they yanked us out of crew rest early, and I'm still trying to get my head together. I really could use some coffee. The ground crew will get some AC hooked into us here in a minute. That'll probably help. Y'all take a seat and stay out of the way. The pilots are still at flight ops but will be out in a minute to preflight us. Then we hit the sky."

"You got it," Santos said, retaking his seat.

As he sat down, the loadmaster said, "Give me a minute to put on some coffee. Then we'll talk about your cargo."

The loadmaster stepped up to the kitchen section of the comfort pallet and set about making coffee. Rather than using the premeasured packages of grounds supplied by Fleet Services, he reached into his flight bag. He pulled out a Ziploc bag containing a blend of Kona and Sumatran coffee he always carried with him on trips. While the coffee brewed, he began to accomplish the departure checklist. During the coffee-making process, the ground crew attached an external air conditioning unit, and it was now pumping cold air into the aircraft. Aside from making it much cooler, the entire inside the aircraft was now foggy.

"Hey, any hazardous cargo on those pallets?" The loadmaster yelled to Santos as he walked to where the Filipino was sitting.

"You mean like explosives and things like that? No, not at all. As far as I know, all of this is just like clothes and papers the President will need when he gets to his destination," Santos got on his feet so he was facing the loadmaster. With all the interior lights of the plane on now, Santos could read the name on the Airman's flight suit: Hamster.

"Hamster?"

Smiling broadly, the loadmaster explained how he'd gotten the nickname from a stewardess who had joined the aircrew in the hotel's hot tub one evening. Upon seeing his hairy chest and back, she started calling him Hamster since he was furry all over like the animal. The name stuck.

"Could've been worse, she might've called me Hairball or something worse."

After the explanation, Hamster proceeded down the walkway on the side of the pallets, performing a quick examination of each one. Usually, he would question everything about the cargo load, requiring the people responsible for the shipment to correct any deficiencies found. It was his job. But today, he was hungover and knew whatever he found he would end up fixing due to the precedence of the mission and who owned the cargo. Unless it looked like it was going to fall apart, he ignored it. As he returned to the forward position in the aircraft, he found Santos still standing there.

"I guess it looks good enough to fly. Coffee should be ready, c'mon."

As he poured the coffee, Hamster began to explain since this was a military flight, there were no stewardesses and such. Before he could get too far into the explanation, Santos interrupted and told him he flew on many military flights and knew how they worked.

Taking a sip of his coffee, Hamster nodded toward the back of the plane, "Super. Go ahead and have a seat. We'll be taking off in a few."

Before walking back to his seat, Santos stirred several spoonsful of sugar into his coffee. As he made his way back to his seat, he sipped the hot, sweet liquid gingerly. Before he sat down, he raised the cup toward Hamster and nodded, "Great stuff, man."

Hamster, who now had his headphones on and couldn't hear what was said, nodded and gave him a thumbs up anyway.

Comfort was the last consideration when a Military cargo jet was designed and built. This went for the seats as well as the environmental controls. As a result, most were cramped, uncomfortable, noisy, and too hot or cold. Shortly after takeoff, the loadmaster sat down in the last row of seats and almost immediately fell asleep. It surprised Santos with all the engine noise surrounding him, he could still hear Hamster snoring.

Santos sat with his arms folded and legs stretched out in front of him. Most of the time, he kept his eyes closed, but occasionally he would open them, staring at the pallets a few feet away. Hidden on one of those pallets was his pistol. Since the loadmaster didn't search him, he was beginning to feel confident incoming customs might not search him either. He was tempted to retrieve the weapon but instead let it remain where it was, carefully hidden.

Santos was on edge. He had not spoken to Madulás for hours, and even though the plane had taken off, he knew it could be ordered to return to the Philippines. He decided his best plan for self-preservation was to continue claiming he was a low-level nobody who knew nothing. It wasn't far from the truth, but he did know enough to be taken into custody and held for some length of time before everything settled down. His goal now was to avoid apprehension by any organization. Being on the loose was his best choice for remaining free.

He dozed for some unknown period when he heard a noise behind him. Upon rising and turning around, he saw Hamster standing at the comfort pallet while flipping through the pages of a checklist. Santos walked toward him, cup in hand, and motioned to the coffee maker.

"Sure, go ahead, there's plenty," Hamster said.

As Santos prepared a cup of coffee, Hamster dropped the checklist and retrieved his flight bag, which he opened and began to search through.

"I picked up this knife from a guy in front of the hotel, he claimed it was authentic, genu-ine tribal Filipino," he explained to Santos as he continued sifting through the contents of the flight bag. Eventually, he pulled out a twelve-inch knife and handed it to Santos. The knife possessed a wooden handle, and the blade stained dark matte so it was not reflective. The length of the blade had a 120° bend in the middle, making it almost look like a boomerang. The bend was functional with the sharp blade on the inside of the angle. If the knife were swung, it would force whatever the blade encountered at the tip or the hilt into the center of the blade. As Santos held the blade in front of him and examined it, he began to nod.

"This one is an authentic *garab*, with a unique style I haven't seen. Most don't have this bend. Having used them to butcher kills in the jungle, it does serve a good purpose," as he handed the knife back to Hamster, he added, "Extraordinarily nice and genu-ine."

"Super, I got it as a souvenir for my nephew. You'd be surprised how much crap we get offered turns out to be fake."

"No doubt," Santos said as he picked up his coffee and returned to his seat. *No, I wouldn't. I used to sell fake crap all the time to survive.* The authentic item could almost always be had for a few dollars more. But, when people wanted to bargain their way down to nothing, they would usually end up with a fake item.

"We'll be landing in about an hour," Hamster shouted to Santos, who turned and gave him a thumbs-up before sitting back down in his seat.

Airman Dormitories - Andersen AFB, Guam

Right at 2200, the beeper sitting beside Dex's bed began buzzing. Without opening his eyes, he reached over and picked it up and manipulated it until the screen was facing him. Opening one eye, he saw the number 2350 displayed. He let his arm fall off the bed and dropped the beeper onto the floor. At this point, he knew he was too exhausted to risk falling back asleep, so he immediately sat up.

A short while later, Dex was standing outside of Ernie's door, banging on it. When the door opened, he was confused to discover all the lights on and his friend standing there in a fresh uniform, wearing a tight-fitting red cap.

In one of their many getting to know you sessions, Ernie had explained the cap was called a *durag*. He wore it, usually at night, to help keep his afro-textured hair from getting too wild. The first thought that ran through Dex's exhausted mind was that it didn't look bad with the uniform.

"What's up, somebody already come by?" Dex asked.

"Nah, I took a quick nap and been up ever since playing Adventure," seeing the confusion on his friend's face, Ernie continued, "Adventure is an interactive text computer game. You roam around inside this huge cave trying to find hints and treasure while avoiding grues, dwarves, and other nasty things that might be down there."

"Grues? Dwarves?" he had played Dungeons and Dragons in high school but had never heard of a grue, "Okay, tell me about it later. We got a 2350 arrival. I figure we should get there around 2230 or so just in case the plane comes in early. We'll go out in the pickup truck first and take a look before deciding what equipment we might need. Cool?"

"Bet. Ready to go when you are."

"Yeah, some of us have been sleeping instead of chasing grues through caves, so I need a few minutes to get a shower and get dressed. I'll come back down and grab you when I'm ready to head out."

Before Dex was even out the door, Ernie was back at his keyboard, furiously typing commands into his game.

Security Forces Headquarters - Andersen AFB, Guam

"What's this?" Gubler asked, pointing to an item on the S.F. blotter. He was leaning on the Desk Sergeant's counter, browsing through the log in preparation for shift change.

"They're using that spot for the cargo aircraft that are part of Marcos' escape," the Desk Sergeant explained, "The C-141 we had out there just left along with all the people. We have another one due in any minute with zero passengers on board. It'll be parked there overnight," he paused to take a sip of his coffee, then leaned back in his chair, "The area will be lit up nicely, so there is no need for extra sentries once the aircraft goes to bed. Already a restricted area anyway. Also, I haven't written it up yet, but we had another report on Super Shakey."

Super Shakey was an urban legend among the Sec Fo. He was described as a wild boar weighing at least 800 pounds, almost as big as a patrol car and with huge tasks that aimed forward rather than curling up. He also had a bad temper. Glimpses of him were caught on the north side of the base from time to time, but no one ever seemed to have a camera with them when needed. Also, even though he was rumored to be aggressive, no one was ever attacked, and most reports were of him running away rather than toward anyone.

"Got it. Anything else flying?"

"Nope. Nothing tonight or tomorrow night, except for the Marcos' Express," as he spoke, the phone started ringing, so the sergeant leaned forward to answer it.

Gubler did like some things about the night shift, like autonomy. With fewer bosses around on slow nights like tonight, he could gain the love and dedication of his troops by letting a few go home early. An excellent way to start his first day. As he waited for the Desk Sergeant to finish his call, he turned to see a young female Airman push her way through the door and head to the shift briefing room, carrying her backpack and weapons. Her uniform and demeanor were sharp.

"Angel Perez," the Desk Sergeant said as he hung up the phone.

"Huh?"

"Her. A good troop from what I hear. Not a complainer."

"I like that."

"Need anything else, Gube?" the Desk Sergeant said as he rose. "If not, I'm heading to the latrine," not waiting for Gubler's response, he grabbed a radio from the charger and turned to leave as if he suddenly had an urgent need.

"Naw, I'm good."

Gubler's first shift briefing was relatively quick. A short introduction, a list of his expectations, then he released two of his troops to go home immediately. He explained he would've had them not come in at all if he had been aware of what the workload was going to be this evening. Gubler then told the remaining Airmen he would spend the shift going position to position to talk with each of them. He wanted to get familiar with what the night shift mission looked like.

Gubler watched as his new subordinates filed out of the room, then gathered his clipboard and backpack before heading to his SUV. Another plus of being on night shift was as one of the senior people on duty, he'd been issued one of the new, fully dressed SUVs the wing had just received.

Chapter 4

The two men sat staring through the windshield of the pickup in silence as they waited for the C-141 to arrive. Ernie was holding the two-way radio that was their lifeline back to the base and fiddling with the antenna.

Dex decided to break the silence, "Do you have like a big treasure you're going for while you're in this cave?"

"No idea, I haven't gotten that far yet. A friend of mine sent me a copy of the game but no instructions or manuals. He gave me a couple of magic words, but I'm waiting on a full list."

"Magic words?"

"Uh-huh, Adventure started as a mainframe computer game on college campuses. If you say the right words, it transports you to different places in the game. It makes play faster once you're further into it by letting you jump from one place to another. Say 'Plugh' and *poof* you appear at another location."

"Plugh? Seriously?"

"Yeah. It wouldn't be much of a magic word if it were easy to guess, would it?"

"I guess not. Does Plugh mean something in the game?"

"Nah, just a magic word for teleportation. He also gave me XYZZY, but it doesn't do anything, at least so far."

"If..."

Both Airmen's attention was suddenly drawn to the east. In the distance, they saw the lights of a C-141 as the aircraft made its approach.

"It'll be at least a half-hour before he gets over here," Dex surmised.

"Bet. You gonna marry her?" Ernie said, abruptly changing the subject.

"I have no fucking idea," Dex said, shifting immediately to the different subject mid-sentence, proof of the two men's deep synergy, "I mean, we're great with each other, and Jessi is the most loyal and loving woman I've ever met. But I know if I get out of the Air Force, I'll lose her. I'm under a year to ETS, and I still don't have my fricking paperwork for reenlistment. I was going to go by the Orderly Room after we get done here to see if I can shake it loose."

"Yeah, it might be best if you settle that first. But don't worry, Barr likes you, and he knows you're doing a good job. He isn't going to let anything bad happen to you."

"Dunno, my last assignment almost ended everything. It was only by the skin of my teeth I got here. You know that."

Indeed, Ernie knew everything about Dex's history. In their first few months here, they became quick friends and remained so. Ernie was always supportive, and Dex appreciated having a positive confidant to talk to.

"Cargo Twelve, this is ATOC. Tail Balls 22 should be parked right at midnight,"

"Gotcha ATOC, what about the load?"

"Lessee looks like you got four pallets, and one passenger."

"Passenger?" Dex said to Ernie.

Ernie was ready for that possibility, "Roger, ATOC. Please let Customs and Immigration know we have a passenger for them to handle. Also, there's only two of us, can you arrange transport back to the terminal for the pax?"

"Cargo Twelve, yeah, we are aware and made arrangements. The pax will deplane as soon as the C-141 is parked and catch a ride in the Follow Me truck.

Neither of the cargo specialists had ever seen Transit Alert get involved with an inbound passenger before.

"Roger, ATOC. I guess everybody's pulling together tonight. Tell TA we appreciate the assist.

"10-4"

"Well," Dex surmised, "If those pallets are built right, we'll be out of here before 0200."

"Yeah, and for this couple of hours, we get tomorrow night off. Five?" as Ernie spoke, he offered the palm of his hand, which Dex slapped.

"Five."

Ernie slumped in his seat and put one of his feet up on the dashboard.

A short while later, the headlights of the Follow Me truck appeared with the C-141 following close behind it. A transient alert Airman parked the truck then jumped out with a pair of light wands to guide the C-141 into the proper parking position. Once he lifted the wands above his head and crossed them in an X, the engines of the C-141 shut down.

Unlike a normal arrival, there were minimal personnel involved in the parking and bed down of tail #0022. A power cart was connected to the aircraft by its crew chief, then the rear clamshell doors of the aircraft were opened.

"Why is he doing that?" Dex wondered aloud. It was unusual for the aircraft doors to be opened unless it was going to be downloaded. Moments later, the Security Forces pickup appeared, and A1C Perez got out of the cab and grabbed a spool of yellow rope. She then began to use it to draw a circle around the aircraft.

Normally, the rope would symbolize a demarcation line where people needing access to the aircraft had to be cleared by the sentry on duty for access. However, this time, it served no purpose as once the aircraft was sealed, no sentry was going to remain in the area. Instead, they would rely on the layered security of the multiple checkpoints en route to the aircraft as a means of protecting it. Once the rope barrier was in place, Ernie and Dex climbed out of the truck and walked toward Tail #0022.

It only took a moment for Angel to confirm the two Airmen had access before allowing them to cross the rope. Dex couldn't help but elbow his friend while nodding toward Angel, "She's kinda cute, man."

"Bet," Ernie said as he glanced back toward her, trying not to look obvious about doing so, "May have to talk her up on the way out."

As they climbed aboard the aircraft, they could hear two people arguing. Once inside, they could see Hamster and Santos facing each other, arguing, with each of them gesturing as they spoke.

"No, man. I'm the courier for this stuff. I have to stay here. It belongs to President Marcos, if you force me to leave, you might be responsible for causing an international incident."

"Look, these cargo guys are going to go through the pallets and make sure they're okay. When they're done, the aircraft will be locked until we come back out here to head for Hickam. No offense, but Marcos is in exile now and holds no power."

Hamster almost didn't say the last sentence of his argument, but he needed the Filipino to obey so he could get the hell out of here and into crew rest. Santos paused and took a deep breath before responding.

"Fine, but I want to be here when it gets closed up and when it's opened up for departure."

Hamster turned to Dex as if seeking approval.

"I don't care, but I don't want him on the aircraft right now in case we have to rebuild something. I don't need the safety write up. How is he going to get to the terminal if the Follow Me truck doesn't want to wait around?"

"I guess he can go back on the crew bus. But I agree with you. He needs to get off the airplane now,", he turned to face Santos, "Have a seat off to the edge of the flightline, and I'll come to get you when we get ready to head out."

Santos was not happy with having people on the aircraft when he was not there to guard his Boss' property, but he had calmed down enough to realize there was little he could do about it. He nodded, giving up the argument. As Santos was walking back to his seat, he saw Hamster's bag sitting on the floor. With the loadmaster busy talking to the cargo crew, he kneeled and reaching into the bag, retrieved the *garab*. As he rose, he slid it into the rear waistband of his pants, covering it over with the bottom of his shirt. He turned, then Santos pushed by the three men toward the door.

"He seemed like a nice enough guy in-flight, but you never can tell what you're dealing with sometimes."

"Gotcha," said Dex, "So, just the four pallets. No hazardous, no sig service, no nothing to worry about. Basically, household goods."

"Yep. The buildup isn't the best, but it worked to get here. I would appreciate it if you guys would throw a few more straps on and tighten it all down."

"Bet. We'll take care of it, no problem," promised Ernie.

Ernie and Dex walked to the back of the dimly lit aircraft. They began climbing around the sides of each pallet to examine where the weak points were and to tighten up any straps that looked loose. Because of the loose tiedown of the nets, the plastic covering on several had worked its way up, leaving the pallet's contents exposed around the bottom.

"Hey, I'm going to go grab some more straps out of the truck. A couple of these could use at least two more."

"No problem, go ahead."

Since the first pallet looked good, Dex moved on to the second and began a close examination. As Dex kneeled on the left side of the second pallet, he noticed there was an ample amount of space between two of the tall wooden boxes on the outside edge of the pallet. From experience, he knew the gap would serve to loosen the nets if the boxes shifted during flight. Moving to the space between the pallets, Dex pushed against the wooden box, hoping it would slide into position. The box moved a small amount before he heard the loud clink of metal on metal.

The sound meant something was loose on the pallet. Dex knew the *something* would need to be tied down and secured before takeoff. It might mean the entire pallet would have to be broken down and rebuilt. Dex sighed as he returned to the side of the pallet and shined his flashlight into the space between the two wooden boxes. At first, he saw what looked like what might be a piece of pipe, but once he reached in and removed it, he realized what he had seen was the barrel of a gun.

"What the hell?" Dex whispered to himself as he turned the Colt 1911 over in his hand, examining it. After identifying the magazine release, he pushed it and was surprised to find it had eight bullets inside of it. He quickly slammed the magazine back into the pistol. He didn't need the complication right now, so he decided to put it off, figuring out what to do with his discovery until later.

Pushing the weapon into his waistband, he climbed back to the front side of the pallet and pushed the two wooden boxes together. Again, he could hear the sound of things shifting in the middle of the pallet. It was not unusual to build a wall of boxes around the edge of the pallet then fill the middle with soft cargo. But whatever was in the middle of this one was not soft.

He grabbed the same box he just tried to move forward and attempted to pull it toward him to widen the gap between it and the wooden box on the opposite side. The net prevented him from being able to move it more than an inch or so, but he hoped it was enough to see what was in the middle so he could figure out the easiest way to fix it.

This time when he aimed the flashlight into the gap, which was now much wider, he was left confused. Rather than the expected soft cargo in the middle, he was looking at the side of another wooden crate. Because whatever was inside was not loose on the pallet, they would not have to rebuild it from scratch. If anything was broken, it was the responsibility of whoever packed the crate. As he began to pull his flashlight out from the gap, a golden glimmer caught his eye. Part of a knothole on the side of the box in the middle had fallen out and provided a small viewport. It wasn't enough to see what was inside, but it was enough for whatever it was to reflect the flashlight's beam.

"Is there a problem?"

"Naw, bro," Dex answered after being startled by Ernie's reappearance, "Just trying to make sure everything is copacetic."

"Is it?"

"Yeah, yeah. We just need to add a couple of straps to this one. The one up front is okay, though."

"Bet."

The two Airmen quickly added several straps to each of the three back pallets, ensuring what was on each would remain motionless. During the entire process, the weight of the pistol kept shifting in his waistband as if it was about to fall. Dex was relieved when they were finished and heading off the aircraft. Loaded weapons are never allowed onboard a military aircraft, so, technically, he could seize it as a safety violation. But if he reported it, he would have to explain why he was snooping around inside the cargo load. For now, he would hang on to it. He could always drop it in an Amnesty Box later.

Once outside of the aircraft, they could see Santos glaring at them through a window on the crew bus.

"I wonder what he's so antsy about," Dex remarked as they walked back to the pickup.

"Well, I guess it is understandable. Yesterday, he had a country. Today, he doesn't."

"I guess I never thought about it like that. Still a little creepy."

A short while after the cargo handlers left, the crew chief closed the doors on the aircraft and boarded the bus. After ensuring light carts lit all sides of the C-141, Angel relayed the status to Gubler. He instructed her to depart from Slot Zulu and grab some chow before meeting him back at the SF HQ. She acknowledged his directions and left the aircraft unattended.

As Dex opened his door, he saw an envelope lying on the floor with his name printed on it. He picked it up as he walked through the door. He headed directly to his sleeping area, depositing the pistol on the shelf of his wall locker and covering it with a towel. After sitting down in the common area and removing his boots, he opened the mysterious envelope and unfolded the letter contained therein. At the top was a sticky note which said, "Sign at the bottom & return to me" with a drawing of a diamond underneath it. The diamond was the added rank insignia of an NCO who was serving as the First Sergeant. Dex lifted the sticky note and read the subject of the letter, "Denial of Reenlistment." He didn't need to read any further, wadding the paper into a ball and then throwing it into a corner.

"Fuck!"

After a few moments sitting in silence, he realized he heard someone talking. His first thought was his roommate Paul might be back from TDY, so he stood up and walked over to his sleeping area in the room. No one was there, but Paul's clothes were scattered all over the floor, indicating he had indeed recently returned. The sound Dex heard was a radio which was left on. As he examined the radio, looking for the off button, the words became more defined, so he listened.

"... and in the continuing saga of Ferdinand Marcos' Philippine departure, the Aquino government released a statement requesting the United States seize and return any and all property transported on US aircraft by the former President, claiming the property belongs to the Philippine people. It was rumored during his final days, Marcos was stockpiling items of high value in case he was forced from the islands. According to the government statement, Marcos is thought to have departed with a large amount of currency and art."

"Nope. Just art of no value," Dex mumbled to himself.

"Additionally, there was a movement of funds between Filipino banks and

those in Switzerland and other countries with strict banking privacy laws. The Philippines National Bank is also said to be completing an inventory of all government owned physical gold holdings. Gold is an easy way of moving wealth without involving a bank. Unlike the United States, it is illegal for an individual to possess gold in the Philippines other than jewelry. This is Air Force Staff Sergeant Frank Thompson, AFN news."

The radio made an audible click as Dex turned it off and returned to his chair in the common area. Looking over, he could see the wadded ball of paper on the floor in the corner of the room. The only thing he gave a damn about losing because of it was Jessica. Without the Air Force, he was just another unemployed high school dropout. The only thing making him stand out in a room full of them was he had skills nobody besides the Air Force needed.

When they'd first started dating, Jessi was forcefully upfront about telling him she had heard too many stories from other women who were taken advantage of by unemployed men and baby daddies. She'd promised herself long ago, she was never going to let that happen to her, even if she wound up alone. He still remembered the morning vividly after they had first slept together and she told him if he ever turned into one of *those*, it was over.

In all of the years he'd been in the Air Force, he had managed to save precisely $2,712.43. It was not going to last long or take him far. As soon as he was out, he would need to find a place to live, utilities, transportation, and a whole lot of other things he didn't worry about now. He closed his eyes, and all he could see was a disaster in every direction. When the visions became too intense, he opened his eyes and stared around the room. Then, as his eyes moved from one place to the next, a twinkle of light caught his eye. *What was I looking at on the plane?*

His mind furiously connected the minor bits of information he possessed, and it led directly to one thing—There might be gold on the C-141. But even better, if there was, there is no way Marcos could make a huge fuss if some of it came up missing. Dex remembered an urban legend about a druggie who went to the police to report someone had stolen his stash. He ended up under arrest after they frisked him and found his stash was in his back pocket. *But the story taught an important lesson—criminals can't count on the law to get back stuff they stole.*

Looking at the clock, he saw it was almost 0230. He was going to have to move fast. As he pulled on his boots, he was trying to figure out how he was going to get access to Slot Zulu without having to do a lot of explanation. A quick yank on the speed laces tightened his boots, and he immediately rose and headed out the door. His heart was pounding in his chest as he jogged from the dorm back to the cargo processing area. At the same time, his mind was busy trying to figure how much gold he could expect, and if it was gold, what his payoff would be.

Security Forces Headquarters - Andersen AFB, Guam

Angel knocked on the open office door where TSgt Gubler was sitting behind a desk. The office was a shared shift supervisor space used for personnel actions etc., so it lacked any personal accouterments which might give away the occupant's history and achievements.

"Hell, come on in. When you're here to see me, if the door's open, you're always welcome just to walk right in."

"Thank you, sir."

"Fine, A1C Perez, I've heard a lot of good things about you. Folks tell me you've done an excellent job since day one and have impressed more than a few of the right people. Because of that, I need to apologize to you right now. When I take over a shift, I make it a point to forgive and forget the history of any bad actors who now make up my team. It allows them a fresh start. Unfortunately for you, to be fair, I have to do the same for any overachievers."

Angel thought for a moment, and then replied, "I'm glad you said so, sir, I think it makes absolute sense to start everyone fresh with the same starting point."

Gubler did not expect that response. He expected her to either get angry or beg to have her achievements considered. Despite his effort to be impartial as he started with a new team, he found it hard not to like her immediately.

"Thank you for understanding. Some people don't. Anyway, my expectations are just like any supervisor. I expect you to do the job to the best of your ability. If you lack something to do it, let me know. It's my job to keep the alligators off your butt. If you're busy dealing with alligators, you're not doing the job. Understood?"

"Easy enough, sir."

"Also, short of accidentally shooting somebody, any mistake can be overcome if you're honest about it. If you try to cover something up and I find out, you've made the only mistake I consider fatal. Understood?"

"Understood, sir."

"Finally, you need to bring me into any questionable situation which might be known or discovered by anyone outside of our team. I do not like surprises. I do not like finding out three days later the Commander is aware of something which happened on shift that I was unaware of, understood?"

"Fully, sir."

"Super, now for the easy part of the meeting. I see you're from Kansas."

"Yes sir, a small town near the Oklahoma border. Kiowa."

The next thirty minutes were filled with Gubler getting to know and understand his new subordinate. The more he understood her and how she would react to things, the better he could guide things from above for her to prevent misunderstandings and disappointments.

As for Angel, it was the first time anyone in supervision ever asked her about where she came from and what she wanted in life. At a time when she found herself in upheaval over her sexual orientation, she was glad to have someone to talk about feelings and attitudes regarding the job. When the meeting concluded, she resumed her roaming patrol near Slot Zulu.

Because of the way he departed, the only identification Santos possessed was his Philippine military ID and driver's license. Without a passport from the Philippines or somewhere else, he could not be admitted into the United States. The State Department had to be contacted to determine if they could accept him as a political refugee. The person who handled such things was not yet in the office for the day, and the local immigration office didn't have anywhere to hold Santos while admission was being worked out.

As a workaround, the base Public Affairs office agreed to serve as his sponsor and ensure he did not leave the base until the matter was settled. Knowing he arrived with no luggage, the PAO took him to the Base Exchange where he was allowed to select up to $100 worth of toiletries and clothing before being taken to transient quarters for the night.

His escort had departed about an hour ago, and ever since, Santos stood by the window, lifting a slat in the Venetian blinds occasionally to stare into the night. As an obedient soldier, he was lost. With no contact from or way to contact his Commander, he had no idea about what to do next. Even staying here was questionable, with the decision being made by some bureaucrat thousands of miles away.

Walking away from the window, he lay down on the bed and stared at the ceiling. He was uneasy about leaving the aircraft unguarded but felt better knowing they sealed it before he was taken from the area. Reaching for the remote on the bedside table, he turned on the TV and flipped through the channels one at a time. Given the hour, he found nothing but static.

Air Terminal Operations Center — Andersen AFB, Guam

One of the things Dex decided on his walk over was to minimize the number of people with which he came into contact. This included people who might just hear something on the radio, so, after retrieving a pickup and toolbox from the freight yard, he went directly to ATOC. Because of the slow night, a one striper was currently in charge. A quick explanation about taking his watch off to reach under nets while working then forgetting to pick the watch up before leaving was quickly accepted. In short order, he was on his way back out to Slot Zulu. After checking his ID, the Security Forces airman at the first checkpoint explained, "The next checkpoint is closed, but it's okay, just go on to the third. With the slow night, the new boss decided to let some folks go home."

"Sounds good, see ya."

Dex was careful to obey the speed limit, even though his time was limited. As one of the few things moving this time of night, he didn't want to arouse any attention. Just being the only thing out there was attention causing enough. As he drove, his mind kept flipping through different scenarios on how he would get the gold off the plane, off the island, and turn it into cash without getting caught and arrested.

Because Jessi's departure date from Guam was before his ETS, the original plan was for her to extend her tour for a few months so they would leave from Guam together. At the moment, reenlistment during an overseas tour would've allowed him to select almost any base in the Air Force as his next assignment. Dex would have used the benefit to choose whatever base Jessi was assigned to next, allowing them to end up in the same place at the same time. The other option, marriage, might have left them on the island for years as the Air Force bureaucracy tried to line up a place to put both of them together. Like many things in the Air Force, it was easier to do it yourself.

As Dex pulled up just behind the wingtip of the C-141, he shut down the engine of the pickup and sat there for a moment. He was still innocent, having done nothing wrong—yet. *Maybe you should just turn around and forget about it. Nope, not my style.* He grabbed the toolbox and flashlight and exited the truck.

His attention was immediately drawn to the tree line just beyond the edge of the pavement by the sound of something moving through the jungle. Dex held his breath. Then he heard the grunts of a wild boar and more noise as the animal ran off into the dense vegetation. *Damn pig.*

The loadmaster used the word *lock* in front of Santos. Normally, it would be called *buttoning up* an aircraft. Technically, the C-141B, like every other plane in the Air Force inventory, did not have locking doors. The reason was simple—if you are in a war zone and you need to get inside an aircraft in a hurry, do you want to wait for someone with the right set of keys to show up? The aircraft also did not require keys to start. Instead, it used a simple mechanical switch, just like almost every military specialty vehicle.

When Dex was standing in front of the door of the aircraft, he stuck the flashlight in his pocket and set the toolbox down. He located the handle, which was recessed inside the plane's fuselage just under the door, and pulled it out. Placing his hands on either end of the eighteen-inch handle, he turned it and watched as the door first moved inward and then lifted slightly. He pushed up on the door, resulting in a space about two feet tall right at the base of the door. This was another of those things he thought about on his way here. If he pulled out the stairs, he would also have to put them back, which would make more noise and maybe draw attention. If he lifted himself, he could climb into the chest-high opening without too much effort.

Once inside the aircraft, he pulled the aircraft door down and then pushed it into place. Now it was impossible to tell from the outside anything was going on inside. Flipping his flashlight on, he began making his way back to the aft end of the aircraft.

He found himself bumping his toes on the devices bolted on the floor and having a much more difficult time moving through the aircraft than normal. He always thought the interior lighting in a C-141 was dim. It was more than adequate compared to what he was dealing with now. He finally established a rhythm to keep himself from running into the evenly spaced hazards inside the aircraft. He was at last positioned before the pallet he was seeking.

Before he got carried away, Dex wanted some assurance what he was seeking was there, so he climbed between the first two pallets. Next, he released the straps he'd put in place hours earlier and began tugging on the wooden crate to recreate the gap. Once the box slid a few inches, he climbed back to the side and shined his flashlight into the gap. This time, nothing reflected. He tried a few angles with the flashlight in an attempt to re-create the conditions as they existed earlier. *My imagination?* It occurred to him if part of the knothole had already fallen out, maybe the rest of it would come out with a little encouragement.

Going back to the front of the aircraft, he found a straw broom and mop tied to the side of the aircraft near the lavatory. Once he was back at his position, sitting at the side of the pallet, he slid the broom's long wooden handle into the gap until it reached the mystery box. Using his flashlight, he aligned the end of the handle with the knot. Grasping the device by the bristles, he began applying a building pressure until it suddenly jerked forward as the knot gave way. Moving the pole out of the way, he quickly picked up his flashlight and shined it into the gap. Now there was a two-inch hole in the side of the box, and something inside of it was returning a gold reflection.

"Shit!" Dex said and then covered his mouth with his hand.

"You better not," a voice behind him said.

Turning, he was relieved to see it was Ernie, "What the hell are you doing here?"

"Well, I just grabbed a shower and was heading back to my room when I saw you take off down the stairs two at a time. Since you were in uniform, I figured something must have come up with the load. I came to help. But after watching you, I'm wondering what the hell you're doing."

"Come here. Take a look at this."

Ernie knelt next to where Dex was sitting. Dex again shined the flashlight down the gap and moved it back-and-forth to accentuate the golden reflection at the other end.

"How did the box get broken?"

"You're worried about the fucking box? Do you know what that is?"

"Something shiny?"

"Use your imagination. All this shit belongs to Marcos. He's running away from the Philippines never to go back after being in control, like forever. Don't you think he would take a piggy bank with him?"

"I suppose, but who knows what his plans are."

"What is the most fluid thing of high value in the world?"

"Oil?"

"Dammit, would you please let your imagination run wild for a minute."

"Fine. Gold? Silver?"

"Exactly. So, what do you think it might be? And I swear if you say oil, I'm gonna hit you with this flashlight."

"Fine, so even if it is gold, what difference does it make? It all belongs to Marcos, not you."

"Not yet."

"Dude, you don't think once he finds out he's missing his gold, he isn't going to raise hell and call the cops?"

"He can't. If he says anything, he's admitting he stole it. Besides, what if we just take some of it. When he gets to the other end, he finds he has some of his treasure but not all of it. He might be pissed, but he doesn't want to risk losing all of it, so he doesn't say anything."

Ernie stroked the side of his face as he considered what his friend just said, then he leaned forward and peered down the gap into the hole at the gold reflection. Unlike Dex, Ernie didn't have a girlfriend who might break up with him if his fortunes suddenly went awry. What he did know was the amount of money he was sending to his grandmother was not covering much more than necessities. A sudden influx of cash could make her life much better and let him have his full paycheck back. Maybe she could pay off her mortgage as well.

"So how much we talking here, serious money like maybe a million or so?"

"Can't tell yet. The news said gold from Philippine National Bank might be missing. Hell, it might be gold coins. We won't know until we open it and take a look."

Ernie nodded for a moment as if deep in thought, then he sighed, shaking his head, "Bet, but if this turns out to be a set of gold cufflinks, I'm gonna whack you with the flashlight."

Without further discussion, the two men began to open one side of the pallet to gain access to the box in the center. This involved peeling back a top net and pressing the side nets down halfway to give them easy access to the boxes on the pallet. Finally, they pulled back the large plastic bag, which encased everything. Dex climbed on top of the front pallet and looked down into the middle of what they just uncovered, and all he could see was the box's top. It was slightly shorter than the boxes surrounding it, with no other cargo placed on top.

"The box is bigger than I thought it was, about three-foot square at most."

"Bet. Is it plywood? What do we need to open it? Some crowbar action, then snatch the treasure and run?"

"I don't think so," Dex reached down and knocked on the top of the box, "I don't think I've ever seen wood like this. It looks like it was put together with lag bolts," Dex suddenly recalled where he left the toolbox he'd brought with him. On the flightline, by the door where it would act as a red flag alerting anyone who saw it something was amiss, "Shit, did you see a toolbox outside?"

Ernie picked it up from where he left it after boarding so Dex could see what he was holding, "Saving your ass again."

"Yeah. Thanks. I must've forgotten to pick it up after I crawled through the door into the plane."

"Uh-huh. You're just lucky I play games requiring me to carry stuff around, knowing I might need it later."

"Yeah, and you know how to handle a grue as well," as Dex said this, he reached out his hand so Ernie could pass the toolbox to him. Ernie then climbed onto the pallet with Dex and took the flashlight from him to assist as Dex tried to figure out what size was needed for the bolts on the lid of the box.

After several tries, he eventually decided on a 1" socket. It would occasionally slip since it was not a perfect match.

As Dex went to work on the second bolt, it suddenly occurred to him why he was having problems finding a match for the bolt, "Why the hell is the Philippines using metric?"

"Not just them, man, most of the world."

"Well, we don't."

As each of the long bolts came loose, Dex would hand them to Ernie, who put them in a pile on top of the pallet. Soon, the twelve bolts holding the lid in place were gone. Dex changed his position so he could reach down and attempt to lift the top off the box. He was surprised when it came off easily.

As Ernie aimed the light down into the box, both men could see the entire top was covered with excelsior packing material. Dex reached down and grabbed a nest of the excelsior and moved it to the side, hoping to expose what it was protecting.

Instead, it exposed what appeared to be several large chrome sprocket wheels, each about twelve inches around.

"Huh," Ernie offered.

"No way, man, what we saw was gold, not silver," Dex lifted one of the sprockets and moved it off to the side and then another. After peeling back another layer of excelsior, he found himself staring at more sprockets. This time, he only lifted the sprocket enough to reach underneath it and, while feeling his way around the next layer of excelsior, felt something that was not sprocket shaped. It was about seven inches long by four inches wide, so he could easily grab it, but it was too heavy for him to lift with only his fingertips at this angle. Shifting positions, he first moved the sprocket away rather than trying to reach under it. Again, Dex blindly felt through the excelsior until he found what he'd discovered a moment ago. Slowly, he began lifting it out of the packing material. It was almost to the surface when his fingers slipped due to sweat, then gravity took over, and he dropped it. A secondary result was that owing to the precariousness of his position—he fell off the pallet.

"You okay?" Ernie said this as he shone the flashlight down from the pallet to where his friend just fell.

"Yeah, I'm fine," Dex said as he came to his feet and began to climb back on top of the pallet, "Can you see what it is?"

Ernie turned the light from Dex back into the open box, and there, he could see under a thin layer of excelsior, was a golden rectangle. A brick.

"Dude, you found gold."

"Freeze!" yelled an unfamiliar voice. This was immediately followed by the sound of an M-16 charging handle being pulled back, readying the weapon to fire.

Neither man had been facing the front of the aircraft. Therefore, they did not see Angel as she walked from the doorway of the aircraft back into the cargo bay. Ernie turned his head slightly, and in his peripheral vision, he could see the familiar Security Forces beret on the person pointing an M-16 with a flashlight held against it. It was aimed directly at him.

"You, slowly climb down from there," then, shifting her attention to Dex, commanded, "You, stay right where you are.

Angel knew the normal procedure was not to walk into a situation like this without backup. But when she saw the boarding staircase was down and the door open on Tail #0022, she knew something was actively going on inside which might require immediate attention. She was too zealous to wait for anyone else to arrive. Once inside the aircraft, she saw there were only two individuals, and both of them were in uniform. She felt secure enough to handle the situation on her own.

Once Ernie was on the flight deck in front of her, she ordered Dex to begin his slow journey off the pallet. Neither man had spoken since she interrupted them. As soon as they were both standing in front of her, she lowered her weapon, and Dex launched into excuse mode.

"Hey, we're here on official business. I realized there was something wrong with the way one of the pallets was secured, and we came out here to fix it before anybody else noticed. After all, you wouldn't want an important plane like this to take off with a bad tiedown job, would you? Of course not, and we didn't want anybody to know, maybe we didn't do our job right. So, we were doing this kind of low-key to keep anyone from noticing. I guess it shows how brilliant you are to figure out someone was inside here since everything was closed up, and there was no way you could tell from the..."

"Stop," Angel was doing her best to maintain an assertive tone in her voice, "I recognize you both, remember, I was here earlier, just like you."

"Yeah, I remember you. We were all out here when it landed. You even checked our IDs," said Ernie realizing there was no way he was going to get to know her socially now.

"Exactly, but you guys didn't clear being here now with the SecFo desk, so when I was driving by and saw the stairs down, I suspected something bad was up."

The comment that the stairs were down, troubled Dex since he was especially careful not to use the stairs. Ernie must have left them down.

"Well, since you caught us doing our job, and you chastised us for not calling the right people, we're all good here?" Dex wanted to get her off the plane as quickly as possible before she saw what they had done to the pallet. Luckily, the front pallet was hiding all the evidence at the moment.

"Probably, but I've got to call my shift supervisor so he's aware of what transpired here. He'd get hot if anyone else noticed this and made a report."

"You gotta do, what you gotta do," Dex shrugged his shoulders as he spoke. Inside he was screaming for her to get off the airplane and leave them the hell alone. Everything would be fine; he was sure of it.

He just needed to keep his cool.

Angel walked from where they were standing toward the door of the aircraft as she took the radio from her belt. Even though she was only a short distance away, Dex couldn't hear her conversation on the radio. Rather than continuing to stand there, Ernie chose to sit in one of the airline seats. Dex glared at him, which confused Ernie.

"You left the stairs down?" Dex finally whispered.

"Yeah, well, I thought we were out here to fix not steal something."

Dex just shook his head at the response.

"I'm sorry, I had no way of knowing what was going on when I climbed in…"

"Okay, my boss said the two of you need to stand by because he wants to speak to you before he closes this out in his shift log. If she had been looking at Dex when she said it, she would've seen his panicked reaction. Now there would be a written record someone was out and onboard this aircraft way outside regular hours. He knew he needed to gain control of the situation somehow.

"Fine, he's on the way out? Why don't we do what we can to speed this up by meeting him outside at his truck? Heck, he won't even have to get out," as he spoke, he walked toward Angel who was blocking the path to the aircraft door. Rather than stopping him, she took a step back and let him pass. Ernie followed, then Angel, until they were all standing outside by the nose of the aircraft. Gubler was still on the way, so Angel returned the M-16 she was carrying to the rack inside her vehicle and locked it. The three of them were standing together in silence when Ernie attempted conversation,

"You from the Southwest?" He knew it was presumptive to assume that because she was Latina, but he needed to start somewhere.

"Yeah, from Kansas."

"Really? I've never been there."

"Where are you from?"

"Maryland. Pasadena, right on the water."

"Sounds nice. Kansas is kinda flat and dusty."

Ernie was about to respond when he noticed her staring off into the distance. Following her gaze, he saw the lights of Gubler's SUV as it made its way out to them. Silence again descended on the three. Rather than parking next to them, or rolling down his window to communicate, Gubler instead parked his vehicle at the required distance from the aircraft, got out, and walked over to the three.

"A1C Perez, are these the uncleared individuals you found on the aircraft?"

"Yes, sir."

"And after discovering these individuals, you searched the rest of the aircraft to ensure there was no one else, correct?"

"Uh"

"Fine, why don't you go and clear the aircraft while I have a conversation with these two."

Angel turned and ran to the aircraft's stairs, quickly disappearing into it. Gubler kept his eye on the two Airmen in front of him while he reached in his pocket and withdrew a small green memorandum notebook. Without looking, he opened to a clean page and then took a pen from his uniform pocket.

"You first," he said, pointing at Dex, "Name, rank, and unit?"

"Randall Dexter Kevan Jr., Senior Airman, Aerial Port Squadron," when Gubler finished writing that down, he pointed at Ernie, who provided his full information.

"So, from what Perez tells me, you two were on board the aircraft trying to fix something you were out here earlier working on."

"That is correct," said Dex

"You didn't clear yourself through security forces before coming out here. Why?"

There was a reason Dex stopped by ATOC on the way out, but he didn't want to drop the card just yet.

"Didn't realize it would be a…"

"TSgt Gubler!" Angel called from the doorway of the C-141 grabbing their attention, "You need to see this."

"Well," Gubler said as he put the pen and memorandum book

114

back in the place he withdrew them from, "I think maybe we need to go see this." Looking directly at Dex, he said, "Senior Airman Kevan, lead the way."

Dex turned and walked toward the front door of Tail #0022, followed closely by Ernie and Gubler. Once they were all inside, Angel led them up the side of the aircraft to the second pallet.

"Is this what you gentlemen were working on?"

"Yes, we needed to unfasten the netting so we could tighten things to prevent anything from shifting around in flight. We were about to start putting it all back together when we were interrupted."

Angel leaned over and spoke into Gubler's ear. He nodded, then pulled himself up on the front pallet so he could see for himself what Angel told him about. For some reason, Dex found himself looking at Angel. He noticed at some point she had unsnapped her holster and was holding her weapon's grip. He knew the world was about to come to an end. From where they were standing, they couldn't see what Gubler was doing, but they could hear him moving things around. Then a low whistle.

"A1C Perez, why don't you have SRA Kevan join me up here?"

Angel looked at Dex and nodded toward the top of the pallet. He obediently climbed up top and moments later was sitting next to Gubler who was looking down on the box and the now exposed bricks of gold.

"I'm guessing you are concerned these might accidentally get shifted around during flight and get broken?"

"Yeah, that's exactly the reason," Dex responded sarcastically to the sarcastic question. At this point, he was exposed with nothing to lose.

"Do you know what it is?"

Gubler leaned back and looked Dex in the eye, "Why don't you tell me."

"It's free money."

"Hmm, to me, it looks like the property of a deposed dictator under the care of the United States government while it is moved from his now hostile home country to somewhere safer."

"But it isn't. It's not his. He stole it."

"So? It's his now."

"Actually, it's no one's right now," Dex paused dramatically, hoping Gubler would pick things up. When he didn't, Dex continued, "Right now, this gold could disappear, and when it is discovered missing, no one can say anything."

Gubler sat silently for a minute as he digested what Dex said. His mind went directly to what the possible value of a single bar might be, and then what four or five bars might be worth. *No idea, but I bet it could wipe out a certain debt,* he thought. He refocused on the present and found Dex staring at him, waiting for some sort of response.

"So how many bars are there?"

"No idea, we just confirmed they were here when we were interrupted," Dex then nodded toward Angel.

"And the two of you?"

"Are the only ones who know about it. Well, we *were* the only ones who knew about it," in an effort to get Gubler to verbally affirm his buy-in, "Now we need to calculate a four-way split?"

The thought of being out from under Wu's thumb and free to leave this place was extremely enticing to Gubler. Yet again, he was faced with compromising his ethics to bail himself out—*Fucking slippery slope.*

"Of course, if you don't want any part of this, you can just take Ernie and I back to the station and write up a report. The gold will go on, and Marcos, who has millions hidden in Swiss banks, will get even more money to add to it. The rich get richer. I kind of wonder how much fucking money the old man needs."

"Not this," Gubler said, finally speaking, causing Dex to smile with the realization a corner had been turned.

"She going to be cool with this too?"

"I don't know, I just met her tonight. Maybe not, she's from a small town in Kansas and was active in her church. Maybe even stealing from a thief would be considered immoral. Why don't we get down from here, and the four of us can have a quick talk before we figure out exactly how many bars are involved. There better be more than four."

"No idea, but the box is deep."

"Let's go."

Chapter 5

Simpson Babineu hated the mundaneness of his job. He was one of two people at INS who processed what was commonly referred to as the clearance of the strange and unusual. Anytime the field ran into a problem with no idea of how to handle it, he would receive a fax and come up with a solution. His Boss told him early on, ninety-nine percent of what he saw was just to be cleared and allowed to come in country. After all, the United States was not worried about being attacked by letting in the wrong foreigner. What he received overnight, interested him.

Being with the State Department, he was acutely aware of what was going on in the Philippines. The day before, he'd prepared and sent a letter that would allow Marcos and all of his staff into the U.S. even if they had no ID whatsoever. The letter should have been used to clear this Santos person who was the subject of the fax. As he read the details, he began to see the same issues the personnel on Guam had seen.

Because of his military ID, they knew he was little more than a low-level enlisted man and not part of Marcos' senior staff. Despite that, the man's name did appear on access lists provided to U.S. military by the PI government. Now he had arrived in Guam, un-manifested and on an unplanned second cargo aircraft, which was not coordinated with the State Department. "Hinky," he thought to himself as he looked over the particulars. The man lacked baggage or hand-carried items, and when questioned for details about the hows and whys, he had no answers beyond being a courier for the aircraft.

Babineu took the file with him, first stopping for a cup of coffee, and walked to the smoking area of the building. He reread the entire file while smoking a cigarette and drinking his morning coffee before deciding he needed to go see his Boss. His recommendation was simple, prohibit onward travel until additional information provided by Santos' home country. He knew, given the current upheaval of the government in the Philippines, it might take weeks. But he was like most bureaucrats and didn't want to do anything with a possible negative result where responsibility could be tracked to him. This way, if he was overridden, the burden became his supervisor's.

On Board C-141B Tail #0022 - Andersen AFB, Guam

Ernie and Angel were sitting in the front airline seats looking up at Gubler while Dex stood off to one side, leaning against the front pallet. After they introduced themselves by exchanging first names, Dex explained why he and Ernie were really out at this aircraft at this hour. Throughout his entire explanation, he kept stressing the money did not belong to Marcos, and there was no way it could ever be reported stolen. Angel sat quietly and listened to what Dex had to say while trying to avoid giving any indication as to what she was thinking. She had been raised to believe if it wasn't yours, you didn't take it, even if it didn't belong to the person who possessed it. You needed to earn what you received in life.

After Dex concluded and he stepped back, Angel waited a moment before asking, "How much are we talking about? I mean in dollars."

Gubler took the opportunity to gain control of the conversation, "Not absolutely sure, but it's probably a lot. After we settle things here, we will unpack the entire box and take count. From there, we'll figure out what the split will be. Also, we can't take all of it," as Gubler said this, he looked toward Dex and could see he was confused. "Look, we're going to take away something from someone who would lose it anyway if it became public knowledge. If we take all of it, he has nothing to lose by reporting it. He might feel like he's getting some level of justice if everyone starts looking into what's missing and why. But, if we only take part of it, say twenty percent or so, he will be prevented from reporting it, thinking he might lose the part he still has."

"That makes sense," Angel said before adding, "sir."

Ernie stole glances of Angel while Dex was speaking. Then he realized the aroma of plumeria flowers he was smelling must've been coming from her hair. He was embarrassed that he figured that out, because it seemed so personal. Ernie shifted in his seat and remained staring forward.

Angel was silent again, trying to figure out a way for her not to be part of this and, at the same time, assure them she would not turn against them either. The truth was, she didn't care what they did, as long as it didn't hurt her and she was not involved.

"What if I say I don't want a cut, but I don't care what you guys do. Once I walk off the plane, what happens… happens. If anyone were to ask me, I could honestly say everything was fine when I left. I will not turn you in, but I can't lie about leaving the three of you on the aircraft if I'm asked that specific question. Would that be okay?"

Ernie, Gubler, and Dex looked at each other, confused.

Dex finally spoke, "But you could do anything you want with your share. You could even donate it to a charity if you wanted to."

"I know. I don't want any part of it at all. Right now, there are just a whole lot of questions as to if this will even come off. You have to get it off the airplane, off the base, find somebody to buy it, and then you have to deal with stacks of cash. Have you guys even thought this through?" It was now her turn to stare at each of them, looking for an answer, "I thought so."

"Look, there are ways things can happen, even on Guam. We

can figure that stuff out later, but if we're going to do it at all, it has to be within the next couple of hours. First, we need to…"

"Do not say another word. I don't want to know. If I'm asked right now, I can avoid implicating you guys without lying. You start talking about your plan, I can't do that. If you guys are okay with me doing this, I'll get in my truck and leave right now. In about two hours, I'll come back on my next rounds." She was doing her best to control any wavering in her voice. Her mind was racing forward, considering alternatives, including a disturbing one where they simply remove her. *Bodies are supposed to be hard to dispose of, but this is probably a lot of money.*

Ernie finally spoke, "That sounds good to me."

Dex and Gubler looked at each other and nodded.

"Fine, then I'll take leave of you gentlemen. I expect to find all of this," she said, motioning with her hands, "put back together and the door of this aircraft sealed with everyone gone."

Without another word, she turned and began walking toward the door of the aircraft.

"You know, if you change your mind before we get it off base, you'd be welcome to come back and take your share."

Angel just shook her head as she continued walking and then climbed out the door.

Dex stared at Gubler a moment, then out of curiosity, asked, "Why, before we get it off base?"

"Because that's when things get risky and when she could be helping us. It's a good breakpoint."

Gubler firmly accepted the idea the treasure was going to solve all of his problems. While dwelling on the thought, he had a flash of inspiration, he thought of a way maybe to solve one of his and his new partner's problems.

"I think I know someone who would convert this gold into cash."

Dex and Ernie looked at him, glad somebody had an idea about how to handle those complexities.

"I'll have to check the possibility once I get off duty. I did notice that these bars have an emblem on them. To avoid traceback, we'll need to figure a way to get it off the bar or even melt them down and reform them into another shape.

"We better think about sanding it off, the melting temperature of gold is over 1,000°C," Ernie said.

"How do you know this crap?" Dex responded to the bit of trivia Ernie interjected.

"Duh, I took AP chemistry. I remember stuff."

Gubler looked at them both and shook his head, "Let's get going."

The Airmen decided to construct a short *bucket brigade* to remove all of the bars from the box. Ernie climbed into the box. After moving the sprocket wheels, he began handing the bars up to Dex, who, in turn, handed them to Gubler. Gubler then stacked them on top of the front pallet.

"Last one," Ernie called out as he passed it to Dex.

Once he received the bar, Gubler placed it on the fourteenth stack he'd created on top of the pallet.

"There you go, thirteen stacks of ten and one stack of seven. One hundred thirty-seven bars total."

Dex shook his head. This is more than even he had expected in his wildest dreams.

"A quarter?" Ernie said.

"What? No. I mean, we still have to get this stuff out of here, get it off base, and fence it. Haven't you ever watched any cop shows? It becomes the law of diminishing returns. The more crap you need to fence, the less they will give you because it gets harder to process."

"How about six each for a total of eighteen."

"Six? I don't know, man. Seems like a lot of risk for a small return. How about ten a piece," Dex countered, then both men looked at Gubler.

"That would be thirty bars in total. Dunno. It even sounds like too much," Gubler rubbed the side of his face with the back of his hand. At the same time, he thought, then he picked up one of the bars and tried to estimate the weight, "These things are about twenty pounds each, you're talking about 500 pounds we would have to move. We can't risk being so visible. How about this, we take half of that, twelve."

"Four each?" Dex clarified.

"Sounds fair to me," Ernie pulled himself up and out of the box, so he was sitting on top of one of the taller boxes, making him level with the others.

"Well, possibly. If we take twelve, and for some reason, Angel changes her mind, we could change the split and still have three each. If she doesn't, then we get four a piece."

Ernie nodded, whatever it took. He figured he didn't need more than one, maybe two, to solve his current problems anyway. Dex was exhausted, and his mind wasn't working. Three or four bars of gold. It had to be enough money for him to get started once his enlistment was over. It should be enough for the first year. He finally nodded after giving up trying to calculate the value. As for Gubler, he figured one bar would need to go directly to Wu, and the others would pay for college educations and maybe a down payment on a house when he got back to the United States. It was everything he would need. As the men looked at the stacks of gold bars sitting on top of the pallet, none of them realized the bars they were looking at were worth over nineteen million dollars at current gold prices.

For speed, they developed a different work routine this time. Dex took a seat in the middle of the pallet and passed the gold bars to Ernie, who re-stacked them in the box, trying to emulate the patterns he'd found when he took them out. Gubler was on the front side of the pallet, and when Dex passed him a bar of gold, he would carry it up to the door of the aircraft. Once twelve bars were stacked, Gubler retrieved his SUV and pulled it close to the aircraft door. He then took the gold from inside the aircraft door and placed it in the back of the SUV.

When all the bars and the chrome sprockets were inside the box, Ernie placed the lid on top. Dex began passing the bolts down to him one at a time so he could return the box to its before state. All was going well until Ernie asked for another bolt, and there were none. Dex had passed every bolt from the top of the pallet down to Ernie, and even after a desperate search could not find another one. When Dex looked down and shrugged his shoulders, Ernie stared back up with concern in his eyes.

"What the hell do we do?"

"No idea, these damn things are metric. I have no idea where to get a metric bolt on this island."

Dex scrambled around the top of the pallet again, feeling around and under the nets in case he missed something the first time. Then he heard it. The metal clanking of the bolt as it fell down the side of the pallet, eventually landing at the bottom on the exposed metal. Ernie peered over the edge of the box and spotted the bolt.

"I got it," then, rather than climbing out of the box to pick it up, Ernie leaned over the edge attempting to grab it with his fingertips. Somehow, he managed to flip the bolt backward, and it fell between the pallets onto the aircraft floor. Once he righted himself, he looked up at Dex, "We're fucked."

Dex stood up to glance back at the rest of the pallets, trying to determine the level of difficulty as all the pallets would have to be slid back to reach the bolt. On the aft side of the last pallet was what appeared to be a sizeable Philippine mahogany dresser and bookcase. The furniture probably belonged to someone on the flight crew who had done some shopping in the PI. Those would have to be moved as well.

"Come on, people, we only got about half an hour before Angel comes back," Gubler said from the doorway of the aircraft, "plus I need to get back on roaming sentry."

Dex knew to move the furniture, slide the pallets back, retrieve the bolt, and put it in place so the pallet could be rebuilt was going to take way more than half an hour. He didn't even figure in the time to put everything else back the way it was.

"We go without it, just start covering it up."

Ernie was confused, but he trusted Dex to know what he was doing and began to climb out of the middle of the pallet, then began replacing the plastic covering. Soon, the two men were reattaching the side nets and then tightening the top net down on the load. Two additional straps, which were first added earlier in the evening, were the finishing touch. They stood back and looked over their work.

Gubler climbed back onto the aircraft while they were busy working and was now standing at the side of the pallet looking up at them.

"Look, Dex, is it right or not?"

"Yeah, it's good."

"Then let's go. Do you remember the second checkpoint? The one that was closed? Meet me there."

"Wait, where's the gold?"

"In my SUV, let's get to the checkpoint, and we can talk about what's next."

Dex turned to make sure Ernie heard what was being said, then nodded.

As Ernie flipped the stairs back into the aircraft, Dex jumped up and grabbed the strap which would allow him to pull the door down. As soon as the stairs locked in place, Dex gave the strap a yank, and the door slid down and into place. Finally, Dex used the handle under the door to pull the door into its frame. By the time they turned around, Gubler was already gone.

Checkpoint 2, Secure Flightline Area - Andersen AFB, Guam

When he saw the vehicle approach, Dex made it a point to look over as it passed to see who was driving. He recognized her immediately. As promised, Angel was on her way back out to Slot Zulu. Just ahead, he could see Gubler was pulled off the road and out of sight behind the Checkpoint 2's guardhouse. In his rearview mirror, he could see the lights of the bread truck Ernie was driving. It was what he'd used to follow Dex out to tail #0022 just a few hours ago.

When all three of them parked behind the checkpoint, Gubler motioned for them to come over to his vehicle.

"You know, I've never been in the back of a police car before," observed Ernie, which made Dex smirk due to his history of being in the backseat of police cars.

"Well, most people try to avoid it." Gubler change his position to where he was sitting sideways and could face both of them.

"Okay, right now, I've got all of the gold bars in the back of this vehicle. I'm a few hours away from shift change over, so they can't remain here long. Unless either of you to have an idea about where to stash them, I'm going to make a suggestion," he waited for both Ernie and Dex to shake their head before continuing, "Fine, I know where there is an unused security building out toward the storage bunker area. There used to be a road leading directly to there, but an earthquake made it unsafe, so now all traffic comes through here. They left the guard shack in place in case things changed. I propose one of you come out and give me a hand with unloading the gold and helping me cover it up. We'll need to get some sort of container when the time comes to move them out," Gubler had no problem leading this discussion, it kept him from having to capitulate anything he was thinking with any ideas of theirs.

"I have an old footlocker I can donate to the cause," Dex said.

"Fine, but before that happens, you need to take some spray paint or something and remove any personal markings on it that might lead back to you. If this stuff gets found, we don't want it to be easy to trace back."

"Agreed."

"Once we have this stuff stored out of the way, we'll give it a day for the aircraft to take off and arrive at Hickam. If anyone is going to pitch a bitch about it, it will happen quickly and ferociously. So, in thirty-six hours or so, we could be ready to sell this stuff."

Leaning forward toward the backseat so he could be included in the conversation, Ernie said, "To who?"

"I'm not sure, again, if you guys got any ideas, say something. If not, I think I know somebody off-base who might know somebody who does something like this. You guys both do know, it will not be free to convert this. We might end up having to pay half of the value as a fee."

"What the hell?" Dex interjected.

Ernie patted him on the shoulder, "Calm down, man, it wasn't like it cost us anything. That would still amount to us ending up with the total value of two or three bars of gold. Hell, that's probably at least $50 to $60,000." Later, Ernie would check the *Stars & Stripes* for the current value of gold, and discover each bar was worth $141,000.

"Everybody okay with the game plan?" After Ernie and Dex again nodded, Gubler continued, "So let's say we meet up at the Arc Light Memorial at 1900 on the twenty-seventh."

"Isn't that kind of out in the open?"

"Yeah," Ernie agreed.

"True, but there are some benches there, and nobody would question people who don't normally pal around together stopping there. If you guys start showing up at my quarters or me at yours, it might not arouse suspicion immediately. However, it'd provide a link if things start to go south," the others agreed with Gubler's logic.

With those details settled, Dex told Ernie to return the bread truck to the shop and then take off. He then followed Gubler out to a guard shack which was set off the road on the way to the storage bunkers. The entry road which used to be there was still visible, although it was obviously unusable.

The two men quickly unloaded the twelve bars of gold and then covered them up with a poncho Dex found inside the truck.

"No lock?"

"Why would you lock an unused building? Don't worry about it. No one has a reason to go inside. All the power and water are off. Just a skeleton left."

Dex was unconvinced, but he didn't have an alternative idea anyway. As his adrenaline drained away, he was overcome by exhaustion, and it was starting to affect him physically. Everything appeared darker to him, and some things seemed to be moving in slow motion. Knowing things were taken care of for the moment, he was ready to head back to his room and get some sleep. As he started to climb into his pickup, his attention was drawn to the jungle. Something was walking toward him. He could hear the crunch of the dead vegetation as each step came toward him. He threw himself into the truck, pulled on the seatbelt, and started the engine. He was ready for this night to be over.

Dex followed Gubler back to the main road, and then when he turned to go back toward the main base, Gubler turned to go in the opposite direction. Before Dex made it back to the freight yard, Gubler was at Slot Zulu again. The sun was starting to come up, and he took a quick look around the area to make sure no details were forgotten. Once he was sure everything was okay, he headed toward the alert area to check on his troops assigned there.

It felt like it took almost two hours before Dex was back in his room, undressed, and lying in his bed. He closed his eyes, and he could feel his entire body start to relax when he heard a key in the door. Refusing to open his eyes again, he could hear the padding of feet entering his personal area. Then the sound of her breathing and rustling of clothes as Jessi undressed before she slipped naked into his bed beside him. He was motionless, enjoying the feel of her nude body against his. She kissed him on the cheek before curling up around him and immediately falling asleep.

Transient Quarters - Andersen AFB, Guam

Outside of old movies, Santos never heard a telephone's bell ring. At first, he ignored the trill of the bells, but because of their insistence, he eventually sat up and looked around the room for the source of the noise. He determined it was the old-fashioned rotary dial telephone sitting on the desk. By the time telephones had become part of his life in the Philippines, they'd already moved on to pushbutton phones with electronic ringers. He slipped out of bed, picked up the receiver, and held it to his ear.

"Santos?" The voice was familiar. It was Madulás.

"Yes, Boss, I'm glad you called me. I made it to Guam with the cargo, but I'm not sure what you need me to do now."

"When do you get to Hawaii?"

"I have no idea. There's a problem. I didn't have a passport with me, so Immigration didn't clear me into the United States yet. Until somebody does that in Washington, I'm stuck here."

Madulás was powerless to do anything about this. He was used to the way things worked when he was in a position of power in the Philippines. He could pick up the phone and make things happen. Now, he was painfully becoming aware he was no longer someone in control but someone being controlled.

"What about the cargo, where is it?"

"Still on the plane, Boss, they didn't take it off. I managed to stay with it until the aircraft was locked, so everything should be okay."

"I guess it will have to do," the disappointment in Madulás' voice pained Santos. He decided not to mention his pistol was now also part of the cargo, "they may not hold the aircraft for you, do you know when it is scheduled to depart?"

"Not exactly, I know the crew I flew in with was supposed to stay with the aircraft all the way back to the West Coast. I think the earliest they could leave would be late tonight."

Santos could hear Madulás' Zippo as he lit a cigarette, then there was a long silence.

"Are you still there, Boss?"

"Yes, just trying to think a few things through. Our situation now is much different than when we were at home. The contacts and professional courtesies I once utilized no longer exist. I knew we would end up in this position eventually, but I was hoping old ties would linger longer than they have. Are you being provided for while you wait?"

"Yes, Boss, they even gave me money to buy a change of clothes and toiletries. They provided me with a meal yesterday, but it is too early for me to tell what might happen today."

"I would expect for a while, they will feed and house you. If I hear anything or can do anything about getting you released, I will do so. To maintain contact, I will call you back, starting in about four hours, which should be noon your time. Correct?"

Santos looked at his watch, "Yes."

"Good, I will call you back then and every four hours until I tell you otherwise. If for some reason, you are not there, I will try back every hour until I reach you."

"What if I'm here, but I don't get a call?"

Madulás sighed, the downside of having an obedient minion was the necessity of providing constant and detailed direction, "If that happens, just stay there. If you don't hear from me for twenty-four hours, do whatever you need to do."

Santos was a bit confused by that last statement. What exactly would he need to do? "Yes, Boss, anything else?"

"No, I will speak to you at noon."

As Madulás placed the phone back in its cradle, he was angered and frustrated things appeared to have fallen apart so quickly.

"Hey," said an NCO, who walked into the room without knocking, "You can't smoke in here. The smell is already all over the building."

Madulás defiantly took a deep drag on his cigarette and then exhaled a huge cloud of smoke toward the NCO, "Forgive me, I was unaware of your rules." He dropped the butt on the floor and crushed it with his boot before walking out.

The Andy South military housing area sat between two of the main north/south roads on Guam. As a result, and due to the low threat condition, the decision had been made by the Base Commander to leave the housing area open. This meant that unlike the main base, anyone could travel in, to, or through the housing area without showing an ID card. Of course, police patrolled the area more often, and there was usually at least one speed trap set up inside the area to prevent thoroughfare cars from speeding.

After Gubler turned in his government vehicle at the end of shift, he picked up his personal truck and began the slog home. It was always his least favorite part of the day, not going home but the drive itself. He was usually exhausted at the end of the shift, and all he wanted was to crawl into bed and close out the world. Just before he turned into the housing area, he noticed a black Buick sedan off to the side of the road. He watched in the rearview mirror as the car got onto the road and followed him after he turned into the housing area. Now, he was fully awake.

Rather than going directly to his home, in case this was some kind of threat, he meandered through the housing area, eventually parking near a playground. Once parked, the other car pulled up beside him. Gubler glanced over and was not surprised to find the windows were tinted to prevent the occupants from being visible. Through the lowered passenger side window, he could see it was Mendoza behind the wheel.

"*Hafa Adai*. The Boss wants to have a meeting."

"Look, I just got off work, can I come down there later?"

Mendoza raised himself in the seat and leaned toward the open window to seem more threatening, "Boss says now. Get in."

Gubler's fight or flight senses were now in overdrive. If he got in the other man's car and something nasty happened, there would be no clue as to why he disappeared and why his vehicle was left at the playground. After forcing himself not to hyperventilate, it occurred to him that Wu might be happy with the news he had for him. As he rolled up his window, he became calmer and more confident the meeting might be a positive thing.

After locking his truck, Gubler walked over to Mendoza's car, opened the passenger door, and got in. They drove to the casino without saying a word. Upon arriving, rather than pulling into the regular parking lot, Mendoza approached a closed garage door. The door opened automatically for him, then they traveled down a ramp, arriving at a small five car parking lot.

"We'll grab the elevator," Mendoza said, guiding him toward a doorway off to the side, "I don't feel like doing the stairs again today."

After the elevator, was a trip similar to his last with lots of twisty passages, finally ending again in the small windowless room with a desk. Once inside, Mendoza motioned for Gubler to sit down, then pulled out his radio and said two words, "We're here."

Looking down at Gubler, Mendoza patted him on the shoulder, "Don't worry, man, this will be an easier meeting than the last one." Rather than taking the seat behind the desk, Mendoza moved off to one side and stood leaning against the wall. He then started to whistle a random tune softly. Shortly, the door behind him opened, and Wu entered the room, immediately taking the chair behind the desk.

"Good day, Mr. Gubler, so sorry to have to bring you in this way, but there must've been some sort of misunderstanding."

"How's that?"

"You see, I've been told you have been moved to the night shift. It might satisfy the requirements to earn your Air Force paycheck, however, it does nothing for me. Things are no longer functioning the way we agreed," Wu removed his glasses and kept talking, "Luckily, there is a moratorium on flights out of the Philippines because of their political situation. Otherwise, something might have arrived requiring your assistance, and this discussion would be much less friendly."

Gubler sat silently, his hands with his fingers intertwined were in his lap. He nodded in reaction to Wu.

"Please let me know when we can resume our normal mode of operation so you can continue to pay off your debt. I will not accept that you can do nothing to change this, especially when you should be highly motivated," Wu did not sense the capitulation he was looking for from Gubler, so he added. "Keep in mind, I not only hold a legal contract for your debt but also an entertaining tape of you and Tala's time together."

Gubler's eyes widened at the mention of the tape. That always seemed to be a secondary concern to everything else going on.

"Mr. Wu, I may have an alternative solution for the money I owe you. But first, I need to ask a few questions. If you would please indulge me," he waited a moment, and then Wu motioned with his hand for him to continue.

"I have recently come into possession of some property— incredibly valuable property. The problem is, this property would need a certain finesse to transition from simple property to actual currency. It is my understanding this casino is owned by certain entities that might have experience in performing such conversions."

Wu winced at the words in the last sentence. Just like the American Mafia denied their existence while still operating in public, the same was true with the criminal elements who employed him. Of course, due to changes in the Philippines, his employment was likely coming to an end. With Marcos out, the Philippine Mafia was looking for new places to operate, and Guam was high on their list. Because of their closer proximity and more brazen tactics, it was probable Wu's organization would fold operations rather than getting into a protracted war. He was already beginning to make preparations for his departure. Of course, all that was irrelevant to this situation.

"I suppose, Mr. Gubler, I might know of individuals who might be able to help you in your current situation. However, what could you possibly be holding, which could be valuable enough to pay off your debt."

"Bars of 99.9% pure gold from a trusted national bank."

Wu smiled and sat back in his chair.

"Twelve bars. At least twenty pounds apiece. So, 250 pounds or so."

Wu knew the actual weight of those bars would be twenty-five pounds, as it was the international standard for banks. The added weight per bar brought the total weight up to 300 pounds. He mentally calculated the total based on today's gold selling price of $352. The gold Gubler was holding was worth roughly $1.7 million.

Gubler sat, staring into Wu's eyes and could tell the wheels were turning in his brain. He also saw the moment when the man decided he would play."

"Mr. Gubler, you realize these types of transactions, even when done between the best of friends, always require some sort of service fee."

"I expected that."

"Now, given the monetary value of the items you're holding as well as issues of who the original owner might be, the fee may be quite high. Perhaps seventy cents on the dollar would be fair."

Gubler went from being hopeful, to crestfallen, to angry in seconds, "It would seem to me, I would be due some consideration from the party handling this transaction as they are benefiting in multiple ways."

"You are not mistaken. There are multiple obligations at play here. I will allow the first bar to satisfy your debt, meaning no service fees. Then, I will take seventy cents on the dollar for the balance."

Gubler stared at the man and thought about it. As he did this, he watched Wu put his glasses back on. Even though he'd only met the man twice, he knew it was a tell. He was about to conclude things one way or another. He was not quite sure what to use as his offer. Still, he knew whatever it was, it would be the last, "I appreciate your offer, but I do have partners in this venture, and their interests must also be protected. I propose a single bar go toward settling my debt, and then we pay you sixty cents on the dollar for the rest.

Wu's broad smile was instantaneous. He then slammed a hand

on the desk then pointed his finger directly into Gubler's face, "No deal on the bar, your current balance is $140K. My cut for processing this transaction is fifty percent based on world gold prices the day we close the deal. You'll be provided cash in circulated twenty-dollar bills immediately. Once done—all of our business is complete."

Gubler was trying to do the math in his head, it was not quite as good a deal for him, but it paid off the balance and left him with enough remaining for a down payment on a house. There was one detail, "The tape?"

"Why, Mr. Gubler, it would no longer be necessary for me to maintain possession of such an item, so I'll present it to you with my compliments at the conclusion of our business."

"Can we finish this in say twenty-four hours?"

"I will need at least seventy-two hours to acquire that much cash and prepare for the transfer."

Gubler rose from his chair, not quite sure what to do before he left. *Do I shake hands on something like this?* This question was answered when Wu also stood and extended his hand. The two men shook, and then Wu motioned for Mendoza to remove him from the office.

Before Gubler pass through the door, Wu spoke again,

"By the way, as a show of my honor in this dealing, I will tell you that the bars you are holding are not twenty pounds but twenty-five. The amount of gold you are holding is fifty pounds more than you thought. I will base my payments on the correct weight. Once again, this is a show of my honor."

Gubler nodded, although it would not be until much later that he realized Wu was giving him an extra quarter million dollars just to prove he was honest. His was reeling as they walked down the labyrinth of corridors back to the parking lot. As they turned one corner, he collided with a small woman wearing a silk robe going the opposite direction. After helping steady her, he looked down into her eyes and saw it was Tala. She gave a quick bow and then continued without showing any recognition at all.

Mendoza returned him to his truck, but before letting him exit, reminded him if, for some reason, the gold deal did not work out, his entire debt might double as a penalty for failing to live up to his arrangements. Gubler nodded, "Don't worry, man, I want this over."

Within minutes, Gubler was home and saying goodbye to his children as they headed off for school and his wife on the way to her job. After taking a shower and climbing into bed, he lay on his back, staring at the ceiling. *If all of this works out, I'll never do something so stupid again.*

US Immigration Office – Agana, Guam

Immigration Officer Joe Lujan read the FAX a second time as he slowly chewed on the bite of doughnut in his mouth. He wanted to be sure he fully understood what the State Department required of them. He shook his head, not only because his office had never handled something quite like this, but also because Washington had made the assumption they possessed the capability to do what they were being asked.

Per the message, they were expected to hold presumed Filipino national Joshua Francis Xavier Santos until the Philippine government could complete a requested investigation. During this period, he was to be treated as a VIP since he may or may not hold or have held a high position in the Philippine government. Even though he was supposed to be monitored, he would not be controlled like a prisoner once all airports on the island were notified to deny him travel and were provided with his picture.

"Did you see this?" Joe asked a coworker, "We're even supposed to supply him with $500 a week until this is settled," then tapping the FAX with his finger, he added, "that's in addition to covering his meals and lodging."

The coworker shrugged and went back to reading the newspaper.

"This is some kind of bullshit," Joe concluded.

With his tirade complete, he prepared to do precisely as he had been told. He first contacted the satellite office on Andersen Air Force Base and informed them the detainee was now their responsibility to monitor until the situation was resolved. Next, he called the base Public Affairs office and asked for their cooperation by letting him stay on base and feeding him at their chow hall. They would also provide him with an identification card that would allow him to go on and off the base if needed.

"Letting him stay on base should make everything easier," Joe concluded as he briefed his supervisor on the actions he had taken.

"Agreed. Just don't forget, if this goes on for more than a few days, he'll want to start exploring and eventually leave the base. Then we lose him among the population here."

It was too late. Joe had already extracted himself from the situation, having successfully handed off responsibility. He was effectively done for the day. Now, he was ready for a leisurely cup of coffee while reading the sports news and consuming another doughnut.

Airman Dormitories - Andersen AFB, Guam

As she slipped the key into the door of her dorm room, she could feel her body aching for a hot shower and a full night's sleep. The day had been both full and confusing. Had she agreed not to say anything when she saw the theft of possibly millions of dollars going on? Then she reminded herself of whose money it was. *Stealing Hitler's piggy bank could not possibly be a sin.*

As soon as she got the door open, she could hear Dawne sobbing from her sleeping area. Walking over, she found her lying face down on her bed, her face buried in her hands.

"What's the matter, babe?" Angel asked. It was not the first time she'd used an affectionate term to refer to Dawne, but it was the first time it felt like something more than friendship.

"It's my Dad," said Dawne as she turned over, "Right before I went into the Air Force, he'd completed chemo for lung cancer, and the doctor said he was all clear. A little while ago, the First Sergeant came by with the message from his doctor saying the cancer was back. Stage four…" Dawne couldn't manage another word, her arms immediately reached out, beckoning Angel to come into them. The two women laid in bed, holding each other without speaking.

Finally, Dawne inhaled deeply and released Angel while trying to sit up.

"I can't do this. I can't just lay here. I need to be doing something."

"Okay. Are you going home?"

"Yeah, the First Sergeant is waiting on some sort of message from the Red Cross, and then he'll approve my Emergency Leave, which will get me a flight to the West Coast."

"And the rest of the way to Michigan?"

"I have to pay for it. No idea what that's going to cost due to the short notice."

"Babe, don't worry about it. I can give you some money."

Dawne turned and looked at Angel, and after a moment of staring into her dark eyes, she couldn't resist the urge and kissed her. Angel returned the kiss, but unlike the other night, she was not in any kind of mood for something like this. Her concern right now was for Dawne's well-being. So, she let the kiss slowly fade away without trying to take it to the next level.

Angel rolled out of bed while saying, "let me check my account, then I can run over to the ATM to pull out what I can."

"Don't. I mean, don't do it right now. Right now, can we just lay back down, and you can hold me? It felt so good. It's still early in the morning, and I can't do anything until the Red Cross message comes in anyway."

"Fine, do you mind if I take a minute to get out of his uniform?"

"No, that's fine. I prefer you out of uniform," Dawne managed a weak smile, trying to make a joke and insert innuendo at the same time. But with her eyes full of tears, there were no words to allow either to work.

Because she was dozing off and on, Angel had no idea how much time passed when she heard the knock at the door. She had just pulled her robe on when the door was thrust open, and a male voice was calling for Dawne. As she walked into the common area of the room, she discovered it was the First Sergeant with Dawne's Emergency Orders. Moments later, Dawne walked out of the same sleeping area to take the orders from him.

The First Sergeant cut his eyes from Dawne toward Angel and then toward the opening to the sleeping area they'd both appeared from, while slowly nodding. He provided Dawne with some instructions on what the Air Force Aid might be able to do for her and left her a card with their contact information. He then turned and left without looking at Angel again.

Dawne was standing next to Angel, reading through the orders, trying to comprehend what this military form meant for her.

"Do you think he knows?"

"What you mean?"

"That we were in bed together."

"Ah. You mean, does he know you were comforting me? Yeah, probably. Does it matter to you?"

"No, I guess not."

"Good," Dawne kissed Angel on the cheek "I need to get going. I've got some things I need to do at the shop before I leave."

"Do you think we could maybe have dinner together tonight, maybe have that discussion we keep talking about having?"

"Sure, if I'm still here. If not, I'll try to take some time when we can at least talk. I know we keep saying that. But I promise we will do it before I leave," Dawne kissed Angel's cheek again before going back into her area to get dressed.

Angel stood in the common area of the room, going over what just happened. Most of all, as she stood there, she wished Dawne had kissed her on the mouth again. The result might've been deliciously different than it was last time.

Chapter 6

Transient Quarters - Andersen AFB, Guam

Santos closed the door to the room and was again alone. A Public Affairs Officer (PAO) and a Guamanian from the INS had spent the last thirty minutes explaining to him what the State Department decided about his status. They covered the restrictions he was expected to follow and provided him with five-hundred dollars cash and a privilege card which would allow him to eat in the dining hall.

He sat down on the bed, trying to figure out what he needed to do next. First, he needed to take a shower and put on some clean clothes. Since he was hungry, he would stop by the dining facility before going to the base exchange. Now that his stay was extended, he needed more clothes and a few other items. Once those errands were done, he would return here and wait for Madulás' call at noon. He would have to update the Boss on his immigration status. The call was not going to be a good one.

Airman Dormitories - Andersen AFB, Guam

Ernie stretched without getting out of his chair and then yawned. He was exhausted. But after lying in bed for an hour, he couldn't will himself to sleep. So, he was sitting in front of his computer, trying to distract himself. He looked down at the keyboard and then typed in a command.

```
> UP
YOU ARE IN A MAZE OF TWISTY LITTLE PASSAGES, ALL
ALIKE.
```

"Damn."

```
> S
You are in a maze of twisty little passages, all
alike.
> W
You are in a maze of twisty little passages, all
alike.
> E
You are in a maze of twisty little passages, all
alike.
```

Ernie groaned audibly, then decided to end it out of frustration.

```
> Turn off lamp
It is pitch black.
You are likely to be eaten by a grue.
> S
Oh no! You walked directly into the slavering fangs
of a lurking grue!
```

Ernie slid his hand down the side of the computer and flipped the power switch off. He had saved the game a few moves ago and could easily start again, but his eyes were burning. Almost as soon as he crawled into his bed, he began reflecting on what had happened the night before. Again. His logical mind said stealing Ferdinand's gold was easily justified.

After all, it didn't belong to the former President. But he couldn't force his conscience to accept the rationale, even though the money would do a lot of good for his grandmother and his family.

He rolled over from his stomach to his back, and for the umpteenth time today, found himself staring at his ceiling rather than sleeping. He looked at his watch and saw it was almost 1100. He knew the dining facility would open in thirty minutes. Rather than continuing to lie there wasting any more time, he decided to get up and eat. *Maybe after I eat, I can sleep.*

The bay orderly had just finished cleaning the shower room when Ernie walked in, making him the first to use it. This was an unusual and unexpected treat, so he took his time and enjoyed the feel of the water and its calming effects. By the time Ernie got to the dining facility, it was already open, and several people were already eating. As he walked to a table, carrying his tray, he noticed a large and out of place Pacific Islander sitting at one of the tables. The man looked up and nodded at him. He nodded in response, then took a seat at an empty table on the other side of the dining room.

Santos speared one of the French fries on his plate and put it in his mouth. As he chewed it, he looked out the window and wished he was at the Red Lips bar instead of here. He closed his eyes and could almost feel the bottle of ice cold, Red Horse beer in his hand. Then, a sly smile came to him as he imagined one of the bar's girls holding his other hand. Opening his eyes, he pushed the tray away and crossed his arms. Because he followed Madulás' instructions, he knew he would not be going back to the Philippines for a long time.

Flight Operations - Andersen AFB, Guam

The Air Force Reserve Captain stood at the Flight Operations counter and scanned the schedule board for his aircraft. He was still technically in crew rest and was wearing a T-shirt and shorts, having just finished jogging. He finally spotted the line with his airplane, Tail #0022, and followed it until he saw the takeoff time was 1300 GMT/2300 local. He studied the rest of the board before speaking to the Ops Officer.

"Since you guys have nothing else flying tonight, any problem if we try to back it up and get out of here an hour or so early?"

The Ops Officer, a Major in a flight suit who was sitting behind the counter reading a magazine, spun his chair around and looked at the flight board.

"Your call. Why the rush?"

"Hawaii has fun things to do, Guam doesn't. If we get there an hour earlier, I can make lunch at the Hale Koa and then spend the afternoon surfing."

"Works for me, I'll get a waiver for breaking crew rest a little early."

"Just tell them we're a crew of Reservists heading home, they'll probably tell you to get the hell out of our way or be prepared to be run over," the Captain laughed at his joke.

"Roger that. Who you fly for in the real world?"

"Eastern Airlines at the moment, but they're having some labor issues, so I might be jumping to one of the others here shortly."

"Gotcha, just save a spot for me. I get out in a year."

"I promise," the Captain replied as he departed the room.

Jack Wu's Office – Happy Luck Resort, Tumon Bay, Guam

Jack Wu had been preparing for his departure from Guam for over a year. Any outsider could see Marcos was not going to hold onto power much longer. Upon his fall from power, a change in the way crime syndicates were allowed to operate within the Philippines was inevitable. It was not Jack's first relocation due to political upheaval, so he knew what was needed to ensure he departed with more than the suitcase of clothes in his hand.

Wu always felt proud of himself for being smart enough to realize the best way to hold on to riches was to distance yourself from them. As a result, none of the cash, gold, and other valuables he'd managed to acquire over the years were on Guam or in the house he owned in Macau. Instead, he used safety deposit boxes in a variety of banks around the world.

Of course, he was sacrificing liquidity by gaining security. Even if a law enforcement agency was able to get a warrant to force the bank to open one of his boxes, the likelihood of them finding more than one, even in the same bank, was minimal. Because he was dealing with physical assets, he hired trustworthy and well-paid couriers to deposit assets into the boxes. Now it was time to task one of those couriers with the responsibility of removing a large sum of cash and delivering it to him in Guam.

By handling the conversion of gold bars to cash for TSgt Gubler, he would make a profit of just over $1.5 million, after paying off the man's promissory note with the casino. A sizable profit for such a simple transaction.

"*Fo XiNan?*" Wu said into the phone when he heard the call being picked up at the other end.

"Yes, Mr. Wu, it is I," in perfect English, with no accent.

"I have an errand for you. Please go to the store and see if you can find me two pounds of American butter," the code was unsophisticated. Still, to a bystander, it would just sound like a simple chore, not a request to retrieve two million dollars.

"I would be more than happy to take care of it for you, Mr. Wu," Fo was hoping the steadiness of his voice would hide both his curiosity and concern over the request.

"Good man, I will see you on Saturday," after saying this, Wu immediately hung up the phone. No need for closing remarks.

Fo placed the phone back in the cradle and stared at it for a moment. He and Wu had met six years ago when Fo was studying to become a Buddhist monk. It was Wu who had given him the nickname *Fo XiNan,* which meant 'Buddhist guy.' Their first meeting was one of grief because Wu had come to deliver the news Fo's father, who had been working for Wu, was killed on the job. Wu, out of a sense of obligation, came in person to deliver the news and to offer the young man, who was now the head of his family, a job as a death benefit of sorts. Wu's hidden agenda had nothing to do with a sense of obligation but his desire to prevent ill will that might've grown over the years to revenge.

Fo's new position of responsibility required him to leave the monastery immediately to take the offer. While he was no longer on his way to becoming a monk, Fo continued to strive for the Buddhist goal of tranquility. In all the time he had worked for Wu, this was the first time he'd been asked to handle a withdrawal. Checking his watch, he knew the local branch of Wells Fargo would not be open for two more hours. Making use of his time, he made flight arrangements, which would have him landing on Guam at 6:00 AM on Saturday.

With the flight arrangements made, he went to his storeroom and retrieved two identical footlockers. One million dollars in twenty-dollar bills would weigh just over one hundred pounds. It was far too much for him to carry on the plane with him, so he would have to transport it as checked baggage. Guam was US territory, and he was arriving from California, there would be no customs or other checks of the bag upon arrival. Even though the footlockers looked incredibly average, each was equipped with high-security combination locks that would take an expert locksmith or explosives to open without the proper codes. Fo prudently bought a first-class ticket so there would be no issue with them being lost along the way.

Santos arrived back in his room just before noon. He spent the time while waiting on Madulás' call putting away the things he'd purchased at the BX.

Noon came and went without a phone call. Santos was apprehensive. Typically, he was in control of the situation or at least knew what was coming next. Now he was in a strange land, with no contacts, and in a situation over which he had absolutely no control. He touched the crucifix hanging around his neck, crossed himself, finishing with a kiss on his thumb. *It couldn't hurt.*

This time when the phone awakened him, Santos knew exactly what it was. He had fallen asleep in the room's easy chair, which left his body stiff as he tried to rise quickly to make his way over to the phone. As soon as he picked it up, he could hear crackling, which indicated long-distance.

"Boss?"

"No. Do not refer to me like that on the phone again. We can't be sure when and if someone is listening. No names. No ranks."

While his boss berated him, Santos looked at his watch and saw it was just after three in the afternoon.

"Sorry," Santos responded and then remained quiet, not knowing what was and what was not okay to say.

"The news from here is not good. Customs seized all of the cargo as soon as the C-9 landed. Now they are going through every box and itemizing the contents before turning it over. I truly expect them to provide the inventory to other people who may want to lay claim to things."

"Understood."

"Do you know if anyone has been on the aircraft since you left it?"

"I don't think so, B..." Santos stifled himself, "It is in a secure area, and the crew will not return to it until they get ready to take off."

"See if you can find out when it will be departing."

The phone then went dead. Santos stared at the handset for a moment before replacing it on the phone. Then a thought occurred to him, and after a quick search of his pockets, he located the business card the PAO had provided him. He dialed the number, but when he tried to discuss getting information about the plane, the PAO refused to discuss it. Instead, he insisted on coming over to Santos' room to speak with him in person.

Once the PAO arrived at Santos' room, the Filipino explained he was afraid that due to his current situation, the aircraft would leave without him, and he might not catch up with his property. As the courier, he was responsible for it. The PAO placed a call to Flight Operations and discovered the aircraft was scheduled for departure. He wrote the information down and then provided it to Santos.

"Do you know if anyone accessed the aircraft since last night?"

The PAO was used to handling high maintenance individuals who were passing through. He wasn't sure if it was a combination of jet lag and climate or the sudden lack of modern communication methods. Either way, people stopping in here suddenly became needy. He knew how to handle them, "I can guarantee you no one has entered the aircraft since you and I saw them seal it up last night. In fact, the only ones who can get back into it are the crew. They are the only ones with a key. Also, it is being protected twenty-four/seven by a highly skilled crew of dedicated Air Force Defenders who will ensure no one who isn't supposed to be there can get close to it."

"Uh, okay. It's just I am responsible, and I don't need anything bad to happen. Especially with the way things are right now."

The PAO spent a few more minutes calming Santos down before he departed. Santos didn't have full faith in this man. He seemed to be more worried about keeping him calm than actually doing something about his concerns.

"Babe, what is this about?" Jessi thrust a piece of paper toward him as she took a seat on the edge of the bed. The paper in her hand had obviously been wadded up then flattened again. He knew exactly what it was.

"Ummpf," Dex groaned, bringing himself to an upright position. He saw she was dressed only in a T-shirt, "What're you doing up?" he said while rubbing his eyes and trying to change the subject.

She immediately stood up, then leaned back against his wall locker while crossing her arms, "Well, Paul was making a hell of a lot of noise getting his laundry done, packing, and then finally leaving again. I gave up trying to sleep and thought I might clean up the room since we have a room inspection. Remember, tomorrow is Thursday? Anyway, I found this crumpled up in the corner and thought I would make sure it wasn't something important before I threw it out," Jessi paused. She wanted him to address the piece of paper and tell her the truth about what was going on. She knew his reenlistment was hanging by a thread. Now it looked like the thread was cut. She wanted to know there was something more to do besides watch him fall into the abyss.

"Yeah, I need to go see the First Sergeant to find out if there's anything I can do to change this. Maybe Barr can help. I know he likes the job I do, maybe he can convince them to reconsider."

Jessi heard the words she wanted to hear. What she did not want to hear right now was that he was about to be unemployed with no prospects. Of course, there were the six months left on his current enlistment to find something else. The question was, would he? She loved him, there was no question about that, but she wasn't prepared to sacrifice herself to another man who couldn't get his shit together. She'd gone down that road once already and wasn't going to repeat the mistakes of the past.

"When will you know anything?" For the first time since she'd started talking, she uncrossed her arms. A sign she might be receptive to something he said.

"Tomorrow. I've been working this Goddamned special mission. It's kept me jamming for the last thirty-six hours." He then remembered the most significant event of last night. It was such a big thing, he wasn't sure why it wasn't the front of his mind. *Exhaustion, I guess,* "There's also something else I'm working on, which should come to fruition sometime in the next few days."

"What?" She asked, taking her seat back on the edge of the bed.

"I'll tell you later. I want to make sure it's all gonna work out first. But if it does, it solves everything."

She looked down into his eyes and knew he was telling the truth, at least as he knew it. There was something big going on. She reached out her hands and caressed the side of his face. Jessi decided then to give him a little while longer to figure things out. When he reached up to stroke the side of her face, she turned, taking his finger into her mouth and swirling her tongue over it. She then changed her position and lay down on top of him.

Lying there for a moment, Jessi enjoyed the warmth of her body on his and the feel of his hands as he caressed her back. She'd never loved a man quite the way she loved him. It was far more than just physical, although that part of their relationship was fantastic. She loved the person he was and the person she was when they were together.

Arc Light Memorial - Andersen AFB, Guam

Angel grew tired of waiting for Dawne to return. When she couldn't sleep, she decided to go for a run to burn off her excess anxiety. From the dorms, she took a route proceeding down Perimeter Road toward the Arc Light Memorial.

The landscape featured a B-52D at its center, surrounded by a ring of lights. A sidewalk surrounded the display along with a parking lot and randomly placed benches. Angel slowed to a walk when she reached it before taking a seat on one of the benches. As she caught her breath, she went over the events of the last day.

It seemed every few hours, she was faced with another life-changing decision that demanded an immediate response. It all felt so out of her control, was she doing the right thing by not reporting the cargo theft in progress she'd discovered? Why did she agree to go along with TSgt Gubler? Maybe she should go back to them and demand her share. Maybe Dawne could use it for her father. The thought caused her to pause. Was she willing to give up everything to help Dawne? She couldn't recall ever feeling this way about anyone else. The decisions she was facing all seemed to require some sort of sacrifice or moral ambiguity on her part—all of them except being with Dawne.

As she rose and began her jog back to the dorm, she decided to speak with Gubler tonight when she got on shift. She would take her share of the gold. And she found it easy to make peace with the decision. The gold didn't belong to the person who would benefit from it, and she wasn't taking it to benefit herself but to help someone else. Sure, there were lots of ways this was the wrong thing, but in her mind, she figured a way to justify it all. She decided she loved Dawne.

Airman Dormitories - Andersen AFB, Guam

After Ernie ate, he was able to sleep for a few hours before his roommate loudly entered the room, having completed his duty day. He lay in his bed and listened as his roommate changed out of uniform and then headed back out almost immediately. The situation Ernie found himself in was just eating away at him. It wasn't the first time he'd followed Dex into a rabbit hole he later regretted. Still, this one had ramifications which might include, what? "Prison." Saying this out loud, served to solidify his resolve about the need to extract himself before things went too far. Or maybe things were already too far along.

Ernie sat up and decided he needed his father's advice before doing anything. He got dressed while his mind busily worked on the way to describe the situation without actually saying what was going on. After pulling on his shoes and grabbing his jar of change, he headed over to the recreation center.

The center provided many distractions for the young single Airmen stationed on the base. In addition, they offered one service not available anywhere else on the island—the ability to call home at a reasonable price. Ernie added his name to the waiting list and then took a seat in the TV room while he waited for his turn. About fifteen minutes later, his name was called over the PA system, and he was directed to phone booth six. At the same time, the person behind the counter connected the call to the number he provided.

"Hello?" His father answered after only one ring.

"Hi, Dad, it's me."

"Son! So good to hear from you. Is everything okay?"

"Yeah, Dad, everything's fine. I just needed to talk to you."

"Well, I'm glad you called. I needed to talk to you too, but I was wondering how I was going to be able to do it without having to go through the Red Cross."

"Well, I'm glad you didn't do that. Somebody else's mom called the Red Cross because he hadn't written home in a few weeks, and it got him in all sorts of trouble. Now he is to go to the First Sergeant's office once a week and write a letter to his mom."

Ernie's Dad laughed, "Well, then it's a good thing I waited on you to call. Although getting a letter once a week from you might not be a bad thing."

"Dad! What were you going to call me about anyway?"

"Well, it's your grandmother."

"Is she okay?"

"Yeah, she's doing fine taking care of those two rascals she has now. But they are taking up so much of her time, they let her go from her part-time job at Kmart."

Ernie's grandmother had initially taken the job at the local Kmart not because she needed the money, but because she wanted to get out of the house a few hours every week. When she became responsible for two children, the money went from something extra to something required.

"Wow, that's not good. I've been sending her a few bucks every payday."

"I know, she told me. In fact, she told me to tell you to stop, but that was before this happened. I don't think she would make it without what you're sending. It's why I wanted to get a hold of you before you heard from her and did anything about it."

"Gotcha. Well, I'm able to get by okay. I'll keep sending it to her."

"I'm proud of you, son."

"Thanks, Dad."

The phone went silent for a moment, just the sound of static across the miles.

"Still there, Ernie?"

"Yeah, Dad."

"Well, why'd you call?"

It didn't matter anymore—things had gone from okay to sketchy. Even though things were okay at the moment with his grandmother, he knew it wouldn't take much to tilt it off the track. Right now, he held the solution in his hand. He just needed to swallow hard and accept the fact he was doing it for the right reasons.

"No reason, Dad. I just missed you."

Ernie had said he needed to talk to him, but his father knew him well enough to know he wasn't going to be able to push whatever it was they needed to discuss, "I miss you too, Son. I love you."

"Me too, we'll talk soon."

After Ernie counted out the change from his jar to pay for the call, he walked back to his dorm room. He thought about playing his game again, but, deciding against it, chose to lay down on his bed. Within minutes, he was asleep.

Security Forces Headquarters - Andersen AFB, Guam

Angel made it a point to show up for the shift briefing a little early so she could speak with Gubler before everyone else came into the room. However, Gubler was late, so her early arrival was useless. When Gubler entered, he glanced around the room before his eyes settled on her. She guessed it would be like this from now on. Every time he saw her, Gubler would be reminded of this turning point in their careers. Even as she sat there listening to him drone on about what issues were left by the prior shift, she felt like every few seconds, his eyes were cutting toward her. When the briefing ended, she rushed toward the front of the room and asked if he had a moment. Gubler lifted his hand to silence her as he waited for the other Airmen to depart the room. When the last person left, he closed the door before asking, "What's up?"

"Since I left Zulu last night, I've been thinking about what happened and the g..."

Gubler interrupted her before she could say it, the risk for discussion while in this building was just too high.

"You mean the cargo. What about it?"

She wasn't sure what she'd expected from Gubler, but she had expected him to be somewhat friendlier. The way he was last night. Now he seemed to be all business.

"Right, uh, I gave it a lot of thought, and I do want to..." She was trying to find an appropriate word that was also nondescriptive.

"Participate?" Gubler didn't have time for this. He was already late arriving for the shift, and she was delaying him even further. He'd worked enough criminal cases to know the bad actor usually began to get noticed when they stopped acting normally and started out-of-character behavior. In the three years on the island, he was never late once.

"Yes," Angel was relieved he said it, "I want to participate in what was discussed."

Gubler's own experience in the security field was fueling his slowly building paranoia. Suppose she made a report to the Office of Special Investigation (OSI) after last night, and she was now wearing a wire. He cut his eyes at her, which betrayed the subconscious suspicion he was feeling. Angel knew the look. She had seen it in her father's eyes when he suspected her of lying about something. Suddenly, it occurred to her what was making him suspicious—*my motive.*

"Something came up with my roommate's family. She is going to need some money—a lot of money to take care of her father. I want to help."

Gubler mulled over the rationale she had given him, and it seemed as likely as any. There were rumors about her and her roommate's closeness, but even if they were just good friends, he always got a good person vibe from Angel. She was the kind of person who would want to help if she could.

"I understand. You okay with how things will be shared?"

Angel nodded without speaking.

"Fine, be at the Arc Light at 1900 tomorrow."

A troubled look crossed her face.

"We need to talk over a few things. It'll also give a little time for some details to be worked out. Nothing major, this whole thing will be over by Saturday night."

She was surprised it was this easy, but when she'd said she wanted out of the arrangement the night before, he had offered her an easy way to come back in, now she had taken it.

"Thank you, TSgt Gubler." She picked up her equipment and

backpack before heading for the door.

Gubler returned to the podium, picked up his notebook, and slipped it into his pocket as he reflected on what just happened. The share for the four would return to the original amounts. It was no problem for him. Even with Wu's commission, there was plenty left over to make the effort worthwhile. He picked up the balance of his equipment and headed for the door himself, happy with the thought that soon he would no longer have any obligation to Wu or the casino.

When he arrived on shift, Gubler checked the status of tail #0022. He was told it had departed early and would land at 0750 Hawaii time. He was still nervous about what had happened, but figured by noon Hawaii time, if any shit were going to hit the fan, it would have done so by then. Gubler smiled to himself as he figured the time difference would be high noon tomorrow.

Chapter 7

Hilton Waikiki Beach, Honolulu Hawaii

Madulás had just dozed off when the sound of the key in the door lock brought him fully awake. He moved from the chair he was sitting in to just inside the bathroom near the front door. He watched as a hand snaked through the partially open door and turned on the light switch before the entrant kicked the door wide open and stepped in. As soon as Hamster was fully inside the room, Madulás put his forearm across the man's throat. At the same time, he injected a syringe of various chemicals into the side of his neck. It only took a few seconds before Hamster was lying in a crumpled pile on the floor.

Looking at the now empty syringe, Madulás was thankful that Customs had been far too busy with Marcos and his upper-level cronies to bother with him when they'd arrived in Hawaii. It had allowed him to sneak half a dozen syringes of a sedative he'd had a college student develop for him. After several human tests that helped him determine the proper nonlethal dosage, he found it to be the most beneficial weapon in his arsenal.

As he regained consciousness, Hamster attempted to move his limbs and quickly found he was firmly duct-taped to a chair. Looking down at his arm, he could see a towel was laid over his arm before the duct tape was applied. He didn't know that Madulás did this to prevent any bruising or telltale signs the man had been restrained from appearing on his arms.

He attempted to open his mouth to speak only to find it was also bound, he assumed by duct tape. The desk lamp was aimed in such a way it shown directly into his face and prevented Hamster from seeing anything in the darkness behind it. He could tell there was motion, and by squinting, he could see what appeared to be metallic dots moving. *No, not dots. Teeth? Golden teeth?*

"Glad to see you are back," a raspy voice from the darkness said. "I've been told you go by the name Hamster. Shall I call you that or is there something else you would prefer."

Hamster attempted to speak, but of course, his mouth was gagged.

"Ah, I beg your pardon. I forgot you are a bit restrained at the moment. Now, I will remove the restraint so we can talk. When our conversation is complete, and if you have been honest with me, I will remove the rest of the restraints. You will be free to return to your normal activities. However, if you attempt to call for help or have lied to me," at this point, Hamster sensed a fast-moving mass in the darkness then suddenly felt the cold barrel of a pistol pressed against his forehead. "Well, I guess it can go without saying, no?" With his mouth taped shut, Hamster drew air in through his nose. The smell of diseased gums and rotting teeth was inescapable, as was his desire to retch from it.

Pulling the gun back from contact with his head, Madulás turned the gun so Hamster could see it, "Do we have an understanding?" Hamster slowly nodded in agreement. Madulás withdrew a knife from his pocket and opened it, cutting the duct tape and then pulling it free from Hamster's head.

As Madulás took a step back, Hamster drew several deep breaths through his mouth in an attempt to clear the stench which seemed to surround this man. His tormentor then took a seat in a chair behind the lamp in the darkness.

"What do you want?" Hamster asked.

"I have some questions about cargo missing from an aircraft for which you were the loadmaster. Tail #0022."

"What are you talking about? I don't know anything about missing cargo."

Madulás leaned forward, but not far enough for his features to be visible to Hamster. He'd used this technique before on victims to plant the image of a wild animal about to pounce from just beyond the edge of the darkness.

"You picked up a load of cargo in the Philippines, and then flew to Guam. After an overnight stay, you brought the plane from there to Hickam Air Force Base. Upon arrival here, you handed the aircraft over to US Customs officials who handled the download of the cargo."

Hamster's mind cleared a little now, so he remembered a little more, "Hey, all I did was babysit the cargo. It was already loaded on the plane in the PI, and nothing happened to it until I got here."

Madulás motions were fast. Hamster didn't realize his inquisitor was upon him until the plastic bag was over his head, and he couldn't inhale as the bag shrunk around his head.

Madulás could feel the man's body trying to move but failing to do so because it was restrained. The sounds which were escaping were minimal, as the man's oxygen quickly ran out, and panic prevented him from being able to form words. Slowly, Hamster's body stopped fighting the restraints as the muscles lacked oxygen to fuel them, and eventually, his head fell forward. Madulás removed the plastic shopping bag and took a seat while the man fought to bring oxygen back into his body.

"Please stop assuming I am stupid or don't know what you did. The cargo load arrived here incomplete. I have seen the inventory completed by the customs officials and it lists a box on one of the pallets contained in an assortment of metal gears as well as one hundred and twenty-five, twenty-five-pound National Bank of the Philippines gold bars."

Hamster raised his head and stared into the darkness in front of him. His expression was blank, which surprised Madulás. It didn't convince him the man had not taken the gold bars, just that he might be an accomplished liar.

"You see, when this box was packed in the Philippines, one hundred thirty-seven gold bars were placed into it, and the lid was bolted down. U.S. Customs included a note that the lid was missing one of the bolts designed to secure it. Someone opened it."

Hamster attempted to speak and instead coughed due to the rawness of his throat. Madulás retrieved a glass from the bathroom and filled it with water, then held it to the man's lips so he could take a drink. He continued to keep it there until Hamster nodded, he was finished.

"I don't know anything about any gold. I don't know anything about a box."

"Well, why don't you tell me about the people who were on the airplane besides you."

"The flight crew?"

"No, not them. Was there anyone else?"

"Yeah, some Filipino guy who claimed to be a courier. Maybe he stole your gold."

Madulás knew he was speaking of Santos, but he didn't feel it was necessary to let Hamster know it. "This Filipino, he was able to break into the pallet in flight, and when he left the aircraft, he was carrying a bag weighing three hundred pounds?"

"No, no. Nobody carried off any bags, you asshole."

Again, Madulás was on Hamster and the plastic bag over his head. Some sense of futile anger motivated Hamster to sit perfectly still rather than fighting against the lack of oxygen. Within a minute, he was forced to attempt to inhale, and when he did, there was nothing except for the plastic bag tightening around his face. Rather than trying to move his arms or legs, he only attempted to move his head from side to side. As he did this, Hamster fought to bite at the bag, which led to Madulás holding his head still as Hamster suffocated. This time, Madulás waited until all motions stopped, and the man's head lolled forward before removing the bag. Hamster did not immediately return to consciousness, so Madulás slapped him on his cheeks until his head moved.

Returning to his seat, Madulás stared at the man for a few minutes, allowing his breathing to return to normal.

"I think you would much prefer this little question and answer period to remain civil, I know I would. So, apologize for your words, and we will continue."

This man is nuts. He knew nothing about any gold. He also knew no one would be looking for him for another eight to ten hours. He was going to have to deal with this man somehow if he expected to stay alive.

"Sorry," Hamster croaked, his raw throat barely allowing him to speak, "He was the only one onboard the plane…"

Madulás knew the man was about to say something else but, for some reason, paused. He gripped the plastic bag in his hand, and when he did, it made a crinkling noise, which drove Hamster to continue speaking.

"Cargo guys. Two cargo guys in Guam got on board to check the way the pallets were built out of the PI. They looked around, added a few straps, and then got off the airplane before we locked it up. They took maybe thirty to forty-five minutes."

"Fine, so now we know about two more people who were on the airplane. When they got off, were they carrying anything?"

"Huh? No, they were carrying nothing. And there was a cop."

This surprised Madulás, "A police officer? You mean like someone from law enforcement or Customs?"

"Neither. A sky cop. Air Force security police. Not too tall, kinda cute. Dark hair and eyes, but she wasn't on the plane longer than maybe five minutes."

"Do you know the names of these people?"

Hamster stared into the darkness at Madulás for a moment, then sighed, "No. No names. We weren't introduced."

"I see. Once these people were off your airplane, you locked it so no one could gain entry until you came back the next day. Correct?"

"Well, not exactly."

Madulás stared at the man and then leaned forward again, parting his lips in a silent growl, "Explain."

"Military aircraft do not have locks on the doors. Anybody who knows where the door release handle is can open the plane and get inside."

Hamster could hear from his attacker's forced breathing he was getting angry.

"But, hey, it's not like everyone has access to the flightline. The base parked us in this special secure area, which only a few people could get into."

"Like?"

"Well, aside from the aircrew, I guess the cargo guys and the cute sky cop."

Madulás sat back in his chair and mulled over the facts he now possessed. He didn't believe Hamster took anything or was aware of anything taken. The guard he spoke of was a woman. Even a woman of large stature could not have carried three-hundred pounds by herself. He withdrew his cigarette from his shirt pocket and lit it.

"Hey, this is a non-smoking ro—" Hamster started to protest but then thought better of it.

Madulás looked toward him briefly before returning to his thoughts. The two cargo handlers had a small bit of time on the aircraft. They could have discovered something which looked interesting and then come back later when there were fewer witnesses. Three hundred pounds could be handled by two people relatively easily. Any more would be cumbersome. It also would've given the two of them one and one half million dollars each, more than sufficient motivation.

Madulás walked through the hotel room and then opened the curtains and drew back the door which led to the balcony. Taking a step out, he took a final drag on his cigarette before flicking it over the rail and watching it fall twenty-three stories to the ground. Of course, he never saw it hit the ground, it was much too far away. Across the horizon, there wasn't much to see. This was the cheap government-contracted side of the hotel, which lacked the beautiful views and instead looked out over parking lots.

He pulled his doubloon from his pocket and began to roll it between his fingers. This was not at all the way things were supposed to work out. During his career, he'd managed to set aside sufficient assets so he could have a comfortable retirement. Now, everything had been seized one way or another. But also, he was being given an opportunity. If he could locate and recover the missing bars of gold, he would have sufficient means for a comfortable existence for the rest of his life. Not the extravagance he'd planned, but comfortable. Also, since he was the only one who knew how many bars of gold were in the box to start with, no one would be looking for the other twelve except him. He allowed his lips to pull back into a smile, which appeared to be more of a sneer. He then heard Hamster cough from inside the room.

As he walked back in, Madulás pocketed the doubloon and withdrew his pocketknife and opened it. He cut the duct tape away from Hamster's legs first, being careful to remove the tape and set it to one side. Next, he removed the tape from his wrists and likewise set it to one side. Hamster was confused and weakened, so he allowed himself to be led toward the balcony without resisting.

"You know, the Philippines is a much more beautiful place than Hawaii."

"Yeah, I like the PI. The women are a lot prettier there too."

Madulás reached out a hand and patted Hamster on the back once, and then on the second pat, pushed him forward. Hamster immediately grabbed for the handrail in front of him to catch his balance. His mind couldn't figure out what was going on when the rail came off in his hand. Then the rest of the latticework of metal came apart in a dozen or so pieces and began to fall toward the ground. He turned and grabbed for Madulás, who simply took a step back as gravity took hold, and the man fell off the balcony. There wasn't sufficient time during the twenty-story fall onto the roof of the restaurant below for Hamster to figure out Madulás had loosened all the bolts holding the railing system. It was information Hamster would never be able to share anyway.

When Madulás reentered the room, he left the door of the balcony open and then gathered up all the bits of tape as well as the plastic bag he'd used to torment the loadmaster. Giving the room a final once over, he wiped his fingerprints from the doorknob as he exited the room. At the end of the hall, he took the stairs down rather than the elevator. Shortly, he was back in his room at the visiting officer's quarters on Hickam Air Force Base. He packed his suitcase in preparation to depart the following morning. It had been many years since he'd last visited Guam.

Angel was the first of the group to arrive at the memorial. After realizing she was the first one there, she decided to kill time by reading the plaque which gave a brief history of the Arc Light mission. Motion off to her left caught her eye, and she looked over to see Ernie and Dex walking toward the monument together. The two were talking back-and-forth and laughing as they walked. *Those idiots*, she thought, *we don't need to be drawing attention to ourselves.*

Rather than speaking to her, the two walked past to a bench where Ernie sat down. Dex chose to sit on the seatback with his feet on the bench. The two continued talking until their attention was drawn to a pickup truck slowly entering the monument area. It was Gubler. Noticing her supervisor, Angel walked to where he was parking and greeted him as he climbed out of the truck.

"Hey, boss," Angel said, continuing to walk toward him.

Reaching into the back of the pickup, Gubler opened a cooler to withdraw two cans of Miller Lite. He opened one and handed it to her before opening his own and taking a long pull.

"Been waiting long?"

"Not so much. I got here ten minutes early on purpose," Gubler stared at her for a moment but didn't speak. "I figured I should get here a little early just to scope to place out and make sure we weren't overly obvious." Her explanation satisfied Gubler's curiosity, so he remained silent, taking another drink of his beer as Dex and Ernie approached.

When he thought they were close enough to hear him, Gubler instructed them to continue walking past his truck and to have a seat on the bench about eight feet away. They would be close enough to hear, but not so close they appeared to all be together.

"Okay, as you can all tell, Angel has decided to join us. This means the share for each of us is now three bars," Gubler paused for a minute to see if anyone wanted to comment.

Since new information was being shared, Dex thought he would add the information he had, "I checked with ATOC and Balls 22 took off two hours early. It landed in Hikam at 0350 our time and was immediately impounded by Customs for inventory. It's scheduled to be released any time now."

Again, no one commented, but they all sat quietly in case anyone else had information for the group.

"Since we were last together, I found a way to convert the gold into dollars. Angel, I explained to these guys last night we were going to need someone to change the gold into currency. The downside is the person doing the exchange wants fifty percent for providing the service."

"What? What about if we just want to take our share in gold bars instead of dollars?" Dex may have been the only one asking this question, but the same thought occurred to Angel and Ernie.

"Dex I told you when we were still on the flightline we would have to pay to convert the gold to cash. You have to know it will be difficult to deal with seventy-five pounds of gold. Add to that, you have no way to explain how you came about it legally. Don't forget, each one of those bars has the imprint of the National Bank of the Philippines. By giving up a little, you still finish the day with right at two hundred thousand dollars in circulated twenty-dollar bills. Those bills weigh forty pounds or so, which aren't hard to move around, and the bills are easy to spend with little suspicion. As long as you don't spend too many in one place at one time, you would never have to explain any of it," Gubler paused. Since he was trying to make it look like the four of them were not together, he couldn't see Dex and Ernie, so he had no way of knowing their body language while he was speaking.

"Fine. We'll go with *your* guy," Dex finally said.

"Look, don't be an asshole. He's not *my guy*. I really don't give a shit who we use. Why don't you go find somebody who will do it for the same amount or less, that way we can go with *your guy*."

Angel couldn't prevent herself from smiling. She knew this was less about Gubler being a pain in the ass and him just being high enough on the food chain that he wasn't used to having things he said questioned or doubted.

"Calm down." Dex's problem with authority figures was about to burst forth.

"Okay, so we've got this guy," Ernie interjected, hoping to calm things down by moving the conversation along, "and we agreed to give him half. You said something about circulated twenty-dollar bills?"

The interruption was enough to slow Gubler's roll. When he was busy explaining things, he didn't have time to be angry about them.

"Right, it means the bills are not too crisp and clean looking, so they won't attract attention. Realistically, you could walk into your bank in Pigs Knuckle, Mississippi, back in the states and deposit them without anyone batting an eye."

Ernie rose to his feet, and Dex immediately stood up behind him, grabbing him by the shoulders. In a soft voice, Dex spoke, "Calm down, buddy. He didn't mean nothing by it."

After a moment, Ernie nodded and sat back down. Dex sat down as well, this time next to Ernie rather than on the back of the seat.

Angel had been listening to all of this and wrote off a lot of bluster going back-and-forth as guys trying to show each other up. She was mentally considering the questions she wanted answered. Now.

"When do we get our cash?"

"On the first, as soon as I exchange the gold for the cash, we meet, and I handoff everybody's share. Then we all go our separate ways."

"Who takes care of the exchange, and what about security?"

Security? Gubler hadn't thought about it. It was a lot of money. He'd seen movies, and sometimes bad guys got robbed in the process of a deal. But he also knew the rules kept him from owning a firearm on Guam. There was also no way for him to check one out from the Security Forces Armory when he wasn't on duty.

"I'll go along to provide security."

Even though they were attempting to look nonchalant, neither of the security forces defenders could resist the urge to stare down Dex for making such a statement.

"You?" Gubler challenged

"Yes"

"Really? What if they have guns?"

"I've got a gun."

"What?"

"A Colt 1911. Is that satisfactory?"

Another hundred questions flooded Angel's mind after hearing his statement. The cop side of Gubler took over as he wondered about the pistol's origins. Neither of them said a word, they just let it go. At this point, they didn't want any more information they would rather not have access to.

"Fine, you and I will go do the transfer on Saturday," Gubler said as he turned back toward Angel, "Anything else?"

"How will we know we got away with it?"

At first, the question struck Gubler as Angel's attempt at being a smartass. Then he realized she was naïve enough to be serious. He was pondering the answer, but before he could say a word, Ernie answered.

"Customs is about to be released to Marcos and Company and somebody is going to go to that box first thing. Once they discover part of their booty is missing, the reaction is going to be immediate. I'd say, if you hear a knock at your door in about sixteen hours, it might be the FBI."

Dex shrugged his shoulders at what Ernie said and then nodded.

"Yeah, as for Ferdinand himself, everything I see the news it says he's more worried about finding somewhere safe to live who won't send him back to the PI. Realistically, the only reach out he has any more is maybe some old friends in the CIA. They would probably show up within a week."

Gubler considered what Dex said and turned to face Angel.

"All of it sounds about right, the only thing which would

probably go beyond a week would be where you came up with so much money out of the blue. I know I said you could probably just deposit it right into your bank, but you should probably do it over several months rather than all at once."

Angel was sure she broke something inside her head when she prevented herself from rolling her eyes at Gubler's last statement. *The man thinks I'm an idiot. No, the idiot man thinks I'm just as stupid as he is.* She finally managed to say, "Understood."

Gubler waited in silence a moment in case there were more questions. When none were asked, he instructed Dex to call him in the morning about picking up the footlocker.

"As soon as I get final times on the exchange, I'll let you know, and we'll set up something to fill up the footlocker and get our money."

"That works," Dex said as he stood up and prepared to leave, "I'm ready to finish this up and move on," he paused for a second in case anyone else wanted to comment. Then he turned and slowly walked away. Ernie followed closely after him, and once he caught up, the two walked back to the dorm together.

"You know, I kind of wish those two guys weren't even involved," Gubler said as he watched them walk away.

"If they weren't involved, we never would've known about this."

"True. See you later, the shift briefing."

"Yes, sir."

Angel turned and walked across the grass toward the NCO Club before turning toward the Airman dormitories herself. Gubler jumped in his truck and went back home for a few hours before returning to base for his shift.

Flight Operations, Hikam AFB, Hawaii

As he walked into Flight Operations, Madulás was disappointed to find a profound lack of Filipinos working there. It was always a possibility. Smartly, he'd decided to wear his camouflage utility uniform in case he needed to deal with U.S. military personnel. Most Americans were not familiar with the rank insignia of the Philippine military. As a result, when they saw the star worn by a Philippine Army colonel, they automatically assumed the wearer was a brigadier general. A colonel received a certain amount of military courtesy, a general even more.

"Sir, can I help you?" The captain behind the desk said as he rose to his feet.

"At ease, Captain. I just came by to see about flight availability to Andersen."

The captain picked up the clipboard and flipped through a few pages, "Normally, we have several a day, but there has been a moratorium on flights destined there." The captain was about to make a comment about the upheaval in the Philippines when he looked up from his clipboard and realized he wasn't sure how it might be taken.

"I see," Madulás said as he scanned the flight board on the wall behind the captain, "What about that one? Departs at 0400. It shows zero seats available, but isn't it possible the jump seat might be empty?"

The captain spun around to see what the general was looking at, and his eyes zoomed in on the 0400 flight.

"Hmm, well, it is a cargo-only mission due to the hazardous material it's carrying. Only military members are allowed on board."

Madulás smiled with his lips pressed together, "I am military, and my country has been a strong ally with the U.S. for many decades."

"Uh, no, that's not what I meant," the captain knew he'd screwed up, "I meant only U.S. military were allowed."

"But not allies?"

The captain didn't have an answer. No one had ever asked about it in such detail in the past. In actuality, the cargo wasn't hazardous. It was only considered sensitive. Something headed to the American Embassy in the Philippines. Yet another reason not to block the general.

"Sir, we have a few hours before the flight. Let me do some checking and see if I can figure out if I can do something for you," the captain said as he picked up the phone.

"A good idea. While I'm waiting, could you provide me with the after-hours number for the Base Commander? He might know a way to expedite my clearance onboard this aircraft. Oh, but look at the time," Madulás clicked his tongue several times while shaking his head, "I really hate to disturb the man at this hour. But I need to be on board a particular aircraft."

"But sir, I am working on it…"

"Indeed. In fact, could I get your full name as well? I want to be sure I let him know exactly who is handling the matter."

The captain glanced at the folder for the aircraft and saw it was flying with a minimal crew, which meant the jump seat in the cockpit would be open. *Not anymore.*

"Sir, to expedite things for you, and realizing your time is important, I've added you to a manifest for the aircraft. You will indeed be sitting in the cockpit jump seat. You should be here ninety minutes before departure with any baggage you have so you can ride out with the aircrew."

"Excellent, I truly appreciate your assistance with this." He paused for a moment as an idea came to him, "Is there a payphone around here?"

The captain picked up the phone from his desk and placed it on the counter, "This phone is AUTOVON, the prefix for Andersen is 315."

At first, Madulás was going to turn down the offer. He often heard the military long-distance service AUTOVON was heavily monitored. But he decided the call was just to transmit some quick arrival information and should not arouse suspicion.

Looking at his watch, he calculated the time in Guam to be 1630. He dialed the number using the prefix the captain provided. After a few seconds, he heard the familiar double ring of an AUTOVON phone call. Santos answered in a voice both suspicious and curious until he found out it was Madulás. The flight arrival information in Guam was passed on. As soon as Santos confirmed it, Madulás hung up. The call lasted less than forty seconds.

Madulás returned to Flight Operations at the required time carrying a small overnight bag, so it was not x-rayed before boarding the aircraft. Due to his status, he was offered a preferred seat on the flight deck, which pushed the loadmaster and cargo courier to the rear of the C-141.

Shortly after takeoff, Madulás closed his eyes, not to open them again until the plane was on final approach. As he departed the aircraft and was taken to Flight Operations on Andersen Air Force Base, the crew was thankful he was not flying further on the aircraft.

"Damn, did you see that guy's teeth? Don't they have dentists in the Philippines?" the copilot asked the flight engineer.

"Dunno, but with where he was sitting, I got a constant barrage of bad breath. Luckily, I was able to move the air vent, so it was redirected away from me."

"That stench wasn't redirected anywhere. It hung in the air on the flight deck from the time we took off until just now. I requested Trans Alert spray the flight deck with some kind of *stench cover* while we refuel."

Santos met Madulás at Flight Operations. He made arrangements with the PAO to get a staff car given Madulás' rank but would have to return it by 1500. Madulás' bags did not have to be cleared with customs, nor was there any immigration check since he flew from one spot in America to another.

After the two men were in the car, Madulás said, "I was able to speak to the loadmaster. He mentioned several people who accessed the aircraft."

Santos immediately stiffened. He'd done his best but was not exactly in control of the situation. Now he felt like his boss was accusing him of failure. Sensing this, Madulás reached out and patted Santos' arm, "No worries. You did what you could. Now, we need to correct the situation. I do not want to use this staff car for anything we are about to do, is there a place we can rent a vehicle?"

"You got it, Boss, I saw one next to the BX. I'll head that way."

"Good, good. You didn't happen to bring your Colt 1911 with you from the Philippines, did you?"

Santos didn't want to admit he lost possession of the weapon onboard the plane. It seemed like a detail best dealt with later. He was opposed to lying but had no problem only giving a selective version of the truth, "No, Boss, I arrived with no baggage and no weapon. The only reason I have clean clothes is because the PAO gave me an allowance. I'm sorry I was not more prepared."

"No worries, I did not give you sufficient time to prepare for your departure. We will deal with it more completely once we've recovered what was stolen."

"Stolen?"

"Yes, customs in Hawaii seized all of the property. When they inventoried it, the count for the gold bars was off by a dozen. So, while the airplane was here, somebody removed twelve bars of gold."

"But who? How?"

"Tsk, tsk," Madulás clicked his tongue, "not to worry, we will rectify the situation. Since all the other treasure is now lost, it is vitally important we recover these twelve bars."

Santos had many questions, but they were now at the BX, and Madulás arranged for a car rental. At the same time, Santos contacted the PAO and informed him he was going to leave the car at the base exchange. Once the baggage was transferred from the sedan to the SUV Madulás rented, they were again on the road. The first stop Madulás wanted to make was the Security Forces Headquarters building.

Once again, the lack of knowledge concerning his rank worked to his advantage. This time, however, rather than being threatening, he was overly friendly toward the bored Security Forces Desk Sergeant on duty. Within a few minutes, he was examining the event logs of 25 and 26 February, he was even provided with a pad and paper to make notes. Madulás scanned through the pages until he located the tail number of the C-141 which transported the cargo from the Philippines. Once he found the correct entry, he discovered the Security Forces Defender who'd worked the aircraft was A1C Angelina Perez. He wrote the name on the pad and then flipped to the back of the event log. He was pleased to see it contained a roster which included the names, addresses, and available phone numbers for all the personnel in the unit. Once he located her on the list, he jotted that information down as well.

Madulás didn't think Angel stole the gold alone. She was a low-ranking nothing who would not have been able to accomplish the theft without assistance. She was just the next person in the chain who could provide them with information. The information would lead him to the location of his property so it could be recovered. Once recovered, Madulás would be off to… where? Events had kept him so busy trying to ensure he kept control of his property, his eventual destination had not been given much thought. *Something for later.*

After returning the event logs to the Desk Sergeant, the two men went back to the car and used the base map to locate Angel's dormitory. Madulás could feel the start of a bad headache. He had not eaten in almost twenty hours, nor consumed his usual amount of coffee. Rather than proceeding directly to the dormitory, the two men went to the snack bar for a quick meal.

Airman Dormitories - Andersen AFB, Guam

Angel moved from lying on her side to her back and then stretched. She'd arrived in the room after shift and found Dawne sleeping soundly. Rather than disturbing her with a discussion of details about her father and upcoming trip to the US, she chose to simply strip down to a T-shirt and panties before climbing into bed with her. Let the discussion wait for the next morning. Lifting her arm in the air, she squinted at her watch and saw it was almost 1630. Angel didn't have to be up at any particular time, as she wasn't working tonight. She was happy to be where she was, next to Dawne and enjoying a moment of peace. Rolling away from Dawne and onto her side, she reached out and took a glass of water from the bedside table. As Angel took a sip, she could feel Dawne's body moving behind her to spoon her in the new position. It felt nice.

Angel shifted her arms and legs until she found a comfortable spot in the bed. Once still, the bed was again in motion as Dawne adjusted herself to Angel's new position. The dance ended with Dawne maneuvering her hips against Angel in an attempt to get as close to her as possible. Outside, the temperature might've been eighty degrees, but they kept the room a cool sixty-five. This allowed for the two of them to be close without overheating.

Angel was still, but she wasn't going back to sleep. She was thinking about the events of the last few days and the meeting at the Arc Light. She was anxious to tell Dawne about the solution for any money problems her father's illness might cause. At the same time, Angel was unsure how she would explain her sudden wealth. It didn't matter. There was time. Dawne was about to leave, and it would be at least a couple weeks before she was back. By then, all the money issues would be settled, and hopefully by then, she would have a story.

As Angel lay there, she became aware of a sensation on the back of her neck. It was soft and warm. It only took a moment before she realized it was Dawne's tongue gliding across the flesh just below her hairline at the back of her neck. Her first action was uncontrolled as she found herself pressing her ass back into Dawne as she shifted her legs and gently moaned. Angel wanted to give in to her urge to roll onto her back so she could enjoy Dawne's tongue all over her body. But she found herself resisting it.

Dawne knew Angel was enjoying the feel of her tongue but

174

preferred to proceed without saying anything to avoid any possibility of being told to stop. Her licking turned into gentle kisses, which proceeded on to her gently biting Angel's neck as she moved from the back to the side. At the same time, she put her arm around Angel while pulling her T-shirt up and out of the way. Dawne then ran her fingertips slowly across Angel's bare stomach just above her navel.

Angel felt her body waking up, not from being asleep but from being touched by someone for whom she held powerful feelings. When Dawne's fingertips moved lower to caressing her just above the bikini line, her moan turned into a low howl. She was letting herself be enraptured. It was as if lightning was slowly streaking across her flesh while she begged it not to find an end. When Dawne's fingertips began to glide lower on her tummy, Angel forced herself to roll away from her while coming to a sitting position at the foot of the bed.

"Well, you're awake," she cleared her throat while pulling the blanket around her exposed body and so she wasn't sitting there almost naked.

"Yeah, and I was ready for some breakfast in bed before you interrupted me," Dawne realized her tone was a bit too mean as her frustration came out.

"Oh, baby, I'm sorry. I still want us to have our talk before we…"

"Before we?"

"Hey, we haven't talked about what happened with you going back to the states, and your father, and…"

Dawne audibly exhaled, the moment having passed once again, "well, everything is set up. I fly out of here later tonight."

"Here, here—or here downtown?"

"Here on base. Getting a C5, I have to be there by 2300." Dawne reached out her hand and placed it on Angel's knee and slowly began to caress her way up to her inner thigh, "Now you know. We have some time?"

Angel reached between her legs and took Dawne's hand in hers. As she did this, she interlaced her fingers with Dawne's, "Yeah, we have some time all right," she kissed the back of Dawne's hand while considering whether the other woman knew how wet she was, "but before we do, we need to talk. But not here. It's only 1630, why don't we go downtown and have dinner at a nice place where we can talk." Angel thought she could see traces of rejection in Dawne's eyes and knew she must belay it. "If we head out in the next half hour or so, we could have plenty of time for dinner, our talk, and even something delicious for dessert," as she spoke the words, she turned Dawne's hand and placed the palm between her breasts. Slowly, she guided the hand down her stomach until it was almost between her legs where she released it.

Angel could see no rejection in Dawne's eyes now, only hunger. Even though she thought better of it, she allowed Dawne to slide her hand under the top of her panties—until her fingertips caressed...

Angel sprang out of bed, leaving the blanket behind her, "Heading for the shower."

"Right behind you."

Instead of immediately getting up, Dawne lay flat on her back and reveled in the moment, feeling satisfied with the plan Angel had created. She breathed in deeply and could smell the scent of Angel's arousal. Even with all that was going on with her father, this was something good in her life—something she needed to enjoy.

After they finished eating, Madulás and Santos headed for the dormitory where Angel lived. Once they figured out which room belonged to her, the two sat in the parking lot, contemplating their next move. While the two men sat in silence, they watched as the door they were surveilling opened. A blonde woman in a robe exited and walked toward the other end of the building using the balcony which ran the length of the floor.

"Is it her?"

"No, Boss. This girl's hair is not dark. A roommate, maybe?"

"Go see what you can find."

"You got it."

Shortly, Madulás watched as Santos appeared on the balcony where the blonde girl had been. He slowly walked past the door where they'd watched her exit, then turned around and walked past it again.

"The placard on the door says she has a roommate named Dawne. That must've been her we saw," Santos said as he reentered the car and closed the door.

"There she is again," Madulás said, nodding upward toward the balcony as Dawne returned and reentered the room.

"Did you see? Her hair was wet. Maybe the shower is down the hall," Santos said.

"Obviously." The thought had occurred to Madulás. Still, he wasn't going to let Santos assume he was the only one who would come to that realization. "We will need to sit here until Angel comes out alone and leaves or Dawne departs leaving Angel by herself.

"You got it, Boss."

Madulás was unaware of how long he snoozed when Santos shook him. He could feel his body bathed in sweat even though the car was idling so the air-conditioner could run.

"Look, they're both leaving."

Glancing up, Madulás could see Santos was correct. Both women were leaving together. Shortly, the two exited the building and climbed into a twenty-year-old beat up Volkswagen bug locally referred to as a *Guam Bomb*. He noticed both of them were dressed up with one wearing a short skirt. It was as if they were going out. After they exited the parking lot, he directed Santos to follow.

Shortly, the two vehicles departed the base and, after proceeding a few miles down the road, made a right-hand turn into the Tumon Bay area. Tumon Bay was not an area visited by most locals or the military. It was primarily the stomping ground for Japanese tourists visiting the island. As a result, the restaurant and entertainment venues were pricey and targeted food and music sought by Japanese.

Santos allowed for two cars to get between them and the two women. It wasn't difficult to follow them as theirs was the only older model vehicle on the strip. The rental SUV the men were in blended perfectly with the vehicles in traffic. After going through a few lights, the car pulled into the parking lot of what appeared to be an Italian restaurant. Santos ducked into the parking lot across the street where the two could observe what the women were doing. After finding a place to park, the women exited their car and walked toward the entrance to the restaurant.

"Keep an eye on them, I'm going to change, and I'll be right back."

Madulás exited the vehicle and then grabbed his carry-on from the back seat. He was displeased Santos chose to pull into a hotel parking lot, but, luckily, next door to it was what appeared to be a small bar. As he walked through the door, he gave his eyes a moment to adjust before walking directly to the restroom. Once inside, he locked the door and changed from the jungle fatigues he was wearing into a pair of shorts and a tropical shirt. After stuffing his boots into his carry-on, he slipped on a pair of flip-flops then walked directly from the bathroom back out into the parking lot. He got back into the passenger side of the car and without speaking a word, pointed through the windshield at the restaurant. Santos nodded then pulled across the road into the lot adjoining the Italian restaurant. Finding an open spot a few cars down from the Volkswagen, he parked, and the two men entered the restaurant.

Madulás was pleased to see the restaurant dining room with quite a few patrons even though it was still early in the evening. It would allow them to hide in the crowd. He asked for a table across from where the two women were sitting. He didn't have to worry about being noticed. The two women appeared to be so self-involved they wouldn't have noticed if the place was on fire. At first, Madulás thought this was curious they would be so attentive to each other, as if they were lovers. The realization made him smile. Now he knew the source of information as well as a way to motivate her to share that information.

To blend in, Madulás and Santos ordered drinks as well as a meal, even though neither man was hungry, having just eaten. They weren't close enough to hear the conversation, but it was easy to tell the two women were celebrating something. When Dawne got up to go to the restroom, Angel was left by herself for a moment. Madulás saw this as an opportunity to set up the next stage. He rose, and as he walked past Angel's table, he pretended to trip, falling to one knee. With Angel distracted, he reached into her purse which was hanging on the back of her chair.

"Oh, are you okay, sir?" Angel said, having stood to help Madulás to his feet.

"Fine, my dear, just getting clumsy with my age, I guess," he grabbed what he knew to be her wallet as he worked his way back to his feet. He looked directly into her eyes to keep her attention on him and not what his hands were doing. Once on his feet, he slid her wallet into his pocket.

"Thank you for your concern," he said, nodding at her, and then he walked off toward the restroom.

Angel sat down again and began fiddling with her napkin. Their dinner plates were gone, and it was almost time to leave. She was excited as she knew it would be a night like none other in her life.

Once inside the bathroom, Madulás removed Angel's wallet from his pocket. He began to search through it, looking for her military ID card. It might've been simpler just to keep the entire wallet, but he didn't want her to notice she was missing something until she got back to base. As he withdrew the card from her wallet, he took a glance at the picture, as with most of these he'd ever seen, it was unflattering. Slipping the ID card into his pocket, he palmed the wallet and then exited the bathroom.

As he walked past Angel's table again, he saw she was still alone. Madulás veered toward it then leaned over and took her hand,

"Thank you again for your kindness, I hope you enjoy your evening," as he spoke in a friendly tone, he dropped her wallet back into the purse which was still agape and hanging on the back of her chair.

Angel was a bit embarrassed by this but nodded at the older man, anxious to be rid of him. Because she was busy with him, she missed

Dawne returning to the table. As Madulás walked away, she said, "I just can't take you anywhere, the minute I leave, you go picking up old men."

"Yeah, that's me," as she spoke, both women returned to their chairs, then Angel reached out and took Dawne's hand. Looking directly into her eyes, she said, "After the last few hours, I realize we don't need to talk at all. Why don't we go home, crawl into bed together, and enjoy what few hours we have left before you have to leave."

As Dawne looked back at Angel, she could see the sincerity in the woman's eyes and could feel the temperature rising in the hand which held hers.

"Let's go."

Madulás barely settled back in his seat when he looked up and saw the women were leaving.

"Put some money on the table. We need to go."

Santos promptly stood up and took a one-hundred-dollar bill from his pocket, which would more than cover the check, and dropped it on the table. Because they needed to be behind the women, the men feigned looking at the decor of the restaurant as they headed toward the door. Madulás glanced over in time to see Angel removing bills from her wallet and counting them out on the table before the two women headed for the door.

Santos and Madulás could hear the doors of the Volkswagen closing as they walked out the door of the restaurant. They proceeded directly to their car and then paused as they waited for the Volkswagen to leave. Santos couldn't help but look around to see what might be causing the delay in the other car's departure. As he glanced through the windows of the cars and over to where the Volkswagen was parked, he could see the two women were involved in a deep embrace.

"Boss, do you see…"

"Yes, I know. It will work in our favor."

Finally, the Volkswagen took off, and the two men followed. The return to the base was done at a higher speed than the trip to the restaurant. When they got to the gate, the Volkswagen stopped in the queue of cars waiting to show their ID to the sentry and gain admittance to the base.

"Shit. My ID is missing."

"You sure?" Dawne asked.

"Yeah, but I know it was in my purse when we took off for town. It must've fallen out in the restaurant. I need to go back."

"Okay"

"Sorry, I know we were supposed to be doing better things."

Dawne smiled at her friend, and then an idea struck her.

"Tell you what, I'll see if I can get one of the gate guards to score me a ride back to the dorm while you go back and pick up your ID. By the time you get back, I should be appropriately undressed, have a bottle of wine opened, and a few dozen candles lit. Sound good to you?"

The idea aroused Angel, then she looked over at Dawne and made a low growl. The car in front of them moved, so Angel pulled up further. She rolled down her window and let the Gate Guard know she was going to have to go back into town to fetch her ID card. Dawne climbed out of the car and showed the other gate guard her ID. While the guard was looking at her ID, she focused her attention on Angel and then winked at her while licking her lips.

Angel whispered, "Tease," under her breath.

"Huh?" said the guard, turning toward her.

"Nothing, okay if I spin around?"

"Sure, go ahead."

Angel pulled just beyond the guard shack and then made a U-turn back to Tumon. Santos pulled into the visitor lot near the gate, and as soon as he saw the VW, he pulled out right behind it.

"How did you know, Boss?"

"Know…?"

"Only the Angel girl would be going back to the restaurant. It will make scooping her up easier."

"I didn't. I expected them both to go back and was hoping only one of them would go into the restaurant, so we could retrieve her on her way out without the other one getting involved. If it had been the other woman, it might have been *bulilyaso*, but this situation is almost ideal."

Angel left her car parked directly in front of the door of the restaurant when she ran inside to retrieve her ID card. Moments later, she walked back out with a confused look on her face. She knew she'd possessed the card when she left the base, and the only place they went to was to this restaurant. Distracted, she didn't notice Santos creeping up behind her. He quickly wrapped his arm around her throat, holding it tight until her body went limp in his arms.

Opening the door of the VW, Santos folded Angel into the seat. As soon as he was out of the way, Madulás leaned in and injected Angel with a sedative to ensure she remained unconscious. Santos pulled out of the parking lot in the VW with Madulás directly behind him in the rental. Santos was not familiar with the island but had seen some abandoned houses in a village named *Yigo*. Lacking any other place to question this girl, he headed there.

Chapter 8

Airman Dormitories - Andersen AFB, Guam

Being part of Security Forces was like being in a large family. Dawne knew that her siblings would never forget any mistake she made, teasing her mercilessly for the rest of the time she on that base. At the same time, she knew if she needed help, she could count on someone coming to the rescue. Dawne was stuck at the gate only a few minutes before a fellow SecFo appeared to give her a ride back to the dorms. As she walked up the stairs toward her room, she could see something was taped to the door. As she unlocked her door, she pulled the envelope addressed to her off and carried it with her inside.

Inside the envelope was a note from her First Sergeant letting her know the flight she was booked on had been rescheduled and was now departing at 2200. The note also reminded her that she needed to be in the Passenger Terminal two hours before departure. Dawne looked at her watch, "Shit.", It was 1935. She had twenty-five minutes to finish packing and get there.

At the bottom was information about a loan he had arranged for her to have available from the Air Force Assistance Fund. Instead of a signature, there was a simple diamond drawn at the bottom. She had heard a lot of things both good and bad regarding him, but the way he had been helping her convinced her the man cared for his troops.

As she began throwing things into her suitcase for a departure that was now happening hours earlier, her mind was also reeling. Most important things first, there was no way Angel was going to get back before she had to be at the terminal. Even if everything went one hundred percent flawlessly, the best she might hope for is seeing Angel wave to her from the terminal as she rode the bus out to the plane. Dawne stared at the disheveled mess in her suitcase for a moment then decided whatever she needed she could get at home. She was going to take time now to write Angel a letter explaining the early departure, her disappointment at having to leave early, and the way she felt about her. As her mind began to put scattered feelings into some sort of understandable order, she spoke out loud and wrote the words, "My Dearest Angel,"

As she inscribed her name across the bottom, Dawne apprehensively looked at her watch, knowing she out of time. She had seven minutes to finish up with her suitcase and walk over to the terminal. Folding the sheets of paper, Dawne slid them into an envelope, sealing it before writing Angel's name on the front. She was going to place it under Angel's pillow when there was a knock at the door, so she dropped it in the middle of her bed.

"If you're gonna make this plane, we need to go now," the First Sergeant told her as soon as she opened the door. She nodded and returned to her sleeping area to retrieve her suitcase. As she threw in a few more items into the bag and zipped it up, the First Sergeant explained he came by just make sure she was notified about the time change. With her suitcase in tow, she followed the First Sergeant out and to the passenger terminal.

Abandoned House - Yigo, Guam

Santos exited the main road into a small housing subdivision, and then took several turns as the roads became more primitive and the houses further apart. He saw a sign labeling one as a DEAD END with a smaller handwritten sign below saying, "Moved to Tamuning. Rosie." While he was not sure exactly why Rosie moved, it didn't matter as long as no one moved back into the house at the end of this driveway since he'd left. The uneven dirt and gravel path went on for almost four miles before ending at a darkened cinderblock building. The front door was standing open, which indicated to Santos it was available for their purpose.

Madulás exited his car and watched as Santos picked Angel up out of the VW and carried her into the vacant house through the open front door. Taking a quick look around to ensure there were no witnesses, Madulás followed him in, pulling the door closed. He followed the sound of Santos' labored breathing and found him in the kitchen where he laid Angel on a long Formica table. Looking around, Madulás found some extension cords and a spool of telephone wire. Without coordinating verbally, the men used the wire and cords to tie Angel's four extremities to the legs on the table. Santos knew what his Boss had in mind.

"Why don't you take a break," Madulás said, aware of his minion's aversion to physically coerced questioning, "Go outside while she and I have a *chikahan*. Who knows, maybe I won't have to get too persuasive."

Santos simply nodded and then headed for the door of the house. He had no desire to watch his Boss question anyone. He had no problem with the screaming or the blood. But there were some techniques Madulás had no qualms about using on a female interrogatee which Santos could not square even with his own warped moral compass. Because of his sisters, he tried to avoid violent encounters with women. If he was outside, and didn't see it, he could deny to himself later it ever happened.

Madulás turned on the kitchen faucet, and after a moment, a trickle of brown water began to flow. He cupped his hands together in the flow and then threw the water in Angel's face. Stepping over to her, he slapped her hard on the cheeks.

"Wake up, baby. Come on, *bebot*, we need to talk," when he saw her eyes first flitter and then open, Madulás began to speak even though he could clearly tell she was confused, "You've stolen from me. Or, maybe it wasn't you, it really isn't important. What is important is where my property is now and what you can do to retrieve it as quickly as possible."

Angel was utterly disoriented. Passing out from being strangled then drugged had wiped her short-term memory. The last thing she firmly remembered was dropping Dawne at the base gate before turning the car around. Anything beyond was blank. As this man spoke, her eyes darted around the room, trying to find something familiar which would give her a bit of reality to grasp. There was nothing. Her throat was dry, but she tried to speak.

"Who are…"

He did not let her complete the sentence before slapping her hard on the side of the face. Madulás was in a hurry and, therefore, unconcerned about leaving marks. This included permanently disfiguring her if that's what it took to get the information he needed.

"Who I am is irrelevant. The only thing which matters is the location of my property. If you don't know the location, then you'll need to direct me to someone who does. Come on. You were such a chattering *taratitat* earlier with your friend. No need to be quiet now."

Her ear was now ringing from being slapped, which added to her disorientation. She didn't understand what was going on or why. He must have seen her and Dawne. *What the hell is this about?*

Madulás was impatient. He didn't have time to wait on her to construct an answer. He slapped her again on the opposite side of the face, and when she opened her mouth to cry out, he stuffed a dirty rag he'd retrieved from the kitchen counter into it to stifle the sound. She could taste paint or something petroleum based on the rag and began to choke and fight against her restraints. But she was tied well, and eventually, she calmed and lay still.

"Now, if you think you can be civil, I'll remove the gag," while looking down at her, Madulás smiled widely so she could see his darkened teeth and golden fangs.

A fearful expression crossed her face, then Angel nodded. Suddenly, things linked in her mind, and she had an epiphany. *Ferdinand's gold.*

"Good," he said as he slowly pulled the rag out of her mouth. She moved her head to the side and spit out bits of paint, sawdust, and other refuse which had fallen into her mouth from the rag.

Looking toward the door, Madulás cried out, "Santos!"

When he appeared, he was instructed to bring the soda bottle from the cup holder in the car. He reappeared moments later with the half-full bottle in his hand and passed it to his Boss as he spun around and left the room in one motion. Santos could see the palm prints on her face and the distress in her eyes. He had no desire to be around as the questioning proceeded.

Madulás unscrewed the cap and then poured a small amount of the beverage into Angel's mouth. The liquid in the bottle was hot since the container was sitting in direct sunlight. At first, she sputtered, but then swallowed it out of need.

Madulás moved to her right side and slowly began caressing the back of her hand. Angel tried to withdraw her fingers, forming a fist, but her reflexes were slowed, and he was able to grab her middle finger and bend it toward the back of her hand. At first, she was going to scream, but then she held her lips together tightly, not wanting the rag returned to her mouth. He then held the finger just short of its breaking point.

"You know, you have nine more of these fingers if this one does not inspire you to talk," he snarled, "You also have toes, they could serve a similar purpose. Tell me where my property is."

"The gold?" Angel squeaked, suppressing her desire to scream.

He immediately let go of his grip on her finger and smiled with his lips pressed firmly together.

"Clever girl," as he spoke, he withdrew a cigarette from the pack in his pocket and lit it. After taking a deep drag, he exhaled the smoke across her prone body. He then clicked his tongue, "I knew you would eventually recall what property we needed to discuss. The property you stole."

She knew the man standing beside her was not Marcos but had no idea who he was or how he was connected to the gold.

"I didn't take anything. I'm not a part of it."

This statement confused Madulás, but he was not going to stop the questioning now that it had begun. She knew something, and right now, he knew nothing. He would keep going until he knew at least what she knew.

He blew on the end of the cigarette until the ember glowed, then lowered it to her cheek. He was careful not to touch the flesh but held it so close he could smell the heat cooking her skin, "You see, you say you weren't part of it, but yet you know about it. The only way you would know is if you were a part of the crime."

"No," Angel said, her voice trembling. When she tried to move her face away from the cigarette, he repositioned it to keep her in agony. Clenching her teeth, she added, "I left."

Madulás withdrew the cigarette and backed up, leaning back against the wall as he stared down at her, "Go on."

"As soon as they found it, I left," she turned and stared directly at him, "I'm not part of this." Many years ago, her father had shamed her when he told her she was the only person he knew who could look someone directly in the eye and lie to them. It had always troubled her that her father thought this of her. Today, she was hoping he was right.

"Fine. You say you're no part of this."

Madulás turned and walked away, exiting the house and walking toward Santos, who was leaning against the car, smoking a cigarette.

"You said you possessed a *garab*? Let me have it." Madulás said.

"You got it, Boss," Santos said as he withdrew it from the back waistband of his pants and offered it. Madulás pulled the knife out of the sheath and examined it for a moment. He then dropped the sheath on the hood of the car and heading back into the house.

Santos shook his head once his Boss was out of sight. The *garab* meant things were about to turn disgustingly messy.

Angel took the time Madulás was gone to sort out what was happening. She had no idea where she was but knew there must be people nearby, he would not have bothered to gag her otherwise. Angel also realized that even if she gave him the information he was looking for, he would probably kill her. The thought made her entire body shudder, then she heard the door open, and Madulás reentered the room.

"Tell me, what did Dawne do with the gold?"

Angel froze, and, in the growing panic, she could feel her heart beating wildly and with such force, she thought he could hear it as well.

"Surprised, I know about your *jowa*—your lover?"

"No! Dawne has nothing to do with this. She wasn't on the plane."

Madulás struck the nerve he was looking for without having to search for it using a variety of increasingly painful methods. He lowered the *garab* toward the side of her head, trying to ensure she couldn't see it. Let the cold steel remain a mystery for now.

"Who then? Tell me," as he spoke, he slid the *garab* between her head and her ear, pushing the blade gently against the connecting tissue, so it made a slight cut. The shallowness of the blood vessels in the area made the small cut immediately begin to bleed profusely. Angel could feel the hot liquid flowing from the side of her head but had no idea what it was from. She was too frightened to move her head.

"C-c-c-cargo guys took it," she took a deep breath and could smell blood in the air. *Did he cut off my ear?*

Leaning forward, Madulás pressed his lips against the ear he cut and whispered, "See how easy the truth is, it wasn't even necessary for me to remove this lovely appendage. Tell me, does Dawne appreciate the simple beauty of it?" Then he flicked his tongue around the edge of her ear.

Angel shut her eyes tightly, but the tears still escaped and ran down the sides of her face as she suppressed the gag from the rancid smell of his breath. *Bastard!* She wanted to scream it.

Moving to her left side, Madulás slipped the *garab* into the neckline of her shirt and then pulled it down, slitting the garment open and baring her flesh. He looked down at her eyes, opened wide, watching his moves. Then he threw the *garab* high into the air, flipping it and then

189

catching it by the handle just as the tip of the blade was about to pierce her sternum. Angel involuntarily yelped from fear and then began to tremble once he saved her.

"The names," Madulás demanded.

"Huh?"

He was silent for a moment as he turned the blade sideways and pressed the edge against the flesh of her stomach. He then slowly pulled the blade across her flesh, shaving the fine hair, "I want the names of the thieves."

Her mind was racing, she'd only met these men twice, and now he wanted her to remember their names.

"Dex and Ernie," she said, exhaling as he removed the blade from against her flesh.

"These thieves don't have last names?"

"I don't know them," she said, rushing the words so he would leave her alone. Instead, he grabbed her left hand. Showing the grace and skill of an expert, he splayed apart her fingers with his left hand as he ran the blade around the bottom of her index finger, cutting through the flesh. Knowing she was about to scream, he stuffed the dirty rag back into her mouth. As a final gesture, he laid the *garab* on her stomach, allowing its cold blade to rest against her flesh. Pushing his face into hers and speaking with great force he said,

"Right now, things are about to go tremendously bad for you. I have cut through the skin around the bottom of your finger. If I were to pull on the tip of your finger, the flesh would come off like a stocking slips off your foot. But unlike a sock, this would rip through thousands of nerves, setting each on fire. Your pain receptors would suddenly spring to life, passing on levels of agony you've never experienced before. The pain wouldn't stop once the flesh was gone. Indeed, it would be multiplied as thousands of nerves scream out in pain. It would not end until either I remove the finger, or you die."

Madulás stood up and looked down at Angel. Tears were flowing from her eyes. She was choking from the rag stuffed into her mouth, but at the same time, he knew she was somehow holding onto a secret from him. He lifted her left hand where she could see it, and then between his thumb and forefinger, he gripped the tip of the finger and bared his teeth at her as he audibly growled. She began to shake her head back-and-forth violently. Without releasing her hand, he removed the rag from her mouth.

"I don't know the names, but I have them. They're in my notebook. It's a small green book. It's in my purse. Please. Don't."

Madulás dropped her hand and taking a moment to stuff the rag back in her mouth, walked outside to the VW to retrieve her purse. Santos said nothing as he saw the man first pick up the bag then dump the contents onto the seat. Madulás sifted through it and then retrieved a small notebook with the word "Memorandum" in gold letters on the cover.

"Put everything back in the purse," he instructed Santos as he went back into the house.

As he walked, Madulás flipped through the pages of the book until he reached the last few pages with writing on them. After reentering the kitchen. He stepped off to the side of the table so he was in her line of sight as he read.

26 February 1986
Slot Zulu
Tail #0022
Two entries: SRA D. Kevan, A1C E. Crenshaw
Supv: TSgt Gubler

"Who is Gubler?" Madulás asked as he entered the kitchen.

Angel forgot his name was listed on the entry as well, "My shift supervisor, he was the one who cleared me off the site."

"Is he a thief too?"

She moved her head to look directly at him, "No."

"*Bebot,* why do you find it necessary to play games and make me hurt you."

He stared into her eyes as he forced the gag back into her mouth, walked to the end of the table and then grabbed hold of her ankles, one in each hand. He leaned forward, running his hands up her legs and then under her skirt. Madulás enjoyed the feel of her now cold thighs as they began to tremble. Then, stretching just a little bit further, grabbed the waistband of her panties, wadding them together toward the crotch. With a single pull, he ripped the garment from her body and then threw them on the floor. He reached forward and retrieved the *garab* and then laid the flat blade against the inside of her left leg. The room was silent except for her labored breathing, trying to inhale while the gag was blocking most of her airway. He slowly slid the steel against her flesh.

"There are many ways to alter you without damage ever being visible. Ways to deprive you of normalcy, which would be invisible to anyone except those most intimate to you. Your lady love—your *kulasisi,* maybe. Of course, those are the same people who would maybe reject you because you are no longer—normal?"

He continued to slide the blade up her leg until he was satisfied the tip was pressed gently against the spot where her inner thigh and groin met. He left it there, then walked back up to the top of the table. He pulled the gag from her mouth and waited for her to stop spitting out bits of paint and sawdust.

"Well?" Madulás said, pulling back his lips in a snarl.

"Gubler's involved."

Now there were three thieves. Of course, he was not convinced she wasn't involved, but if she knew where the gold was, she would have given it up instead of the names of the others.

He stuffed the gag back in her mouth. Madulás was finished, having extracted everything he needed from her. The only question remaining was whether he killed her now or just left her there to die if she wasn't discovered in time. As a firm believer in destiny, he always preferred the second option. Of course, just because it was an option it didn't always mean it was a possibility. He'd once left a man eleven miles into the Philippine jungle rather than executing him on the spot. Of course, because the man was bleeding in an area where both wild boar and leopards hunted, it was unlikely the man would survive. But it'd been possible.

Once outside, Madulás lit a cigarette and retrieved his bag from the rental car. After a brief search, he withdrew the syringe and handed it to Santos. "This should keep her out for at least twelve hours. Also, clean up anything that might leave a clue we were here," he then dug Angel's ID from his pocket and handed it to Santos, "Leave this behind as well."

Santos took the items, nodded, then walked toward the house. As he reached the door, Madulás added, "Oh, and retrieve your *garab* from between her legs."

Santos tried to turn before the look of disgust crossed his face, but he wasn't quite fast enough.

"Don't be a *kulelat*. There's barely any blood on the knife, and I didn't use it on her there anyway. Wipe off any fingerprints and then leave it here." Madulás slipped her notebook into his pocket and withdrew his doubloon. For the moment, he was satisfied to stand there, rolling it between his fingers as he smoked and waited on Santos to finish.

Santos made his way directly to the kitchen and stared down at Angel, who was now covered in sweat with her flesh exposed and the side of her face bloodied. Because the sun was going down, her visibility was limited. Angel heard the sound of someone coming in but was surprised it wasn't Madulás there to assault her again. She tilted her head back until she could see Santos standing at the head of the table. As her eyes pleaded with him, Santos had the shocking realization of why she looked familiar. Her dark hair and eyes, along with the composition of her face and her small frame, reminded him of his younger sister. He suddenly felt ill. He needed to fix this.

When Santos opened the door of the house to leave, he ran into Madulás about to enter.

"Why are you taking so long?"

"Boss, I wanted to make sure it was cleaned up like you said."

Madulás pushed his way past Santos and walked directly into the kitchen. There he saw Angel's body lying perfectly still, eyes closed. He walked around her body as he examined the woman lying there. When he got to her feet, he pulled on the bindings to ensure they were tight. All appeared to be in order.

"Why did you remove the rag from her mouth?" Madulás asked when he noticed it was no longer there.

"Once I gave her the shot, she was asleep. No need to keep it there."

Madulás glanced around and saw the rag sitting on the kitchen counter, then retrieved it. He forced her lower jaw down and inserted it into her mouth then slapped the side of her face gently as if he was approving the job.

"Let's go."

The two men walked out of the house. Santos closed the door behind them. As he walked toward the VW, he grabbed a leaf off a banana tree beside the front walkway, then used it to wipe the blood off of his *garab*. Dropping the foliage, he searched his pockets and withdrew the keys to Angel's car along with her ID. Without getting in, he stuffed the keys and ID under the driver's visor. After examing the *garab* for any more traces of blood, he slipped it into the sheath he retrieved from the hood, then tossed it onto the floor on the passenger side.

"Everything good?"

"You got it," Santos said as he walked over to the rental car and got in.

As soon as the older man climbed into the vehicle, he turned and looked at his Boss for instructions.

"You said you were assigned an escort who was helping you at the base?"

"Yes, the PAO."

"Good." Madulás looked at his watch briefly and then frowned before saying, "Let's go back to the base. It's too late to call this person now, but we'll speak to him first thing in the morning. We have the names of the Air Force people who accessed the plane. They are the ones who stole my property, so we need to find out what they did with it."

It took only a moment for Santos to understand what was being said, he nodded and began the drive back to Andersen Air Force Base.

Anyone who knew Dex casually knew what his interests were. Often, he would jokingly say he only worried about the three S's—Sleep, Sex, and Something to eat. Those who knew him better, like Jessi and Ernie, knew about his interest in and talent for photography. During his tour in Europe, he'd managed to acquire a small collection of high-end photographic equipment. While he was there, he'd learned the rudimentary skills of how to use the it. When he arrived in Guam, he had turned those skills into art.

Jessi and Dex enjoyed a wonderful afternoon together, after several confusing days when he'd been acting like anyone other than himself. He knew spending the day with her would take his mind off everything else and allow him to relax before the final steps of converting the gold into cash. Cash to create his future.

Except for a small picnic pavilion, Tarague Beach was one of the few undeveloped places of beauty on the entire island. The reason was not lacking in want by developers, but it was located on a secure Air Force Base. The beach was a vast expanse backed by a colossal coconut grove and then tall cliffs left from the island's volcanic origins. Except on holidays, the beach was seldom crowded, and even if it was, it was possible to walk further down the beach to find some private space even on the busiest of days. It was what they did today.

After retrieving a backpack full of photography equipment and a small cooler, the two walked down the beach and around a rock outcropping. There, they found an isolated piece of the world. Several weeks before, Dex had convinced Jessi to let him photograph her nude on this section of the beach. It was an enjoyable time for both, and Jessi had enjoyed the undivided attention he'd given her. Then, just as they were packing up to leave, two Security Forces Defenders had come around the outcropping on patrol. Even though they hadn't been caught, Jessi swore she would never pose naked there again.

Today, Dex was hoping to capture some images of coconut crabs and some of the more exotic insects. Even though he was no expert on either, he found the photos interesting to look at, and he had even given a few prints of them away as gifts. He was hours away from having a secure financial future, maybe he could find a future in photographic art.

After their day together, they returned to Dex's room. They spent from late afternoon to early evening dozing in each other's arms while listening to music. Now, at just after midnight, Jessi awoke to find Dex had taken a shower and was putting his uniform on.

"Why do you have to go to work, Babe?" Jessi pleaded with Dex as she lay in the bed, watching him put his boots on.

"I'm not going to work, well, not work, work. I have to meet somebody about something that happened at work."

"At 0200 on your day off, and in uniform?"

Dex turned and looked at her. With about half an hour to be where he needed to be to meet Gubler, he probably could've used that time to explain to her what was going on. But Dex had no desire to do it now. He loved Jessi, he could see a future with her, but right now he didn't want anyone to mess with the decision that he'd already made. He couldn't think. If he spent some time thinking, he would abandon the entire plan. He knew he couldn't do it. If he abandoned what he was doing, he would lose Jessi. By failing her, everything good that was going to happen in his future was lost too.

"I'm going to see Barr, okay?"

Jessi readily accepted it and saw his going now as something positive, not more strange behavior which had popped up over the last few days, "Good. I'm glad you're doing it then, still not sure why you couldn't do it at a more agreeable hour."

He walked over to her and kissed her before saying, "We're

vampires, we work at night—this is the most agreeable hour."

Smiling, he kissed her again before turning and leaving.

Someday I'm going to hell for lying to that girl.

Security Forces Headquarters - Andersen AFB, Guam

Dex took a quick look around before climbing into the passenger seat of Gubler's government SUV.

"I hope this won't take too long," Dex said as he looked in the back seat of the vehicle and saw his old footlocker there.

"Quick out, quick load up, then quick back in. The action will take about half an hour at most, but it's going to take at least that to drive out there and back."

The two men didn't speak again until they arrived thirty minutes later at the abandoned guardhouse where they'd left the gold. After both of them got out of the vehicle, in a moment of silence, both heard the faint sound of an animal rooting.

"A wild boar must be nesting out here," Gubler concluded.

Looking around and peering into the jungle, Dex said something under his breath before motioning to Gubler to proceed toward the abandoned guardhouse. Gubler stood his ground, staring at Dex.

"What the hell was that?"

"Something a local told me when I first got here. You always get the permission of the *Taotaomona* before you enter the jungle."

"Yeah, but we're not entering the jungle."

"Well, this is sort of the jungle. It used not to be a jungle but is turning back into it."

"So why didn't you do this the other night?"

"I don't know. It just seems more appropriate to do it tonight. I figure at this point, we've been lucky so far—I don't want to piss anybody off now."

Gubler considered Dex's words for a moment and then nodded without further comment. He retrieved the empty footlocker from the backseat of the SUV, and the two men proceeded to the dilapidated building. After throwing back the poncho covering it, they began to retrieve the gold and neatly stack the bars in the footlocker. Once they were finished, the men used the handles at either end of the footlocker to carry it back toward the SUV. Gubler motioned for Dex to set the footlocker down so he could open the back of the vehicle.

"Why not just stick it back in the backseat?"

"Don't want to risk fucking up the upholstery," he motioned for Dex to pick up his end of the footlocker again. But, when he did, the handle broke off.

"Shit," Dex said.

"Yeah, so much for getting the blessings of the *Taotaomona*."

"The handle just broke off. It looks like the footlocker's still in one piece. I'll pick it up from the bottom."

They picked up the footlocker again and slid into the vehicle.

Dex nodded, and the two men climbed into the SUV then headed back toward base. As they pulled into the Security Forces parking lot, Gubler pulled his car keys from his pocket and handed them to Dex and then pointed through the windshield at his truck.

"Just follow me, we're going to go down by the fuel storage area near base housing. There are some streetlights to help us see," seeing the concern on Dex's face, he added, "The road is basically abandoned at night."

Dex nodded as he took the keys from Gubler and then exited the SUV. A few minutes later, they were parked on Plumeria Boulevard underneath a streetlamp. Within moments, the transfer was complete.

"What now?" Dex asked as he slid the footlocker further into the back of the truck until it was at the cab. Once it was in place, Gubler covered it with the poncho they retrieved from the abandoned guard shack.

"Follow me back to the SF parking lot and park it where it was, then give me the keys. When I leave in the morning, I'll take it home and wait to hear from my contact. I'll try to get us at least an hour before the meetup, so I have time to get word to you."

Dex was unsure how the next step was going to work. It all sounded a little flaky, but he nodded rather than arguing about it. After dropping Gubler's truck off, Dex took a look at his watch and saw it was almost 0400. Rather than going back to his room, he went to early breakfast. He was skeptical about what was going to happen next, and the uncertainty led him to believe he wasn't going to get regular mealtimes today.

Abandoned House - Yigo, Guam

As soon as the sound of the tires rolling over the gravel faded away, Angel turned her head to the side and used her tongue to force the rag out of her mouth. With the obstruction gone, she could breathe again and paused to gulp fresh air into her hungry lungs. As she lay there, she considered why this Santos person would do what he did to help her. He said something about his sister, but she didn't fully understand what he meant by it. All of it was irrelevant, all that mattered was he had not killed her, and he left her in a position to escape.

The house was now completely dark with the sun down, but somehow, her eyes adjusted to what faint light was coming in through the windows. Using a great deal of effort, she lifted her right hand, and as she did, she broke the single piece of brittle wire holding it in place. Santos had scored the wires so they would break easily when pressure was applied. It was lucky for her Madulás hadn't tested the binding. She used her right hand to free her left and, for the first time, could see what her torturer had done to the finger on her hand. Clearly, he'd sliced around the entire circumference at the base, which would've made his threat of removing all of the flesh from the finger possible. She hoped she might find a bandage or some tape in the car to serve as a temporary dressing.

Now, with both hands free, she sat up and untied the bindings holding her ankles. The extension cords were thick, and while they held her in place tightly, the knots fell apart as soon as they were loosened. She shifted position, dangling her legs off the side of the table. As she prepared to stand up, she realized she was no longer sweating which could be an indicator of heatstroke. To the best of her recollection, she hadn't had anything to drink in almost six hours. Before that, most of what she'd drank was alcohol. Sliding herself off the table, she landed on her feet. After standing there for less than a minute, she was overcome by dizziness and collapsed unconscious onto the concrete floor.

When she regained consciousness, Angel felt something caressing her cheek. Slowly raising her hand to it, she realized it was just a gecko and grabbed the lizard, gently tossing it across the room. She was suffering from temporal disorientation. Her surroundings were pitch black. She didn't know if it had been minutes, a few hours, or maybe a full twenty-four hours later. She attempted to stand up and was greeted by stiffened muscles. Those symptoms told her she had been there for an hour or more, at least. When she was on her feet, she slowly made her way to the front door of the house and opened it. Angel could see the sun was beginning to brighten the sky to the east, and there was no moon in the sky. Dawn. *No. What about Dawne?*

With the immediate threat to her gone, she was taking her time trying to feel her way back into reality. The sudden thought of Dawne in danger placed her entire being back into a state of full anxiety. She walked quickly down the walkway to her car, and after getting in the driver seat was frustrated to find her keys were not in the ignition. She then recalled what Santos told her about leaving it under the driver's visor. Pulling the visor down, the keys and her ID fell into her lap. She quickly inserted the key into the ignition and turned it. When the interior lights of the car came on, a reflection in the passenger-side footwell caught her attention. She retrieved the *garab,* then, withdrawing the knife from the sheath she examined it for a moment before stashing the entire assembly into the door pocket of the car. *I'm no longer defenseless*

Due to the combination .of darkness and having never been in this area before, it took her almost forty-five minutes to find her way back to the main road. It was a mix of ego and prudence which drove her decision to perform a quick clean up before attempting to go through the gate. Once on the main road, she drove directly to a twenty-four-hour Winchell's Doughnut house. Except for a single employee, the place was empty as she proceeded from the front door directly to the bathroom. There, she washed the blood from the side of her face and tied the tattered ends of her shirt together to hide the fact the shirt was sliced from her body. The finger on her left hand was incredibly sensitive, and she attempted to wash the wound gently, knowing she was going to have to go to the clinic to have it properly repaired. With the basics done, she looked in the mirror and could clearly see the burn on her cheek and bruises were now appearing. By the time she pulled through the gate at Andersen Air Force Base, she had calmed down and was waved through by the sentry without question.

After clearing the gate, she glanced at the dash clock and saw it was 0600. If everything went according to plan, Dawne's C-5 would have taken off five hours ago. Unless for some reason she'd missed the flight. Rather than going to the dorm, she went to the passenger terminal, and once there, to Flight Reservations. After being told about the early departure of the aircraft, the rest of her time in the terminal was spent being repeatedly told that they would not confirm who was on the C-5 when it took off. Giving up in exasperation, she stormed out of the building. On her way back to her car, a Navy seaman in a crackerjack uniform caught up with her. He said he'd seen a woman get on the C-5, and after exchanging description information, Angel was satisfied it was Dawne.

With her primary concern abated, Angel went back to her dorm room to take a shower and change before trying to get in contact with the other three in the conspiracy. When she entered the room, the lingering scent of Dawne's perfume engulfed her, painfully reminding her of the missed night of passion. She saw the envelope with her name printed on it lying on her bed straightaway. She knew it was from Dawne, but since Angel knew she was safe and others were at risk, she opted to read it later and stashed it under her pillow before heading to the shower.

Gubler's Quarters – Andy South, Andersen AFB, Guam

Gubler had been up since sunrise, unable to sleep. His body was reacting to a combination of continually rotating shifts and the anxiety over the upcoming exchange, which hopefully would solve all of the other problems bothering him. As he sat at his kitchen table drinking a cup of coffee, the sound of a vehicle driving past his home set off his internal sense of danger. Taking his cup with him, he went to the kitchen window and peered out for the source of his apprehension. He saw a black Buick slowly driving past as the driver lowered his window and looked directly at Gubler. He then gave a slight nod and threw a wadded-up piece of paper into his front yard before proceeding on.

Gubler immediately knew Mendoza had left him instructions for the exchange. Trying to suppress his panic, he quickly walked out the front door. When he was about to pick up the message from the dew-covered grass, he heard a familiar voice behind him.

"Don't you hate those asshole locals?"

Gubler turned to see his neighbor sitting on his stoop, smoking a cigarette.

"Yeah, real jerks."

"The guy even had the balls to roll down his window and give me a dirty look as he threw the trash out. I should've gotten his plate."

"How long you got left?" Gubler said, changing subjects.

"Twenty-five and a wake-up. They pick up household goods on Monday."

"You're going to Fairchild, right?"

"Well, it's what the first set of orders said, now I'm heading for someplace called Grissom in the cornfields of Indiana," shrugging he added "Anyplace has gotta be better than here."

Gubler felt he could get away with nonchalantly picking up the piece of paper now, he did so and slipped it into his pocket without glancing at it.

"Well, good luck. Maybe Mary will let you get away with smoking in the house at the new base."

Instead of verbalizing an answer, his neighbor merely grunted, took a deep drag on the cigarette and shook his head.

After reentering his house, Gubler returned to his seat at the kitchen table and flattened the crumpled piece of paper on the table in front of him. As he sipped his coffee, he read the dark black text printed on the paper.

Yona
Left at Lujan art shop

The next instruction was to turn right on a particular road. Then a series of directions both left and right eventually ending on a walking trail bordered by coconut trees a half-mile off an unpaved road. Next to the final arrow on the map was the time.

4:30 PM

It was too complicated for him to memorize and destroy, now he was left holding a vital piece of physical evidence. *Shit.* He read the instructions one more time before neatly folding the page and sliding it into his pocket.

Since he was going to a location he'd never been before, and since most of the island's roads were iffy at best, he knew he would have to depart at least an hour early to ensure he arrived on time. Subtracting another fifteen minutes to allow time to reconnoiter the location, he needed to have Dex in the car and on the road by 1515.

Jack Wu's Office —Happy Luck Resort, Tumon Bay, Guam

Wu was aware Fo had arrived over an hour ago, but was still surprised when he heard a knock on his door. Almost immediately after the knock, Mendoza opened the door and stuck in his head.

"Fo is here."

Wu motioned with his hand for Mendoza to bring his courier into the office. As the two men struggled to bring in the footlockers, Wu removed his glasses, then closed and stacked up the ledgers he was working on. He stood and walked toward Fo, embracing the man.

"Welcome, my friend."

"Thank you. It is good to be here, especially after such a long journey."

Wu looked at Mendoza and nodded, indicating he should retrieve refreshments. He motioned for Fo to have a seat in the chair in front of his desk before returning to his desk chair.

"Any problems?"

"No, not at all. Everything was smooth. I have to say I prefer flying in here as opposed to going to a location where I have to deal with customs."

"Yes, there are some advantages to it. But I fear with the recent changes in the Philippines, the power structure on this island will be changing, and soon it will be time for me to depart and find a new home base."

"Really? I'm surprised to hear they would be so bold as to attempt to push you out."

Wu waved his hand toward Fo, "Quite often, the way things work out is not always the way one would expect. Besides, I think it is

204

time I look for a home base that will also allow me to transition into retirement. Guam was never anywhere I wanted to stay for a long time."

"I guess I can understand, it is not exactly Macau is it?"

Wu laughed at the reference just as Mendoza reentered the room and served tea to the two men.

"You will stay for a few days to catch your breath before heading back, yes?"

"I can. I have nothing pressing right now on the West Coast. Thank you for the invitation."

"Always. If you will forgive me, I do have some business I need to attend to immediately now that I'm in possession of my *dairy products*."

Fo immediately jumped to his feet and held out his hand, "I understand, perhaps we can get together again before I depart. Dinner, maybe?"

Wu took Fo's hand and shook it, "Yes, we must do so. Mendoza will take you anywhere you need to go, and of course, you have a suite here available for your use."

Mendoza and Fo left Wu's office, leaving the two footlockers, each containing one million dollars behind. Fo told Mendoza he first wanted to go to his room to freshen up before doing a bit of touring. Dutifully, Mendoza delivered him to the main hotel desk and, after identifying him, allowed the staff to take over responsibility.

Upon returning to Wu's office, he could hear an argument going on behind the closed door. Mendoza stood for a minute, holding his ear against the door to listen and determine if he should intercede. Once he was able to identify the voice Wu was speaking with, he opened the door. He stepped in to find the two standing face-to-face, obviously arguing. Mendoza's sudden appearance caused both Wu and Tala to suddenly go silent.

"Should I remove her, sir?"

Wu sat down, then put his glasses back on, "Yes. It seems Tala failed to realize the amount she owed the casino was accruing interest as she worked off her balance. So, rather than paying it off today, as she assumed, she still owes several more months of service."

Tala, who was standing directly in front of Wu's desk, pounded her fists on the desktop before dropping into the chair and burying her face in her hands as she cried.

Wu considered the crying woman in front of him for a moment, "I know. One of my employees from the West Coast is in town for a week. You will stay in the Entertainment Room while he is here and be at his beck and call for anything he wants. I know you have a great many talents, Tala. Perhaps if you please him well enough, I will deduct these nights from what you owe rather than just taking them as a penalty for your disrespect." Wu nodded to himself in approval of his idea, then looked at Mendoza, "Deliver her there, and see she strips out of this unacceptable outfit," the disgust in Wu's voice almost dripped from every word as he referenced Tala's outfit of Levi's and Lynyrd Skynyrd T-shirt, "and into something more suitably subservient and erotic."

Wu then stacked up the ledgers scattered across his desk and handed them to Mendoza with instructions to return them to the top shelf of the safe and retrieve the videotape from the second shelf. Mendoza took the ledgers and then lifted Tala by her arm and guided her from the office. As soon as the two left, Wu opened one of the footlockers and removed seven blocks of currency, placing them on his desk. Each one contained one thousand twenty-dollar-bills with a value of twenty-thousand dollars. He sat down and withdrew a form from his desk drawer. Wu had already recorded the transaction in his ledger book. This form would be given to Mr. Gubler as a receipt, showing his entire debt to the casino had been paid off. Once he signed the receipt, he folded it and placed it inside an envelope. He would give it to Gubler along with the videotape later in the day when the exchange took place. There was another knock at the door. This time a cash courier came down from the hotel's accounting office and retrieved the one-hundred and forty-thousand dollars which paid off Gubler's debt.

Once Tala and Mendoza reached the Entertainment Room, he unlocked the door then pushed her through it.

"Get out of those clothes and take a shower. You smell like cigarette smoke."

Tala turned and walked toward the bathroom compliantly. Mendoza knelt down in front of a large aquarium set against one wall. Opening a concealed door in the base he revealed a safe. He spun the dial several times, then turned the handle and pulled the door open. After placing the ledger books on the top shelf, he retrieved the videotape and then secured the door. He'd just closed the door below the aquarium and stood up when Tala reentered the room naked.

She walked directly to Mendoza and pressed her body against him while wrapping her arms around his shoulders and said in a sultry voice, "You remember, the first night I was here? You were my first. You were so loving, so gentle. Why don't you tell Wu you want me, and I be just for you? I live with you and be there all the time. I take good care of you, like your best girlfriend."

Mendoza reached up and took her by the wrists forcibly, removing her arms from around him while taking a step back and pushing her to the floor.

"I may have been the first, but there have been too many since," he stared directly into her eyes, without emotion then paused for a moment in case she wanted to respond. Tala was silent.

Chapter 9

Angel took a long shower, trying to wash away not only the grime but the invisible stench Madulás' touch had left upon her body. She was doing her best to suppress the memories of what just happened. Still, as she glided the soap over various parts of her body, she found herself being haunted by flashbacks from the night before. The shower served to revive her, but along with the revival came renewed fear not only of what she'd just survived but the unknown threats ahead. Once out of the shower, she found the speed of her actions accelerating even as she tried to force them to be more deliberate.

Angel didn't know Ernie's last name, but she knew where his dorm room was located. As she stood in front of his door, she leaned forward and pressed her ear against it. Nothing. Then, she gently knocked. The cut on her finger was throbbing, reminding her it would soon need professional attention. After a few minutes without response, she knocked harder, and the door was suddenly thrust open by a half-asleep Ernie wearing a pair of gym shorts and a T-shirt.

Angel didn't say a word as she pushed past him into the room. Ernie was confused by her arrival but was glad his roommate was out so they could speak freely.

"Uh, so why are you here?"

"I met someone last night, someone who is more than a little bit angry about his missing property."

"You're kidding, right? Marcos is back on Guam?"

"No, not Marcos, some other guy. He didn't give me his name. There were two of them—the guy in charge and some guy named Santos who helped me escape."

"Escape?"

Angel was about to tear into Ernie when it occurred to her, he would have no way of knowing what she had been through in the past eighteen hours. She looked around the room and took a seat.

"Have you got something to drink? I'm parched."

Ernie nodded and went over to his refrigerator and withdrew a beer and Coke. He held both toward her to let her choose. To his surprise, she took both. Ernie moved some laundry off another chair then took a seat in front of her.

"Want to tell me what happened?"

Angel pulled the tab on the Coke and lifted it to her lips, draining the entire can before sitting the empty back on the table. Next, she twisted the top off the bottle of beer and took a sip of it, wiping her mouth with the back of her hand.

"I was out at dinner last night with my roommate when I was kidnapped."

"Wait, someone kidnapped you right in front of your roommate? The news must be all over base by now."

"No. Just shut up and listen. I was at dinner with my roommate, but when we were heading back to base, I found my ID card was missing. When I went back after the missing card, I left her at the gate. That's when I was kidnapped," she paused and took a long pull from the bottle of beer.

"I don't know exactly what happened, but at some point, they grabbed me, and when I came to, I was tied up in an abandoned house, and this old guy with black teeth kept asking me questions about what we stole," she pointed at Ernie with the beer bottle, "What *you* stole."

Ernie wanted to interject a correction that she was also involved, but he held back. Instead, he went to the refrigerator and retrieved a beer for himself. After he'd opened it and taken a sip, she continued.

"He kept asking about where the property was and the names of all involved. Kept saying things in Filipino, I think."

"What did you tell him?"

She held out her hand and displayed her bandaged finger, still bleeding, "I might be loyal, but I'm not going to lose a finger for you."

The reality of the blood on her finger made Ernie take a good look at her for the first time since she entered the room. Both of her wrists appeared to be bruised, probably from being tied up. Her cheeks showed the clear imprints of the hands, which struck her repeatedly on both. There was a small trickle of blood down the side of her neck, and circular burn on the side of her face was bright red. *I wonder what damage I'm not seeing.*

"When I was sure he was going to hurt me bad, I gave them your first and last names, and Gubler's too," her voice trembled as she spoke, and then she took a drink of her beer in an attempt to calm herself.

"What happened with your roommate?"

"She's okay. She left early this morning for the World. Her father's sick."

"Well, I guess that's good, but it doesn't sound like it should be good."

"Once I told the old man what he wanted to know, he left. Then he sent Santos back in to give me a shot. I guess to knock me out. Instead, he loosened my bindings and told me where he left my car keys. As soon as the two of them left, I tried to take off but passed out due to dehydration, I guess. I woke up a few hours ago, grabbed a shower, and now I'm here."

"Who else have you told about these guys?"

"You're the first. I only knew where you lived because I saw you leaving from here a few times. I have no idea which room is Dex's. Since Gubler lives in Andy South, it made sense to try and get a hold of you two first."

"Bet. Give me a minute to get dressed, and we'll head down to Dex's room and see what he thinks we should do next."

This struck Angel as strange since between Dex and Ernie, Ernie seemed to be the one more calculating and thoughtful. *Why would he want*

Dex to decide what to do next?

When she didn't immediately respond, Ernie took it as acceptance and went to get dressed. Upon returning, he reached down and picked up his beer and drained it.

"Ready when you are," he said to Angel.

She immediately rose and followed him out the door then down to Dex's room. Ernie gently knocked twice on the door before turning the knob and opening it. The two walked in, closing the door behind them.

"Yo, Dex. We got a problem, man," Ernie announced in a low voice as he and Angel took a seat in the common. Moments later, Dex appeared, rubbing his eyes, more than a bit surprised to see Angel there with Ernie.

"What the hell?"

"Did you swap out the gold yet?" Ernie asked, to which Dex immediately responded by waving his arms to alert him the three of them were not alone. Glancing into his sleeping area for a moment to confirm Jessi was still asleep, Dex stepped forward and took a seat on the coffee table in front of Ernie and Angel. With the three of them huddled this close together, they could speak in a low voice and not be heard by Jessi.

"I haven't heard anything yet, supposed to be this afternoon sometime. What's up?"

Ernie nodded toward Angel, and she began to speak. She repeated the story she told Ernie about being kidnapped and questioned. When she was done, Dex was silent.

"Some kinda shit show, huh?" Ernie said in an attempt to break the silence and force the conversation forward.

Dex nodded without saying a word.

"Look, if you're just gonna sit here, we probably should get down to Andy South and let Gubler know what's happened."

Dex just continued to nod, not saying a word. Finally, he stood up as if he had come to some resolution.

"We can't tell Gubler until after the exchange."

Ernie and Angel both stared at Dex as if they didn't comprehend what he was saying.

"It just doesn't do any good to tell him beforehand, one more thing to worry about. This exchange is going to be complicated enough. Getting it done solves two things," as he spoke, he raised one finger in the air, "Once we've handed off the gold, we no longer have it. If they ask, we tell your two friends who we gave it to, then we're done, and," raising a second finger beside the first, "the cash we're getting is untraceable. If these guys hassle us, we go to the cops while we still keep our spoils."

Neither person in his audience seemed to like or understand what he was saying.

"Look, we're not equipped to take out two experienced bad guys. Our only choice is to get them off our tail, and the easiest way to do it is to put them on someone else's. Failing that, we let the cops take over. Maybe the bad guys get taken out by them."

He looked from Angel to Ernie and knew he still had not changed either person's viewpoint.

"I guess one of you has a better idea?"

Silence.

Ernie cleared his throat, and then spoke, "The only thing we need to agree to right now is not telling Gubler. Once the exchange is complete, we can tell him what happened then worry about the next step."

Angel nodded in agreement, and when Ernie glanced toward Dex, he saw him rolling his eyes before finally nodding as well.

"Look, we got a plan, and after a night of getting the crap beat out of me, I'm starving. Can we get something to eat?"

"Yeah, yeah," Dex said as he disappeared into his sleeping area, "Give me a few to get dressed."

After getting dressed, he retrieved the Colt 1911 from its hiding place in his wall locker and looked at it. He knew how to fire a pistol, having qualified with a thirty-eight. He felt reasonably confident he could handle this one, but as he turned it in his hand and looked at it, his body was chilled. If the situation arose requiring him to point this at someone, he might have to fire it. Right now, at this moment, he wasn't sure if he could do it. He began to return the Colt to its hiding place when he thought about how the situation was vastly different this morning than last night. Instead of hiding the weapon, he slipped it into the back waistband of his pants.

When the three were standing outside of Dex's door, he inserted the key and locked the room. Usually, he felt no need to lock it, but right now, someone was looking for him, and he didn't want them to find Jessi. Another idea crossed his mind as he stood there, and Dex removed his name tag from the door.

"We should do that too," Ernie said to Angel, who nodded in agreement.

"Meet you guys downstairs," Dex said as he took off down the stairs and into the parking lot.

The three of them climbed into Angel's VW and went in search of lunch.

Transient Quarters - Andersen AFB, Guam

Madulás' snoring irritated Santos, but that wasn't why he was awake so early. Since he was a lower-ranking man, Santos was left with the couch while Madulás got the one bed in the room. After a night of tossing and turning on the sofa, at sunrise, Santos lifted one blade of the Venetian blinds in such a way it stuck in place so he could gaze out the window. He wasn't paying attention to the people he saw walking by. He found himself daydreaming about his family. His sister in particular.

By now, the girl from last night should've managed to untie herself and find her way back to civilization. This meant their presence just became exponentially more dangerous. But those thoughts only troubled him momentarily. What bothered him was how easily he did precisely what Madulás told him to do. This was nothing new. He had been working for the man for years and immediately obeyed every order given. Also, she was not the first female he would have violently attacked, but this girl struck an emotional chord like none before. Angel reminded him of his sister, and whatever bits of remaining ethics or morality he possessed would not allow him to do such things while staring into his sister's face.

Strangely, he felt reassured there were limits to what he would do when ordered. His soul was not lost. This realization also meant he was no longer capable of following all orders he was given without contemplating them. This time, the boss would never find out, but what about next time? What would the reaction be from his Boss? Would it get him killed?

Likely.

He was distracted by noises from the bed as the old man turned over in his sleep. Santos closed his eyes and let his mind wander. This was a time of great upheaval. Maybe it was time to seek a new destiny. Given all the things he had done in service to Madulás, he knew he would never be able to return to the Philippines. So, where could he go? An even deeper question would be how he could go anywhere with only a few hundred dollars in his pocket.

"Santos."

Madulás was awake.

"Yes, Boss?"

"Contact the Public Affairs person you spoke of, let's see if we can find the people with the three names we have."

"You got it."

"Tell them we want to give them a personal thank you from Marcos for their efforts during this difficult transition."

As Madulás considered the next step toward retrieving his gold, he began to think about the next steps in his own personal journey as well. His actions, even if the bodies were never discovered, were not the kind Marcos was going to be able to forgive. He was a deposed leader and lacked any power other than that begrudgingly given to him. If one of his soldiers began to cause problems, the easiest thing to do would be to disavow knowledge and allow their prosecution. As of now, anything that happened to benefit him would likely be as a result of his own actions. He stared across the room at Santos, who was talking on the telephone.

Santos was going to be something else Madulás would have to take care of. Even if he were able to retrieve all of the gold, it would not be enough for two people to re-establish themselves in the Western world. The thought of wasting a dedicated resource troubled him, but not as much as what it would cost to maintain it.

"Boss," Madulás looked toward Santos to see him standing there with his hand covering the telephone mouthpiece, "I keep pushing him to find out where these guys are working, but he insists he wants to come along and take pictures for the base newspaper or something."

"Well, that's not the way I would prefer it, but I guess we'll just have to roll with it. Let him know we can be ready in an hour."

Santos concluded the telephone call, and then the two men began preparing for the day.

A short while later, the phone rang, and Santos picked it up. The Airmen who handled the aircraft were not currently on duty, but they were scheduled for later in the day. The PAO would be by to pick them up and take them over to the cargo terminal at the appropriate time.

"So, it would seem we have a little time. Do you know if there is a Philippine gift shop nearby?"

Santos thought for a moment, "I think there is one over near the base exchange. It's kind of small."

"That's okay. I thought we might pick up a small keepsake to present these Airmen with to prevent too many questions from being asked."

"Understood, Boss."

The two men completed the short drive to the base exchange and were pleased to find there was a Filipino gift shop as part of the mall of shops surrounding the main store. Madulás selected three display frames with miniature replicas of Filipino *garabs* and tribal knives. Each frame was made up of four rows of three, Santos was amused to see the knife he had earlier was one of the knives represented. Of course, the shop was also selling several replica *garabs* but none with the razor-sharp blade that was a trademark of the knife.

Before returning to their room, Madulás purchased some ornamental stationery from the base exchange. Once they were back in the room, he would use this to create a letter of appreciation he would sign with Ferdinand Marcos' name. The words were not as flowery as Marcos might have used, but then Madulás tended to be more matter-of-fact when he wrote. After creating the three letters, he slipped each into an envelope and placed them in the bag with the knife displays.

Santos found a soccer game on TV, and the two men sat waiting for the next step in their retrieval mission to occur.

Airman Dormitories - Andersen AFB, Guam

As soon as Dex was inside the room, he spun around to close the door quietly. Slowly, he turned the lock and secured the room, trying to be as quiet as possible. After tucking the Colt 1911 in between the cushions of the couch, he walked toward his bed. He saw Jessi lying there, facing the opposite direction, and slowly exhaled as he got undressed.

"You realize you and Ernie made so much noise coming up the stairs you woke me up before you ever opened the door."

Dex squinted and shook his head, "You got me. I guess I can't ever be a cat burglar of any place you live. So, how about if I just climb in bed with you instead?"

"Sure," she flipped the bedding back, giving him a view of her naked backside, "come snuggle me."

Dex dropped the last of his clothing on the floor and climbed into bed behind her, pressing his naked body against hers.

"Ugh, you smell like you've been drinking beer and eating *kelaguen*."

Without saying a word, he jumped out of bed and grabbed his toothbrush. As he brushed his teeth, he spun the lid off the mouthwash bottle. After pouring the mouthwash into his mouth, he gave it a quick swish before spitting it in the sink. After he wiped his mouth off with a towel, he dashed back to bed and Jessi. Once his naked front side was pressed against her bare backside, he wrapped his arm around her and slowly exhaled. A few moments of silence passed before Dex slowly began to slide his hand down her stomach and between her legs.

"Not yet," Jessi said as she grabbed his hand and placed it back on her stomach, "I want to know who Angel is and what's going on between you and whoever this Gubler person is."

Dex was not an athlete, but he understood what people meant when they suddenly got a muscle cramp in the middle of running or swimming. He realized what was going on in his mind right now was the mental version of a cramp. He felt a sudden pain, but at the same time, his mind needed to react and do something. He was just powerless to force it to happen because he couldn't make his brain work.

Jessi realized ambushing him like this probably wasn't the best way to approach him. Still, she was angry because he had obviously been keeping secrets, and it was something they swore they would never do to each other. After giving him what she considered ample time to respond, she spun around within his arms. She forced Dex onto his back, then straddled him, looking down into his eyes. She pulled the blanket around her shoulders. After all, this wasn't supposed to be about him staring at her naked body. It was about him telling her the truth.

Finally, she broke the silence again, "You don't have anything to say?"

"I do, but I just don't have a way to explain it all. I can tell you by this time tomorrow it will all be over, and things will be better than we ever could've hoped."

A confused look crossed her face, then she asked, "Does this have something to do with your reenlistment?"

"If only, I still need to talk to Barr about that. But when this works out, none of that will matter anymore."

At first, she was angry. Now she was hurt because it was apparent he was hiding a lot more from her than she already knew about.

"You son of a bitch!" as Jessi said this, she climbed off of him and stormed into the room's common area. After wrapping herself in a blanket, she sat down on the couch. As soon as she did, she began to beat herself up mentally. Why was she still there? Why didn't she storm out the door and back to her room? Why is she still giving him chances? She wanted to cry, not out of hurt but out of frustration. *Dammit, why do I love him?*

Dex peered around the corner at her sitting on the couch and considered his next move carefully.

"Do you remember the other night when I went in because Marcos was escaping from the Philippines?"

Jessi nodded as she repositioned herself on the couch, pushing herself into one corner so he could sit at the other end.

"Ernie and I wound up handling a second aircraft that only had cargo on it," as he began to explain, Dex took the open space on the couch and sat down facing Jessi. Then, it suddenly dawned on him. The person who had been on that C-141 was Santos. He was the one who saved Angel. *I'll figure it out later.* "Anyway, I was listening to the news after we worked the airplane…"

Dex carefully wove the entire story for Jessi. She sat silently without asking questions or reacting to what he was saying. Instead, she just stared at him with this awful hurt look in her eyes. He couldn't tell if she was judging what he'd done or that he even considered doing what ended up happening. Dex was explaining the arrangements Gubler made when Jessi finally spoke,

"Do you realize when you guys get caught, you're all going to Leavenworth?"

She paused for a moment to allow him to answer, and in the silence, it suddenly occurred to her she was now an accessory after the fact. *What the fuck do I do?*

Dex immediately launched into the logic of how stealing from a thief was not really stealing, and there was no way for the victim to report what happened without implicating themselves in a bigger crime.

"You see. Nobody can come back on us." As soon as the words came out of his mouth, he realized not only could they, but they had.

Just as he convinced Ernie and Angel to keep the secret of Bad Teeth and Santos from Gubler, he decided to set that part aside for the moment with Jessi as well.

"So, anyway, Gubler is supposed to get with me today so we can swap the stuff out for the cash. Then the only thing left to do is to split up the cash."

Even though she was mad, Dex was convincing. As she sat and let her mind mull over everything he said, it made sense.

In the silence, Dex immediately began to ponder how he was going to tell her about the threat that remained. Then he noticed Jessi shifting uncomfortably then reaching between the cushions of the couch and carefully withdrawing the Colt 1911. Even though she was holding the weapon gingerly between two fingers, she had been raised in a house that owned guns and knew how to use them. She tilted her head and stared at him, waiting for the explanation.

"Remember, I just told you how I found something on the plane, and it's how this all started? That's what I found."

Jessi then took the gun firmly in her opposite hand, slid the bolt back, and after ensuring the chamber was clear, quickly examined it to include extracting the magazine and counting the number of bullets. Dex had no way of knowing, but the inclusion of the Colt 1911 as part of the scheme bothered her less than anything else she'd heard all morning.

"Nice Colt 1911. Why do you have it?"

Figuring if she were comfortable with guns, she would be comfortable with his explanation, he told her the truth, "I'm going to be the security during the exchange. Gubler will take care of getting things transferred, and I will just hang back in case anything goes wrong. He said these guys are trustworthy, but it never hurts to have some insurance."

"As long as you understand if you point it at somebody, you're ready to shoot them."

"Yeah, I kinda got that."

"If you're ready to shoot them, you also have to be ready to kill them," Jessi's voice was flat and unemotional when saying this. He wasn't even sure she was the same woman he had been with for the last year.

"Gotcha."

Lacking anything else to do with it, Jessi slid the Colt back between the cushions. She then stared at Dex for a long time, thinking about everything he'd just said and where they were now.

"I don't want to know anything more about this. At this point, if it all falls apart, I can claim I didn't know anything. And even though it would break my heart, I would walk away from you because I'm not gonna be part of what happens next. Understood?"

Dex nodded as he looked at her. He realized he'd never felt anyone in his life love him the way she did.

Jessi stood up, then dropped the blanket before walking toward the bed. She turned back and looked him in the eyes for a moment before saying, "If you got stuff to do later, you better get in here and love me now."

Airman Dormitories - Andersen AFB, Guam

Dex dragged himself from the bed to the door, opened it a crack, and upon seeing it was Gubler, motioned for him to enter.

"We gonna do this thing?" Dex asked as he walked to the center of the room and turned around to face Gubler.

"Yeah, we need to be on the road in about fifteen minutes. Can you make it?"

"Sure, have a seat."

Ten minutes later, Dex appeared from the sleeping area wearing jeans and a T-shirt. He walked over to the couch where Gubler was sitting then slid his hand into the crevice to retrieve the Colt 1911. Gubler's eyes went wide when he realized what he had been sitting on.

"You know, most people keep those things in a safe."

"Yeah, well, I don't have a safe. Maybe later today I'll have the money to buy one," as he spoke, he slid the gun into his waistband and then pulled his T-shirt over it.

"Let's hit it."

As the door slammed closed behind the two men, Jessi closed her eyes and said a prayer for Dex's safety. She wasn't sure why she kept moving beyond her self-established limits for him. Deep down, she knew, in the end, he would be worth it.

As Gubler drove through the gate heading south, Dex looked over his shoulder into the back of the truck. The edges of the poncho covering the trunk flapping in the wind as they drove.

"You just left it sitting there?"

"Sure, it doesn't look like anything. Why would anybody mess with it?"

Dex couldn't argue with the logic. He pulled out a cigarette and held it out toward Gubler, seeking approval.

Without breaking his attention from the road, Gubler nodded and said, "Yeah. Go ahead but roll the window down."

Dex rolled down the window before lighting the cigarette, then took a piece of paper Gubler was now offering him.

"The directions. You can play Nav as well as security."

While Dex took a drag on his cigarette, he read over the directions. Of course, they made no sense without being at the various turn points. When he finished, he idly stared out the window, looking for the distance sign for Yona.

"We're going to get there a little early. I wanted us to have time to look around so we are familiar with the location," Gubler stared out the windshield without ever turning toward Dex.

"Got it."

"The way I figure it, we find a place for you to hide while I do the exchange. If things look like they're going sideways, you pop up. If everything goes as planned, you come out afterward and help me carry the money back to the truck."

"Sure," now that Dex was aware of it, it was bothering him that Gubler never looked toward him, "Do we have a problem?"

"Huh?"

"Well, we've been riding along for a little bit now, and you haven't once taken your eyes off the road. I guess it's okay if this is driver's ed, but it isn't the way normal people drive."

Gubler turned his head and stared directly at Dex. After a few moments, he turned his attention back to the road.

"I don't have any problems, except I'm cruising around with a footlocker full of stolen gold in the back of my pickup. Oh, and the guy riding with me is carrying an illegal, stolen pistol," Gubler made a show of turning directly toward Dex before he said, "Nope, not one damn problem. Do you have one?"

Dex wasn't sure how to react, so he sat in silence. After several moments passed, Gubler returned his attention to the road and audibly exhaled.

"I'm running through what we're about to do over and over again in my head, trying to figure out any issues I might've missed. Okay?"

"Yeah, I guess so. By the way, we turn just up there, by Lujan's Art Shop," Dex said, pointing to the shop's sign just ahead.

Exchange Site – Near Yona, Guam

The meandering directions took the two men to the remains of a house overlooking an empty valley and backed by a small hill of volcanic rock. The one advantage of the location was they could easily observe the road they arrived on for Wu's approach. The only parts of the house remaining were a concrete pad with a single-story cinder block wall on one side and a half-height stone wall running the full length of the pad adjacent to it.

Gubler and Dex lifted the footlocker, avoiding the broken handle and then carried it onto the concrete pad, placing it near the half wall. Both men began to look around for a good spot for Dex to position himself so he was concealed but could still see what was going on. After a few minutes, Dex saw a place up the hill where there was a small outcropping of volcanic rocks.

"How about there," Dex said as he pointed out the spot to Gubler.

Gubler saw the spot and nodded as he continued to look for something better, but his search was interrupted by the sound of car tires on a gravel road. Looking through the trees below, he could see a black SUV climbing the road.

"I guess your spot is what we'll go with. Get in position and pay attention. If this goes bad, it's going to go bad in a hurry," as Gubler said this, he walked back onto the concrete pad and stood beside the footlocker. Using what little time was left, he made sure he could see the position they'd identified for Dex. Then he paced out the section of floor around the footlocker, making sure it was also visible to the outcropping. Satisfied, he took a position next to the footlocker, waiting for Wu's arrival.

The SUV came to a stop next to his truck, then Mendoza and Wu stepped out of the vehicle. Wu walked directly toward Gubler while Mendoza retrieved a gray nylon duffel bag from the back.

"Ah, Mr. Gubler, greetings. I trust you were able to find this location without too much difficulty."

"No problem at all, you provided great directions. I assume everything is ready to go on your end?"

Wu stepped in front of Gubler and thrust out his hand, "Yes, yes. Let's get right down to business."

Wu reached into his suit jacket for something as Mendoza continued to patrol the concrete pad, looking up at the hill above and surrounding area for anything that looked out of place.

"So, is this your building spot for your next casino?" Gubler said, trying to distract attention from anything but himself.

Wu nodded and smiled as he withdrew an envelope from inside his coat, "Well, no. As I understand it, this was the home of the gentleman I replaced. It was destroyed during Super Typhoon Pamela," after glancing at the envelope for a moment, he handed it to Gubler, "This is a receipt for all monies you owed the casino. Since I expect this transaction to go smoothly, I took care of that bit of business so you would not find it necessary to return to the casino."

Gubler opened the flap of the envelope and pulled out a small receipt showing he paid the casino one-hundred and forty thousand dollars with the remark 'Paid in full' handwritten on the bottom.

"Also, today's current gold price is…"

"Three-hundred and fifty-two dollars an ounce," Gubler finished for him.

Wu smiled and nodded, "Which of course leaves me owing you seven hundred and five thousand, seven hundred and sixty dollars after deducting what you owed the casino and my commission. As a sign of my generosity and to make it easier, I've rounded up to an even seven hundred and six thousand dollars," Wu motioned for Mendoza to bring the bag over to where they were standing. As soon as he was standing beside Gubler, he allowed the bag to slip off his shoulder and fall to the ground.

Gubler then leaned over and opened the footlocker.

"Here you go, a dozen bars of ninety-nine-point nine percent pure Filipino gold, each weighing in at twenty-five pounds. Three hundred pounds total." He looked from Wu to Mendoza before adding, "We good?"

Mendoza withdrew a small electronic instrument, slightly larger than a pen, and after kneeling in front of the footlocker, pressed the end of it against the top bar. A blue light flashed, followed by a beep. He then proceeded to test each of the other bars. When the final beep sounded, Mendoza nodded up at Wu.

"Indeed, we are good."

After Mendoza shut the footlocker, he reached over to the shoulder bag and pulled an object from the outside pocket. As he stood back up, he handed the object to Wu, who immediately passed it on to Gubler. It was a videotape.

"Our final bit of business. I guarantee you this is the only copy of the video, so you are free to do with it what you like. Perhaps even an occasional private viewing to remember your uniquely erotic evening with Tala," as Wu said this, he tapped the tape with his finger.

Gubler stared straight into Wu's eyes, surprised the man would say such a thing, but at the same time, wondering if perhaps he should look at it just to see what did happen.

During his entire time in the Air Force as a Security Forces Defender, Gubler had only ever fired a weapon at the range. Not once had a situation ever arisen which caused him to discharge a weapon on the job. Today, before he ever heard the sound, he saw the shock and surprise in Wu's eyes. The sudden realization. Then, he saw Wu's lapel shift as a hole suddenly appeared, followed by a small blast of red. Finally, he heard the silenced crack of the shot as Wu began to collapse in front of him. Before Wu hit the ground, three more shots were fired, hitting him in his torso.

Gubler reacted instinctively, dropping to the ground, and scanning for the source of the shots. Mendoza's reaction was also rapid and intuitive as he scooped Wu off the ground and half carried him to the SUV, leaving the footlocker they came to retrieve behind. Within seconds, the SUV was spraying gravel as it sped off.

With no further shots being fired for several minutes and the apparent target having departed, Gubler stood up, still scanning for any obvious threat. Then he saw three men in dark suits walking toward him. Even though he knew it was the wrong thing to do, he stole a glance up the hill and could see Dex's silhouette near the outcropping.

"Friend," Fo called out in English, "no need to be afraid. Our quarry is no longer here, and we have no business with you."

As the three got closer, he could see the two shorter men each possessed a rifle slung across their shoulder. The three paused at the edge of the concrete pad, and then Fo spoke again, but this time in a language Gubler was not familiar with,

"Kayong dalawa, kunin ang kahon at ibalik ito sa aming sasakyan. Sasalubungin kita doon sa isang iglap."

The two shorter men then walked toward Gubler. He was tense as they got closer, one of them nodded to him before reaching down to take the handle of the footlocker. The second man began to reach for the handle on the opposite side but found none. Without saying a word, the two men tipped the footlocker forward and then sliding their hands under, picked it up by the bottom. Gubler was confused. If they were going to rob him, they should have also taken the nylon bag of cash.

Realizing the question Gubler was not asking, Fo spoke, "Ah. No, we'll not be taking that. Let's call it payment for your silence. You and your friend," Fo pointed to the location where Dex was hiding, "I think it's a fair exchange, and it will put an end to any further dealings between us. Agreed?"

Gubler's mind was scrambled, but he understood the words being said, and in the end, he and his friends ended up in the same place they would have regardless of what happened. So, he nodded.

"Well, it seems we have concluded our business. If you would please stay here for another ten minutes or so to prevent our being seen leaving together, I will bid you a good day."

Gubler nodded as he watched the man walk away in the same direction as the other two.

"Okay, so what the fuck?" Dex had already come down from his hiding spot and was now standing next to Gubler. Once Fo pointed directly at him, he saw no need to remain hidden.

"You know, I'm not exactly sure," Gubler looked down at the nylon bag then noticed sitting next to it a smashed videotape. He must have fallen on it when the shooting started. Gubler picked up the tape, and after crushing the case more completely, withdrew the spool of videotape and slipped it in his pocket.

Entertainment Room —Happy Luck Resort, Tumon Bay, Guam

Mendoza helped Wu through the door, dropping him on the bed before attempting to loosen his tie. He knew his Boss was in bad shape. His shirt was completely soaked in blood, and so much blood was flowing from the man, the front of his pants were also soaked in red. Things were so confused during their escape, it only just occurred to him he failed to pick up Wu's glasses when they fell off in the middle of the firefight.

"Jack, I'm going to get a doctor. Just stay here. Try to be calm."

Looking down into the man's eyes, he could not see any cognition at all. He was surprised Wu's eyes were open and could only hope he understood what he just said. Before he left, he grabbed one of the pillows and stuck it under Wu's head before slamming the door behind him on the way out.

Tala heard the noise from inside the bathroom. Having been imprisoned there overnight, she had no desire to confront Mendoza or Wu. She slowly walked into the room and stared down at Wu's bloody body on the bed. She had seen enough gang killings to know even with the best medical care, it was unlikely Wu would survive the night. She walked to the door and tested it to see if Mendoza failed to close it properly. It was secure. Then she heard a scuffle, shouting, and shots being fired in the hallway outside the door. Silence followed

Her mind began to click into gear, and the first thought was to avoid becoming part of what was playing out by hiding in the bathroom. Then it occurred to her if Wu was injured, and Mendoza was by himself, someone more powerful was responsible. A moan from the bed caught her attention, and she walked over and looked down at Wu.

"We must escape this place," Wu said in a hoarse voice.

Tala looked toward the door then back at Wu.

Even though Wu was losing his fight with consciousness, he knew what was needed, "There is a key in the safe."

"Then, I need the combination."

"Spin the dial to the left three times to the number forty-three."

Tala got off the bed and walked over to the aquarium, kneeling in front of it and opening the hidden door which concealed the safe. She looked at the safe's dial and followed Wu's instruction. Once the number forty-three was in proper alignment, she asked for the next number.

"Spin to the right four times to twelve."

Even though it was unusual to increase the number of spins, she did as she was told. Wu then provided her with the next number, which followed two spins to the left. She verified the number and waited on the next instruction but was met with silence.

Getting up from where she was kneeling, Tala walked over to the bed. He was lying there, his mouth slack-jawed, with drool running down the side of his face. *Was he dead?* Her heart began to pound in her chest. Without the rest of the combination, she could not retrieve the key and exit this room before being discovered. What did discovery mean? Wu's death was inevitable, but for her, it meant continued sexual slavery. She slapped Wu's face, trying to bring him back to consciousness but without success. She slapped him repeatedly and then began to pound his chest out of anger. How could the beast die without freeing her?

She stood up and returned to the safe but kneeling and staring at the dial provided no answers. This safe was unlike any other she'd ever encountered. The number of spins and direction seemed to be random. She knew if she moved the dial, she was more likely to ruin what had been entered thus far rather than guessing the correct number. Then she heard a cough. Dashing back to the bed, she noticed Wu's eyes were now open, and he was trying to swallow. She lifted his head to help him breathe, and after a few moments, he nodded.

"The last step is to turn the dial to the right until you reach the number eighty-four."

She immediately jumped off the bed and again knelt before the safe, slowly turning the dial to the right until the number eighty-four was under the indicator mark. Tala then attempted to turn the large handle on the front of the safe. It would not move. The safe was still locked. Carefully, she took the dial between her fingers. As she applied pressure to the handle, she slowly turned the dial back-and-forth as if she wanted to seat the number eighty-four properly. Then she felt it, the dial was in the correct place, and the handle suddenly moved downward, and the door came open.

She pulled the door completely open and stared inside. Hanging from a hook on the door was a solitary key she assumed was for this room. But she knew there were other items inside the safe, and one of them needed to be taken care of, or else whatever she did next would not matter. She pulled a stack of ledgers from the top shelf and looked through them until she found the familiar red book she knew contained the record of her debt.

"Tala. Tala! Stop playing around, girl, get me help."

Tala stood up with the ledger in her hand. She realized there was no way to mark the debt paid in a way that would not lead to the new owners of the casino tracking her down to extract what they felt was due. She also knew if she tore a page out of the book, it would lead to questions, and questions might lead back to her. She needed the book to be destroyed in such a way it would take a long time for the transactions it contained to be recovered if at all. That was when she noticed a duffle bag on the floor next to the safe. She unzipped it and saw the saran wrap sealed blocks of cash inside. She didn't need to know how much was there, but just by looking, she knew it was enough to start a new life somewhere else. Somewhere far from Guam.

The sound of gurgling from the bed drew her attention. It amazed her Wu was somehow, still managing to cling to life. She quickly made several decisions then put her incomplete plan into action. She would have to think the rest of it out as she went. First, she needed to take a shower and rinse the blood off her hands and body and put on fresh clothes.

When her shower was complete, she attempted to lift the duffle bag and found she could not. She removed the cellophane-wrapped cash blocks one or two at a time until she felt the bag was of a weight she could handle. As Wu continued to mumble incoherently, she tore open the blocks of cash she had removed, spreading the loose bills around the room. As she did this, it occurred to her she was going to use thousands of dollars of their own money to free herself from this place. Once she scattered the final block of cash, she retrieved the key from the safe and slid it into the lock on the exit door.

After retrieving a book of matches from the cigarette box on the bedside table, she struck one. She then opened the ledger book containing the page with her debt, and as she held the match to the page's edge, it immediately began to burn. She laid the book on the floor in front of the safe and waited for a few moments until it was completely engulfed in flames. Items in the safe were now beginning to burn as the scattering of bills spread the fire around the room.

Tala picked up the duffle bag and headed for the door. She was about to turn the key when she heard his voice again,

"Why are you doing this? I treated you well."

Without dropping the duffle bag, she walked over to the bed where Wu lay dying. Looking down on him, she spit on his face before leaving the room for the last time.

After making sure the door to the room was securely locked, she turned to see Mendoza's blood-covered body lying on the ground against a wall. She gingerly stepped around it as she walked determinedly toward the rear exit of the casino.

Chapter 10

Air Cargo Terminal – Andersen AFB, Guam

Ever since the PAO picked up Santos and Madulás from transient billeting, he was regretting setting up this presentation. Madulás did not present the kind of appearance expected from a Colonel. His uniform was clean and pressed, but his behavior and appearance did not speak of a professional military officer. He had already been told the TSgt he wanted from Security Forces was not going to be present as he was unavailable. He was just hopeful the other two would be in place when they got there, and this presentation could be taken care of swiftly.

When the PAO walked into the Air Cargo Terminal, he was lost. Unlike the passenger terminal, no signs were there directing to various functions. Usually, the only people entering the terminal were those who were working there. He was able to wave down a young Airman who was walking past and asked to speak to the supervisor in charge. After the Airman scurried off, the PAO turned and apologized for the delay,

"In just a minute, we'll have the shift supervisor here, and we can locate the Airmen involved," the PAO was shouting due to noise of the machinery and activity within the cargo yard. "They're working a night shift, so they should be just reporting for duty."

Madulás squinted at the PAO and then nodded.

"I'm going to step outside for a smoke, come and get me when you have things ready."

After he departed, the PAO moved closer to Santos so he could be heard.

"I'm not sure what all is going on between you and your Boss, but the INS people from town asked me to pass this on to you," as he spoke, he withdrew an item from his pocket. "Based on your history as part of the Marcos' administration, the United States is giving you a temporary limited-validity passport which will allow you to enter and exit the United States for the next two weeks. I hope this will get you where you need to be. If you check with Flight Operations, they'll tell you about flight schedules to Hickam or wherever you want to go. The letter inside the passport authorizes you one flight from here to the States at U.S. expense."

As he took the passport from the PAO, Santos opened it and looked at the photo. It was a few years old but from his official Philippine government file. He never ceased to be amazed at what the US government was able to get done behind the scenes. Closing the cover, he realized he suddenly had options he never even considered before. He was no longer shackled to Madulás but could now determine his future for himself.

Looking up, the two men noticed the Airman walking toward them with an older NCO.

"I'll let Colonel Madulás know we have the person in charge." Santos turned and walked outside to retrieve Madulás, who was smoking a cigarette while watching the cargo handling equipment moving in and out of the building.

"So, where are our honorees?" Madulás as soon as he was within earshot of the PAO.

"Not quite sure, Colonel, I'm sure TSgt," the PAO scanned the approaching man's uniform to make out his name, "Barr is here to tell us."

Once Barr joined the other three, the PAO performed introductions even though he had never met Barr before.

"So, were you working the aircraft that night as well?" Madulás asked.

"No, sir. Senior Airman Kevan and Airman First Class Crenshaw handled the aircraft. Kevan was the senior man on the team. He had all the necessary qualifications to handle the aircraft with a substantially reduced team. The rest of my team had been busy earlier in the day handling the first aircraft on which President Marcos arrived. I'm sorry to inform you the two men you want to meet were given the night off since they worked the second aircraft by themselves. I know it isn't what you wanted to hear. They will be in tomorrow night if you want to set something up."

"So, we have no heroes to celebrate. Is there no way to contact them?" anyone who knew Madulás would realize his jaw was beginning to tighten, and his patience was thin.

"Before I walked out here, I tried to get a hold of them but could not reach either one. The two men are friends and tend to be together even off duty." The truth was, Barr had not even attempted to get a hold of either Airman, this was not the kind of thing Dex or Ernie valued. He decided they would enjoy the uninterrupted time off more.

"Ah, I see. Disappointing. Perhaps, if we waited a while?" Pulling the doubloon from his pocket he began to slowly work it through his fingers. He was using it as a tool to distract himself, not wanting to show the Americans he was getting angry.

The PAO glared at TSgt. Barr.

"I, uh, really don't think it would do any good sir, both men tend to be out and about when they are given time off, they probably won't return to base until much later tonight."

Madulás nodded his head while pursing his lips. The four men stood in silence together, waiting for Madulás to make the next move or say something.

"I guess since they're not here for me to present the plaques directly, I will have to rely on you to take care of it for me," as he said this, he handed two of the letters he had written to Barr while motioning for the plaques Santos was holding, "Such a pity, I had told President Marcos I would personally ensure these men were recognized properly." After handing two of the plaques to Barr, he gave the third to the PAO, "Please ensure the Security Forces NCO gets his as well." He then handed him the remaining letter.

Madulás shook hands with Barr and immediately turned around and headed for the door. Santos began to follow but then stopped in between the door and the two remaining men who were still talking.

When the three arrived at billeting, the PAO exited the car and opened the door for the Colonel while Santos exited on his own. When the Madulás was out of earshot, the PAO leaned forward and said to Santos, "By the way, you have twenty-four hours to get off base before you turn into a pumpkin."

The expression on his face showed Santos was confused.

"Never mind the pumpkin part, just me trying to be funny. If you need anything before you leave, give me a call."

As soon as Santos walked into the room, Madulás pounced on him with questions, "What were you talking to him about? Did he have questions about me? The man proved to be utterly worthless. Now we have no idea where these thieves are, and our time is running out."

"It's okay, Boss. I heard the PAO and Barr talking. The two guys we're looking for, they live in the dormitory near the BX."

Santos had been smart enough to give Madulás something else to think about rather than allowing his paranoia to run wild.

"Good. Let me get out of uniform, and then we can take a walk over there."

Barr just watched his three visitors depart when he got a call on the radio, he was to report to ATOC.

"ATOC, this is BK-Three. What's up?"

"BK-Three, we got a rep from the DPAA team standing by. He wants to speak to you.

"Rog, ATOC. Which way are they going?"

"BK-Three, heading in."

"I'll be there in five mikes."

Before climbing into his truck and heading to ATOC, Barr dropped the plaques and letters off in his office.

Gubler and Dex were walking toward Ernie's room when they heard his excited voice,

"That's it, that's it! We're through the maze."

"Well, at least we know a grue didn't eat them," Dex said as they turned in front of Ernie's room and knocked on the door. Gubler was confused. *Grue?*

Seconds later, Ernie thrust the door open and, after taking a quick look, walked back into the room where Angel was sitting at the keyboard of his computer.

"She's killing this game, and she's never even seen it before today."

Angel looked up at Gubler and Dex, who had just walked in. Then all four fell completely quiet for a moment.

"Well?" Angel finally said.

"It's done," as Gubler said this, he took a beer Dex offered.

"There's something else you need to be aware of," Dex said, looking over at Angel.

Gubler placed both hands around his beer bottle and then looked at Angel sternly, "Well?"

Dex did not appreciate what Gubler was doing and sought to take some of the heat off Angel. "While everything was being arranged for today's swap, Angel met Bad Teeth and Santos."

"Santos? Bad Teeth? What the hell are you guys talking about?"

Angel began to relate for the third time the tale of her kidnapping and questioning. Each time she told the story, it seemed to have a cathartic effect, calming her down and forcing her to realize the past danger was over, even as she possibly faced more. Gubler listened attentively and, like the others, asked no questions as he began to comprehend what happened. When she finished speaking, the room fell silent for a few minutes while Gubler played events over in his mind.

"So, Bad Teeth was in charge, and Santos didn't take any part in the questioning and even tried to help you escape. Right?"

"Pretty much," Angel said, taking a sip from her beer.

Gubler let the thoughts play around in his head for a few minutes in the silence.

"I'm going to bet Bad Teeth is part of some personal commando squad of Marcos'. But it seems kind of blatant for him to show up here and start grabbing people. I'm willing to bet they don't have a whole lot of time to settle this. Their operations window is closing fast," as he looked around the room, the other three nodded, "Well, it doesn't stop what we're doing. We just need to be aware bad guys might be following us."

"Bet. Now we gotta split it up and get the cash the hell out of here." Ernie said as he high-fived Angel.

"Yeah, the quicker we get it off the island, the better I'll feel." As Dex spoke realized he needed to take care of one detail. Now. "I'll be right back." Dex then disappeared out the door.

He quickly walked up to his room and using his key, entered. Jessi was not there, but the room had been cleaned up, so he was pretty sure she was okay. Taking the Colt 1911 from his waistband, he slipped it back into his wall locker before returning to Ernie's room.

"See, boss, there he is!" Santos said this, pointing through the windshield up to the walkway where Dex was making his way from his room to Ernie's.

"Good." As Madulás lit a cigarette he rolled the car's window down, "Let's see where he goes."

The two men watched through the windshield, as Dex returned to Ernie's room, where he entered without knocking.

As Dex walked in, he caught the tail end of Gubler's condensed version of what happened earlier during the exchange.

"And after his buddy helped Wu get into the car, the three guys in suits who had shot at him walked up."

Dex wanted to move on to the next item of business, so he

inserted himself and shortened the story even more.

"In the end, those guys told us to take the cash, they took the gold, and here we are."

"So, where is it?" Angel asked

"Locked in the cab of my truck. With Bad Teeth and his buddy running around, this might not be the best place to count everything out."

"How about we go out to where we stored the gold?" Dex asked.

"Not a bad idea. No one can get to us without the right clearances, and no one will bother us while we do it. Works for me. How will we all get out there?"

"Well, the cab would hold three, and then we could put one in the back of the truck underneath the poncho." Dex theorized as he turned to look directly at Ernie.

"No way, man."

"Yeah, he's right. The guards wouldn't let it go through like that anyway," Gubler said.

"Why don't we just take my VW?" Angel asked.

Gubler looked at her for a moment, then shrugged his shoulders, "Didn't know you had one. If you're okay with it, I could drive to make it easier getting through the checkpoints."

"No problem, we can do it."

"Why are we sitting here?" Dex asked.

All four stood up at once, those who had beers finished them, and Ernie saved his game then shut down the computer. As the four walked out of the building and toward Angel's car, Madulás and Santos ducked down in their vehicle to avoid being seen. Gubler first stopped by his truck to retrieve the nylon bag, then climbed into the driver seat of the VW. As they sped out of the parking lot toward the flightline, Santos and Madulás rose to watch them depart. Madulás didn't say a word but pointed through the windshield, telling Santos to follow them.

As the VW moved down the road, Gubler was attempting to familiarize himself with the new vehicle,

"No rearview mirror? Really?"

Angel shrugs her shoulders and said, "The car cost me one hundred and fifty dollars. I'm surprised every time it starts."

Gubler adjusted the angle of the seat, but he still couldn't see out of the passenger side mirror. The driver side mirror wasn't much better with one side corroded so severely he couldn't see a reflection. In addition to the lack of mirrors, the extra heads in the backseat also blocked the view behind him, Gubler found the driver side shade offered zero protection from the setting sun. All of this made it easy for Santos to follow them without being noticed, even though the Filipino was inexperienced at tailing another.

When Gubler approached the first checkpoint and slowed down, Santos did the same, maintaining a wide berth. Of course, since Gubler knew the people on duty, they immediately waved him through without question. When Santos pulled up to the checkpoint, he was not quite sure how he was going to proceed. Rather than demanding identification, the sentry asked if he was with Gubler. Santos nodded and was waved through.

Abandoned Guardhouse – Andersen AFB, Guam

As Gubler approached the abandoned guardhouse, he turned the wheel without warning, surprising Santos, who spun the wheel on his car, taking it off-road and into a patch of tall grass. Madulás, who had been silent during the entire drive, preferring to chain smoke one cigarette after the other gave Santos a stern look.

"Can you at least see what they're doing from here?"

"Yes, Boss, they are all out of the car now. One of them has a gray nylon duffel bag. There's some sort of structure there. They appear to be heading toward it."

"Dammit, don't just sit there, let's go," as he prepared to exit the vehicle, Madulás retrieved his Colt 1911 and slid the action back on it, putting a round in the chamber.

"You got it," Santos said as he climbed out of the vehicle and followed Madulás toward the guardhouse.

Once all four were inside the guardhouse, Gubler realized he underestimated how cramped it was going to be.

With sweat beginning to pour off his body, Ernie asked, "Tell me again why we couldn't do this in my air-conditioned dorm room?"

"Because the four of us should never be seen together," Gubler snapped at Ernie. "Also, out here, nobody can get at us, we are guarded by the Air Force's best, so we can get this done without interruption and witnesses.

"We need more bags," Angel observed and, without saying another word, returned to her car and retrieved four nylon bags from the VW's trunk. Upon returning, she passed the bags out, saying, "I got these at the base gym for some promo they were doing. Good thing I grabbed extras."

Dex looked at Gubler and began unzipping the gray bag, "In the end, how much did we wind up with?"

"The bag is supposed to have seven hundred and six thousand dollars in it."

Angel did the math in her head, "Hey, that's way short. There should be like another hundred and fifty K or so."

"There was. The money comes out of my end, it was to take care of a private matter." Sensing a question was coming, he added "That's all you need to know."

"Fine," Dex said. He made a quick count of what was in the bag and announced, "It looks like we have thirty-five cellophane-wrapped blocks and three bundles with purple bands."

Angel looked up from a piece of scrap paper where she had been doing the math, "Looks like the three of us get two hundred eleven thousand five hundred dollars and Gubler gets seventy-one thousand five hundred dollars."

"Which amounts to ten of the blocks plus eleven thousand five hundred dollars in loose cash for the three of us." after Ernie said this, he went silent for a moment to consider what he said, "You know, I don't think I've ever even seen eleven thousand five hundred dollars in loose cash in my entire life."

All four of them were chuckling and agreeing with Ernie's statement when they heard a sound from deep in the jungle.

Gubler looked into the jungle, and seeing nothing, turned back to the group. Trying to defuse the tension, he commented, "Must be Super Shaky here for his cut."

The other three, having heard the rumor about the giant boar, nodded and laughed again but not as profoundly. Dex reached into the big bag and grabbed two cellophane blocks at random and handed them to Ernie, who then put them in the nylon bag he was holding.

"So, you idiots trade almost two million dollars in gold for less than half?"

The voice startled all four of them as they turned toward the open door of the guard shack where Madulás was now standing. He motioned with the gun he was holding as he spoke, "You. Close the bag," Dex did as he was told, zipping the bag up.

Madulás looked from person to person, and then grinned when he recognized her face, "Well, if it isn't my *wafa* toy. So glad you made it for the finish. But I do not see your *jowa*. She couldn't make it?"

"Just take the money and get the hell out of here," Dex said as he handed the bag to Madulás.

Madulás pulled the bag's strap over his shoulder then pulled his lips back, baring his wild animal like fangs, "Boy, do you not understand? Your *bulilyaso* has sealed your fate. I'm taking the money, and none of you live beyond today."

Madulás stepped back from the door and then motioned for the four to come out of the guard shack. Each of the four walked through the door, one at a time, holding their hands up. Soon, the four of them were lined up against the front of the guard shack. Madulás stepped in front of them, his back to the jungle.

"I spent my life watching you American children come into my country thinking you controlled it," Madulás patted his chest with his pistol as he spoke. "I controlled it. I would still control it if you did not interfere. What kind of idiocy are human rights? Humans deserve no rights. The *yorme*—the leaders get to determine what rights are given. Then, after your country steals my power in a coup to put Aquino in charge, you decide I don't deserve to keep all I've worked for my entire life?"

Angel saw the fronds behind Madulás slowly moving. Something was back there in the jungle, and it was slowly coming this way.

Madulás took his doubloon from his pocket and began to rub it between the fingers of his free hand as he continued to speak about the unfairness of the last few years as Marcos' grip on power began to fail. None of the four in front of him said a word as he spoke, but each within their thoughts was considering how to regain control of the situation. The gun was the single factor allowing this one man to control the four of them. After realizing the hopelessness of trying to come up with the plan for regaining control, Dex slowly exhaled while making a silent request to the *taotaomona* for assistance. *Couldn't hurt.*

Madulás then pointed the gun at each of them, one at a time going from right to left. Gubler could see the gun was already cocked. All the man needed to do was pull the trigger to kill any one of them. That was when Ernie's attention was drawn to the motion behind Madulás, Angel was already watching. Suddenly, the humongous boar cleared the undergrowth, quickly closing the distance between it and Madulás.

It all happened so quickly, Madulás had no opportunity to move before the boar's tusk looped through the strap of the nylon bag and pierced his midsection from back to front. Madulás looked down and watched in horror as the pointed end of the tusk appeared through his midsection. The extended scream was not human. As the force from the animal pushed the man forward, he released the items in his hands, with the gun falling harmlessly to the side and the doubloon hitting Angel in the chest before falling to the ground.

The four watched in shock as the boar lifted Madulás off the ground, shaking his body from side to side, the body becoming limper with each lunge. The boar then raised his head and let loose a mighty scream before it turned. Pausing, it stared at the four with one eye. It was as if the boar wanted to brag, showing off the profile of what it just did. He completed his turn and began to walk away into the jungle as the victor. Once it was hidden under the fronds again, they could hear the sound as the boar trotted deeper into the jungle.

"What the fuck?" Dex said as he shook his head.

With the tension of the moment and imminent danger suddenly gone, Angel found herself unable to control the desire to laugh.

Gubler was speechless. He kept staring toward the jungle, waiting for whatever was going to come next to come from there.

Ernie looked at Dex and then at Angel, suddenly realizing all four of them were okay. He felt an immediate but odd calm.

"Well, it would seem we just had the last of what we thought we were going to get taken from us."

Ernie turned and walked into the guardhouse, returning with one of Angel's bags in his hand. Lifting it, he said, "Well, not all of it. We have two blocks in here. Forty thousand dollars?"

"Indeed, it is," said Dex, "I think we say fuck it, go back to the room, have a beer, and figure out how we're going to split the bit we have left."

Everyone nodded as they turned and began to walk back to the VW. While they clambered into the car, Angel ran back to retrieve the doubloon. She then went into the guardhouse to retrieve the unused nylon bags as well. As she was walking out, she heard a noise in the jungle and looked. There, she saw Santos. He appeared to have one of the cellophane-wrapped blocks in his hand and was trying to sneak away. Angel closed her eyes and nodded as if to say—this makes us even. She turned and left without saying a word.

Airman Dormitories - Andersen AFB, Guam

On the way back to the dorm, they stopped at the Shoppette and picked up two more six-packs of beer to ensure there was sufficient libation on hand. Once they were all back in Ernie's room, he opened the nylon bag and pulled the two remaining blocks of cash out and set it on his coffee table. Angel reached into her pocket and took out the doubloon she retrieved then placed it on top of the blocks. Gubler retrieved Madulás' Colt 1911 and set it on the blocks as well.

"Well, this looks like all we're left with," Gubler said, trying to prompt discussion.

"You know, I'm not a cop, but I've seen a lot of cops on TV. There are probably at least a few dead bodies that would trackback to this gun. Hell, there are probably a few on the gun I picked up earlier as well. I don't think any of us should keep those. I think both of them need to be destroyed."

"You're probably right. If everyone agrees, I'll get rid of them on my way out of here. I'll throw them off of Pati Point. No one is allowed to swim there due to the Buff that crashed."

The other three nodded in agreement.

Dex knew he had skills to sell things, but he also had the ability to communicate convincingly. "Everybody got into this for a different reason—their own reasons. Maybe rather than just dividing this amongst everybody, since there's not a lot left, we should tell each other why we needed the money. Then we can jointly decide how best to divide things up."

Each of them, in turn, confessed to the others why they got involved to begin with. Dex went last, and by the time they got to him, his reason seemed trivial compared to the others, so when it was his turn, he lied and said he just wanted the cash.

Angel attempted to summarize, "Okay, Gubler did this because he owed some money, but it's already taken care of, so he doesn't need to play into this," she looked at him, and Gubler nodded.

"Dex was in it for nothing specific, so..."

"I don't need any of what's left. You guys split it."

"Fine, Ernie needs this for his family. I want the money to help a friend, which is sort of like family but not the same thing," Angel paused for a moment and took a breath before saying, "Ernie, you need it for your real family. You should keep both blocks. Send it to your Grandmother. She needs it for those kids. It's the best use of what's left."

"What about you? I can't take everything from you."

"I'll take the doubloon. It must be worth maybe a couple of thousand dollars for the gold value alone. Maybe more since it's old. Either way, it will be a good start for my friend. I didn't promise her anything specific, so it will be a pleasant surprise regardless of the amount."

She picked up her beer bottle and held it out. Each of the other four clicked their bottles with hers to show their agreement.

Gubler drained his bottle and then immediately stood up and asked Dex to retrieve the other Colt 1911. He did so, and within thirty minutes, both guns were sitting on the ocean bottom a few yards away from tail # 0630 off Pati Point.

Later, as Dex held Jessi's body against his, he felt at peace for the first time in a long time. Yes, he was still battling things like not being allowed to re-enlist, but he could own that. It wasn't something he felt was unfair being done to him.

Chapter 11

As Tala made herself comfortable in the window seat, she knew she would remain on edge until the plane took off. It'd only been a day since she'd escaped from the casino, and because she was disconnected from events there, she had no idea if she was being pursued or not. Now, she held hope for her future, *if this damned plane would ever get off the ground.*

When she saw the large man coming down the aisle way, she was hoping he would go past her to a seat in the back of the plane. But then he paused, checked his ticket, and made his way to the seat beside hers. He spent a few minutes tucking his bag under the seat in front of them, fastening his seatbelt, and playing with the air vent before even acknowledging her. A quick nod, and then he focused on what was going on in front of him.

Tala took out a Tagalog movie magazine and flipped to the first story.

"*Filipina?*" Santos asked in Tagalog after noticing her reading material.

"Yes."

The curt one-word answer did not put Santos off, "Where at in the PI?"

Again, she provided a short answer and attempted to give her undivided attention to the magazine.

Santos leaned close to her and whispered in her ear, "So, are you an escaping bank robber on the run?"

Tala laughed nervously and then considered Santos for a moment. Over the years, her instinct had served her well, and, surprisingly, the man sitting next to her set off no warning lights. She then leaned toward Santos and whispered,

"I'm a spy. I'm in pursuit of a double agent sitting up in first class," she then nodded toward the front of the plane.

Santos laughed and shook his head, "Seriously? Every time I see James Bond, he's flying first class. What are you doing back here in Coach?"

With the ice broken, the two of them began to have a conversation in earnest. Within a few moments, both of them said they had no desire to speak of the past or why they were leaving, what was important was what was in front of them. Tala told him she was headed for Spokane, Washington, in a surprising coincidence, Santos confessed he was headed there as well.

Airman Dormitories - Andersen AFB, Guam

In the two weeks that passed since they divided up the proceeds from Madulás' gold, fortune had befallen most of the four.

TSgt Gubler received notification of his next assignment and was busily getting his family ready for the move. They were headed to Nellis Air Force Base, Nevada. After recent events, Gubler had written off gambling forever, but being stationed at a military base within minutes of Las Vegas' hundreds of casinos meant temptation would be constant.

Because Guam was part of the United States, Ernie was able to use the US postal system to simply mail the blocks of cash to his grandmother. For the first time in his life, he lied to her, explaining the money was gambling proceeds. After a promise from him never to do such a thing again, she accepted the money without further questions. Upon receipt, the wise woman set up two accounts to take care of the college education of her grandchildren. She then used the balance to pay off her bills and establish a savings account to help her care for her charges until college. Ernie's father not only called him to tell him how proud he was of what his son was doing for the family, but the next three letters Ernie got from him also gushed over what he had done.

Angel took the doubloon to a gold shop in town who luckily refused to touch it, referring her to a coin shop instead. When she went to the coin shop, she found out the extraordinary value of the doubloon. At the same time, she found out how difficult it would be to sell the coin due to the limited number of them available on the open market. After haggling with the owner, he agreed to give her half the value of the coin in exchange for no questions being asked.

Angel immediately sent one-hundred thousand dollars to Dawne to help cover the medical bills for her father's care. The amount covered most of what was due. At her mother's insistence, Dawne sent an enormous care package back to Angel, along with an emotional thank you note.

The only downside was that because of her father's continued treatment, the Air Force reassigned her to the nearest base rather than having her return to Guam. She and Angel made plans to get together upon Angel's return to the United States. After all, there was a conversation between them still waiting.

The one person who walked away with nothing was the one who discovered the gold to begin with—Dex. When he explained to Jessi how the four decided to split the small treasure that was left from the caper, he was surprised by her reaction. The woman who insisted she would only stay with a man with a job and a future dropped those requirements. Instead, she chose the man she loved who was generous enough to take care of his friends who needed it despite his own tenuous future.

Angel found herself spending more and more time with Ernie as the two played computer games together to pass their off-duty time. It was in Ernie's room that Jessi found them, "Hey, either of you guys seen Dex? I just got off and figured we would grab some dinner. You two want to come?"

Ernie spoke without looking up, "He came by here a little while ago and said he was on his way to the Commander's office." Pausing to look directly at Jessi, Ernie added, "The man was in blues—I couldn't believe it."

Jessi furrowed her brow, getting called into the Commander's office was never a good thing. *Probably something to do with his denied reenlistment.*

"Okay, maybe I'll go over there so I can walk him back."

Commander's Office - Andersen AFB, Guam

"I was told you wanted to see me, sir?" Dex said as he stuck his head through the doorway of his Commander's office. The administrative troops had all departed for the day, so there was no one to announce him formally. Dex did not like coming to this office and liked it even less when he was forced to put on his blues to do so.

"Yeah, Airman Kevan, come on in."

Dex walked in and stood at attention directly in front of the Commander's desk. He was preparing to salute and provide his reporting statement when the Colonel waved his hand and motioned for him to sit down.

"I want you to know I denied your reenlistment. It was based on several things you did and did not do in the past year."

"Understood," *He brought me here so he could browbeat me?*

"Yeah, well, TSgt Barr pleaded heavily in your defense. He talked about your improvements and your master level skills on the job."

Dex nodded. He knew Barr liked him.

"Well, it wasn't enough. I didn't think you should remain in the Air Force. Not everybody's cut out to do this, you know?"

"Yes, sir."

"Anyway, those missions from a couple of weeks ago where we handled Marcos' skedaddle from the Philippines? I was unaware you were put in charge of the entire mission by yourself with just one subordinate. Had I known, based on prior performance, I would've forbidden it."

Why does he keep pausing? Get on with it and let me go.

"Well, apparently somebody outside of this unit noticed your good work and saw fit to write a letter of appreciation for your efforts."

"Who?" the word escaped his mouth before he could stop it.

"President Ferdinand Marcos. Incredible, right? He sent a deputy back here to present the letter to you, didn't you get it?" Dex shook his head, "Well, it doesn't matter. Barr got a hold of the letter somehow and then decided to pass it on to the Base Commander. I will tell you right now, I don't appreciate being stepped over. I also don't appreciate having to explain to the Base Commander why I chose to deny your reenlistment when you apparently do your job so well."

"Anyway, the Air Force needs good people. You're proving yourself to be good people. You need to sign this letter," he spun a sheet of paper, letting it fly through the air from one side of his desk to the other. "Provide the date you want to have your reenlistment performed so we can get the paperwork set up."

Dex rose and picked up the letter of reenlistment. As he stood looking down at it in disbelief, the Colonel became impatient.

"Take it with you, you can read on your own time. Have it signed and back to me within three days." The phone on his desk began to ring.

"Thank you, sir. I'll get this right back to you," Dex said as the phone continued to ring.

"Dammit!" the Colonel then picked up the phone, "Aerial Port Commander."

Dex listened to the one side of the conversation he had access to. The Colonel was giving one or two-word answers, and there was no way Dex could make out what the conversation was about. After several minutes of this, he hung up the phone.

"That was TSgt Barr. He needs you out on the flightline now."

"But sir, I'm not dressed…"

"I said now. Go out the back door, and Barr'll swing by to pick you up."

Dex came to attention and saluted the Colonel, holding it until the Colonel looked up and returned the salute. Dex executed a crisp about-face and exited the office. He walked quickly down the hall and then took the door on the flightline side of the building, walking out just as Barr was pulling up.

"Well, look at you, pretty boy, all dressed up," Barr said after he rolled down the window.

"Yeah, I don't clean up half bad." Dex then walked to the passenger side of the vehicle and climbed in. Soon, they were headed down flightline toward a C141 parked in the distance.

"Seriously, thank you for sending the letter to the Base Commander, I guess the good General called the Colonel, and now I get to reenlist."

"Well, how about that. Here I thought you were just another scuzz-bucket."

"Oh, I am. I'm just a scuzz-bucket worthy of reenlistment. What is this all about?" Dex asked peering at the C-141 ahead.

"You worked these DPAA missions before."

"Uh, no."

"Uh, yes. DPAA, the Defense POW/MIA Accounting Agency. Remember?

"Not that I recall. Wait a minute, you mean those science guys headed to Vietnam to find the remains of our guys and bring them back?

"Right, the DPAA."

"Fine, fine, the DPAA. What does this have to do with us right now?"

"Well, a little while back, it occurred to somebody this place is the first American soil those remains land on."

"Yeah, Guam. Where America's day begins."

"Yeah, more than just a marketing slogan. It's true. So, some of the folks here decided Hawaii shouldn't be getting all the glory getting to do the repatriation ceremonies for the remains."

"Fine, so we're going to go do some ceremony?"

"No, actually the VFW does the ceremony. This one is kinda special. I thought you would want to be here for it."

The two men finished the ride in silence, and then Barr pulled his pickup truck near the aft end of the C-141B where half a dozen older men in VFW caps were standing in formation while one of them was reading from a book.

"This time, they found five sets of remains. From what I heard, one of them was a complete set, which is extremely unusual."

Dex nodded and continued to watch through the windshield when he noticed an older gray-haired man wearing tiger stripe cammies and a jungle hat walking toward the vehicle.

"Come on, I want to introduce you to someone," Barr said as he got out of the vehicle.

Barr walked toward the man and stretched his hand out. The older man took it and shook vigorously. Dex walked up just behind Barr, and the man presented his hand to him as well, so Dex shook it.

"Dex, this is Dr. Harold Przygocki. He is the chief of the DPAA team. Doc, this is Senior Airman Randall Dexter Kevan. Junior."

Upon hearing the suffix of Dex's name, Dr. Przygocki's eyes lit up with recognition and excitement.

"You know, my job has me spending months in the lab before I can tell a family I've settled a mystery they may have lived with for decades. I think this is the first time in my career I'm able to speak with authority almost immediately and maybe provide some comfort just as quickly."

Dex looked toward Barr, visibly confused, his eyes pleading with Barr to provide some sort of explanation.

"Dex, it would seem Dr. Przygocki found your father's remains."

At first, Dex was visibly excited and then immediately angry, "Yeah, well, don't deserter's bodies show up too from time to time?"

Dr. Przygocki reached out and placed his hand on Dex's shoulder, "My boy, I think we need to have a talk and straighten out part of what you think you know with the truth I'm holding right now." Przygocki looked up at Barr as if he was making an inquiry, and Barr got the gist immediately.

"Why don't you two use the cab of my truck to sit and talk for a few minutes, I'll go over and get the rest of the paperwork cleared for this aircraft."

Dex climbed into the driver's side of the truck, and Przygocki climbed into the opposite side after retrieving a soft-sided briefcase. After thumbing through it and pulling out several files, he set the briefcase on the floor and then patted the files on his lap,

"These files are everything we received from the Pentagon in the way of information regarding First Lieutenant Randall Dexter Kevan. Senior. Now, pay attention, and I'll provide the rest of the information we discovered once we were on the ground near the Laotian border." He paused for a moment to allow Dex to nod acknowledgment. "This map shows the last known coordinates for your father. He was the Company Commander for a group of men brought in to perform an observation after an Arc Light mission."

"Wait, Arc Light like that Arc Light," as Dex spoke, he pointed in the direction of the memorial.

"Yes," said Przygocki nodding, "in fact, the mission cell was to originate from right here on Guam."

For the first time, Dex began to pay close attention to what this man was saying.

"It was his unit's mission to record the effect of the B-52 strike and then to return to their home base. However, due to the crash of tail number 0630, the mission was canceled. This left your father and his men close to enemy lines. They were unable to EVAC because the weather changed, leaving them without airlift. So, they proceeded to walk back to an approved landing zone. Based on witness statements, the FAC that was leading them to the LZ got disoriented and instead led them directly into an enemy camp."

"Holy shit, so he was killed because the other guy got lost?"

"Well, no, not exactly. His men got into a firefight with a much larger force. According to witnesses who were there with him, he decided to draw the enemy away from the exit route so his men could escape."

"Is this why everybody thought he was a deserter?" as Dex began to realize what was being said.

"I suppose so, if they didn't have all of the information. Dex, your father was a hero. Without his bravery, perhaps all of his men would've been killed. What makes this particular case unusual, is I was able to meet with three of the men who were on the opposing side during this firefight. They were the ones who guided me to where I recovered the remains. Those soldiers also supplied statements as to the valiant way your father fought as he drew the enemy away. It was not until I explained the situation to them that they were even aware there were more troops in the area."

"The guys who killed my father took you to his body?" Przygocki was used to seeing this reaction. In many cases, the location of American remains was provided by men who fought on the opposite side but not necessarily in the battle where a particular person was killed. "You have to understand, the war is over. It has been over for a long time. These men are no longer soldiers, but out of a sense of honor, they want to do what they can to help bring American families peace by returning these remains to their home country. You should be grateful."

"I guess. I just have to get used to all of this." Dex's mind was spinning.

"One of the men who guided me to the remains was there when he was buried. When time permitted, the Viet Cong would wrap American remains in a poncho and bury it using Buddhist blessings."

"I don't even know how to ask, but after all this time, there wasn't anything to see was there?"

"No, frayed bits of uniform and skeletal remains. Because the skull was intact, I was able to make a comparison with dental records and confirm the identity on-site." As he spoke, Przygocki pulled a small plastic bag out of one of the files, and upon opening it, dumped its contents onto the dashboard. A set of corroded dog tags landed in the pile. Picking them up, he handed them to Dex.

"Normally, you would receive these when you came into our lab in DC. We would give you a slideshow of sorts, explaining who we are and what we do, and then let you view the remains if you wanted to and then present you with any property found. I think we can cut the red tape."

Dex stared at the two pieces of metal in his hand, running his thumb across the face the dog tag, he could feel the indents where the metal was printed with his father's name, blood type, serial number, and religion. None of that mattered to him. For the first time since he was six years old, he was holding something which had been close to his father. Now he knew his father was not a deserter but a hero.

"Oh yes, I also have this," as Przygocki spoke, he reached into his briefcase and pulled out a long cylindrical object, which he put on the dashboard. "Do you remember if your father smoked cigars?" Dex shrugged, shaking his head in response, "No matter. This cigar container was found near the body and, in all likelihood, was your father's. It was not unusual for people who did not smoke cigars to carry them. They were often given as good luck charms or a way of saying congratulations. If your father did not smoke cigars, it is likely his Commander gave him that one."

The two men sat in silence for a moment, Dex clutching the dog tags in one hand and the cigar tube in the other.

"Well, as a result of me finding these remains, and the fact the remains were found inside the country of Vietnam, I have already been in contact with my office at the Pentagon. The Army will be releasing your father's G.I. insurance with interest to you immediately."

Dex's father had left a way for him to fulfill his dreams. "Also, because we have three eyewitness statements regarding your father's valor and courage, I'll be submitting him for at least a Silver Star. Your father saved more than a dozen men and sacrificed his own life by taking on a much greater force to do so. Ordinarily, that would have satisfied the requirements for a Medal of Honor. The issue we have here is the only witnesses I have were the enemy in the battle. I'm not sure exactly how the Pentagon would look upon it."

Dr. Przygocki often encountered the silence of a family's reaction at this moment. For the survivor, the past and present were suddenly colliding, providing answers to questions which had gone unanswered for decades. He wanted to do his best to honor it, but his time was limited.

"If you would like, you can come over to the aircraft and pay your respects. It'll probably take six months for all the paperwork to be done and the remains released to you once I get them back in the lab at the Pentagon. This will have to do for now."

Dex didn't say a word but nodded, and the two men exited the truck, walking over to the C-141B parked on the ramp. The rear door of the aircraft was open, and on the ramp were five individual boxes, each covered with an American flag. They were not coffins but simple wooden crates used to move the remains from the field back to the United States. Przygocki walked over to one of the crates and nodded toward it. Dex knelt beside the box and saw his father's name on the tag attached to the side. He slowly reached out a shaking hand, placing it on the flag-covered box.

Dex whispered, "Dad, I'm so sorry. I've missed you so much..." Given the emotion of the moment, his throat closed up, and he couldn't utter another word. But instead laid his face on the box and shared a moment with his father seventeen years after losing him.

Arc Light Memorial - Andersen AFB, Guam

Even though it was approaching twilight, Jessi could see Dex sitting on a bench in front of the B-52 on display. His body appeared to be still as he stared off in the distance.

"Hey, you," she said, walking up from behind him and wrapping her arms around his shoulders, "It's been forever since I've ever seen you in blues, you look good."

He gave a gentle grunt and reached up and grabbed her forearm with his hands, squeezing it.

"Ernie said something about the Commander calling you into his office hours ago, then you vanished." She moved from standing behind him to take a seat next to him, leaning her head on his shoulder. *It must've been awful for him to be this quiet.*

"You know, this has probably been one of the best days of my entire life."

"Really? You look so happy and celebratory," she accented this by giving him a gentle punch in the ribs.

"No, really it is. You know why Commander called me in?" He waited a moment to allow her to shake her head, "He approved my reenlistment."

"Oh, Babe, that's terrific."

"Yeah, apparently President Ferdinand Marcos wrote up a nice little handwritten letter of appreciation. Somehow it got to Barr and Barr passed it on to the Base Commander who convinced the Colonel to change his mind."

"Marcos sent you a letter?"

"So, I've been told, although it was probably written by Bad Teeth as part of the scheme to find me. Anyway, it's all signed, sealed, and delivered. All I have to do is acknowledge it and set a date for the ceremony."

"You are going to do it, aren't you?"

"I don't know."

She pulled back and looked him directly in the eyes. There was no mistaking the look of confusion on her face.

"You see, while I was in the Colonel's office, I got a call sending me to a repatriation ceremony out on the flightline."

"You mean those ceremonies the VFW comes out and does when they're bringing human remains back from Vietnam?"

"Yeah, that's it. I met the guy in charge of the team, Dr. Przygocki. Nice enough, guy. He and Barr work together now and then when he flies back-and-forth into Vietnam. Anyway, when they sent the manifest ahead for this trip, Barr recognized one of the names. After a quick conversation with Przygocki, he told Barr he wanted to meet me."

"Okay," then a sudden epiphany hit Jessi, "Is this something about your Dad?"

"Not exactly, it *is* my Dad."

Dex went on to recount what had happened when he went out to the C-141 a few hours ago, to include the ceremony and all of the extra stuff Przygocki told him.

"He told me he got my Dad's G.I. insurance released, and I should get a check in a day or so. Then as soon as he gets back to DC, Przygocki's going to submit my father for a medal based on what he found out."

"All this time, you never knew he was a hero?"

"Yeah, but now I do," he lifted his right hand, which was clenched in a fist, and slowly opened it to reveal a pair of corroded dog tags, "They're my Dad's."

Jessi reached out and gently touched the tags with her fingertips, she too felt the sudden reality of Dex's father.

"Przygocki gave me this too," Dex picked up the cigar tube from the bench, where it was resting against his hip. "Aside from his bones, it was the only identifiable thing left."

"Do you remember him smoking cigars?"

"No, but according to Przygocki, a lot of these things were presented back-and-forth between officers in appreciation of this or that. Some were given for luck. If that was the case—it didn't work."

Dex had been trying to keep his composure. He was hoping if he made a joke, he might be able to get off the borderline between laughing and crying. He failed. Jessi immediately knew what was going on inside the man she loved, and she shifted position, taking him into her arms so she could comfort him.

"Jessi, I have been mad at him for over half my life. I never knew. I was blaming him for something he did that made him a hero. The worst part of it is, I understand why my mom lied. It was the only way she could cope. But it left me with such a fucked-up attitude toward life, the military, all of it. Until today." As he spoke, he wiped his eyes with his fists and pulled his face back from hers so he could look at her, "Today, it's all fixed. Today, I know the truth," the tears started to flow again, so Jessi pulled his body to hers and held him.

The two of them sat there in each other's arms until the twilight faded and the darkness enveloped them, and the lights of the memorial came on.

"Come on, Babe, let's get out of here before we get eaten alive by the bugs." Jessi pulled back from him and changed her position so she could stand up.

"No, wait. All the shit with finding out about my Dad and being allowed to reenlist—those were things which solved problems. I know there is more to my life than just problems. There is the best part of my life, which is you." She turned to face him as he spoke, and tears began to fill her eyes. This time, not for the pain she was sharing with him but for joy, "Jessi, I want to be with you for the rest of my life."

Jessi allowed herself to fall forward, back into his arms, and they kissed.

Epilogue

Two days after the Air Force ceased strip alert operations in April 2020, renowned ornithologist Dr. Alicia Fortis was given access to the northern jungles on Andersen Air Force Base. The area was previously restricted with no civilians allowed to enter. Fortis had been on Guam for the last eight years, searching for the Guam Rail.

The Guam Rail was a flightless but fast-running bird with a narrow body adapted for running through thick marsh grass, weeds, and underbrush. It was one of three native bird species left on the island. Before there were biological import controls, warehouse owners introduced Philippine rat snakes to Guam to help stave off the rodent population. Once the snakes ridded the island of rats, they found the Rail to be an adequate replacement food source since it could not fly. The snakes were believed to have eaten the Rail into extinction. However, starting in the early nineteen eighties, there were rumors of birds dwelling at the north end of the island on the airbase believed to be Rails.

Armed with the rumors and using her reputation, Fortis hoped she would be given access to the jungles on the base. In the years prior, many base commanders had given her access to various sections of the base, but none of them ever gave her access to the northern jungles near the flightline. Until now.

Stepping into the steamy jungle, Fortis and a group of graduate students were now performing a grid search of the previously unavailable and untouched wilderness using two-way radios to coordinate their efforts. Carefully and slowly walking each square inch of the jungle looking for signs of the Guam Rail.

Her radio crackled to life as she heard one of the student's shout, "Dr. Fortis!" over the radio.

"This is Fortis. What is it?"

"I don't have a way to describe this. It's huge. You need to see it."

"Where are you?"

"About two klicks northeast of where you are."

"On my way."

Fortis quickly got her bearings and then headed off to the northeast from where the student called. When she finally saw the outline of the student through the jungle, she slowed her pace and became more careful and deliberate in the way she was walking through the jungle in case there was something that need not be disturbed. Then, she stepped into a wide clearing.

The jungle floor, rather than being a dark mishmash of various decaying vegetation, was instead a light-colored blanket that looked as if it were painted on the ground. Kneeling, Fortis scratched into the surface, revealing the original material was a lighter green than what was on the top muted by time and weather.

"It's over here," the excited student called from a few feet ahead.

Rising, Fortis walked toward the student and then saw it. As an ornithologist, she was used to seeing the skeletons of birds, but what was presented in front of her now looked more like one of the whales she had seen in the Smithsonian Museum of Natural History. From one end to the other, it must've measured at least three meters. The rib section was huge, and she was almost sure she could walk through it if she stooped over. The massive skull had huge, thick tusks.

"This surprised the hell out of me," the students said.

"Yes, I can see why. Based on the skeleton, this beast must've weighed in it almost four hundred and fifty kilos. I've never seen a boar even half the size. It probably dwelled here for decades without ever

260

being seen."

"But what is this stuff all over the ground, it seems to cover the entire area."

"I don't know. It looks like a paper of some sort that has rotted and mildewed over the years until it no longer looks like sheets of paper. I can't tell if anything was printed on it or not. I have no idea why it's here. I don't think boars build nests." Fortis laughed at her joke.

"Look, there are more bones over there," the student pointed to an area off to one side, and the two of them walked over and kneeled to examine it.

"Probably just the leftover bits from its food storage area."

"Boars are carnivorous?"

"Omnivore, I believe." As Fortis said this, she rose to her feet, "All swine are omnivores. But what do I know? I do birds. Which is why we're here. Did you find any sign of the bird?"

"Uh, no. I found this right at the end of the segment I was reconnoitering. No sign of the Rail."

The radio crackled to life, with an excited voice shouting something about finding a nest.

Dr. Fortis turned to the student and told them to mark this area complete, and the two of them walked together to the south toward the location of the student claiming to have found a nest of a Guam Rail. On the way out of the clearing, the student tripped over a fallen limb, flipping bits of decayed vegetation in all directions. Without looking back, the two of them headed off.

It is possible to be in sections of the Guamanian jungle so thick almost all daylight is blocked out. It gives the feeling of being in a constant state of twilight. But even in those sections, when the wind blows, and the trees sway, bits of sunlight fall between the fronds and sometimes extend all the way to the floor of the jungle.

This bit of jungle, now quiet again from the molestation of man, was enjoying the bit of sunlight peering through the trees and down onto what was once hundreds of thousands of dollars in U.S. currency before it mildewed and rotted. As the light danced across the section of the jungle floor that was just disturbed by a student's tripping, the sunlight hit the golden teeth still attached to a decaying skull. Soon, it would completely vanish with the only thing remaining the *taotaomona*, silently protecting the jungle.

Glossary

Note: This glossary is meant to be a simple translation of the words which may have been used in this book. All words are *Togalog*, except where noted. There may be other possible unintended meanings based on regional or tribal uses.

albor- borrow

anda- money

bebot- chick, babe

bulilyaso- a failed plan

Chamorro- (Chamorro) indigenous peoples of the Mariana Islands

charot- "I'm just kidding!"

chibog – mealtime

chika – "What's up?"

chikahan- a conversation

dedo- dead

dehins- don't

dekwat- to take without the owner's knowledge

ermat- mother

erpat- father

hinde- no

jowa- lover

kelaguen - similar to *ceviche* with the meat being cooked by the marinade rather than heat

keri- can do

krung krung- crazy, nutty

kulelat- the one in last place, loser

kulasisi- mistress

matsala- thank you

mumshie- Mommy

mumu- ghost/spirit

praning- crazy

swabe- smooth, suave

syonga- stupid

taratitat- a talkative person, a chatterbox

taotaomona- (Chamorro) the people of before, ancestral spirits that inhabit the earth along with the living jungle spirits

tigok- Dead

tsekot- car

tsibog – mealtime

wafu- handsome

wafa- beautiful

walwal- intoxicated

yorme- head of a town or city

From the Author

I hope you have enjoyed reading this book. You can always find an up-to-date list of my Evan Davis tales and all of my other books, at my website: **www.valkyriespirit.com** Also...

Sign up -- Be the first to know when there is a new release by signing up for the Email Newsletter. I will only send emails when there is book news and will never release your email to others, ever. To sign up drop a line to newsletter@valkyriespirit.com

Review it --- Consider posting a short review with the vendor where you found this book. Reader reviews help others decide whether they'll enjoy a book.

Connect with me -- I'd love to hear from you, please stop by my Facebook page for updates on new titles, cover previews, and general discussion: www.facebook.com/TheRealSheldonCharles/

shel@valkyriespirit.com

Three Paperclips & a Grey Scarf

"…author Sheldon Charles captures the brutality of the battlefield and the true strength of brotherhood with sharp, visceral prose and a stark level of realism. At times tragic but always gripping, there are also moments of whimsical musing about life and fate that would resonate in any genre. Told from the unique perspective of a writer forced into his own story, this action-packed novel has just as much brains as brawn." **Self-Publishing Review**

Blood Upon the Sands

"This thrilling and exotic adventure juxtaposes philosophical dilemmas with nail-biting moments. Charles has created an incredibly vivid world where his characters can play and struggle and learn. This is more than a basic novel of good guys taking down a bad guy; this novel shoots across the bow of systemic and perennial issues that deserve serious attention in the real world. Thanks to Charles' unforgiving eye for seeking truth, fearless style of expressing hard ideas, and photographic heart that can seamlessly transport readers to far-flung locales, *Blood Upon the Sands* is a masterful international thriller." **The Independent Review of Books**

"★★★★★…it is the caliber of Charles' writing that makes this espionage thriller so involving. The book's length is substantial, but once opened, the action and events and premises are so compelling that pausing the experience is not likely. Highly Recommended – Sheldon Charles is a superb weaver of stories!" **Grady Harp, San Francisco Review of Books**

From Within the Firebird's Nest

"… Charles renders all his characters believable and endows them with fully-realized backstories… Charles also skillfully balances all the structural elements of his complex plot, maintaining tension but never adding unnecessary complication or filler… should appeal to fans of Cold War espionage great Robert Littell, and leave readers eagerly awaiting Evan's next adventure." **BlueInk Review**

Evan Davis' first adventure, in eBook & Audiobook.

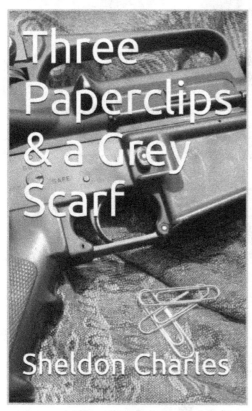

Writer Evan Davis desperately needs to find his muse to finish his book. As the impossible deadline approaches with a virtually nonexistent wordcount, his agent presents him with a unique reprieve: Gain a delay by becoming a press embed with U.S. troops going to Central Asia. Davis sees it as an unlikely place to rediscover his muse but lacks any alternative. After being presented with an odd luck talisman of three paperclips by a friend, he travels with his assigned unit to Afghanistan. There he is out of his comfort zone and pushed into a world where friendships are vital, and lives are on the line. His problems pale in comparison to what these brave men must face daily. As Davis begins to write about their daily hardships, he rediscovers his love of the written word. He also finds a use for each of his talismans, as they save his life and those of the men he comes to regard as his team; soldiers who promised each other they would all make it home in one piece.

Follow Evan's journey as he finds his muse in the most unlikely place under the most extraordinary circumstances.

Hired by *Al Hakim*, a Kuwaiti horse breeder, to improve the world's bleak perception of his beloved country, Evan Davis enters Kuwait with six months to produce articles about its people and culture.

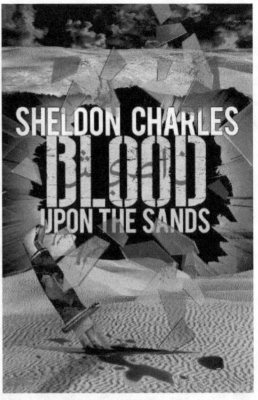

A journalist by necessity, Evan soon forms a close bond with his employer and his interpreter and cultural guide. But when some shocking information is anonymously put into his hands, his eyes are opened to the plight of an entire people group. He must choose between a newly formed friendship and exposing a tragic truth to the world.

With a sinister and sociopathic ex-KGB assassin sowing hatred against the down-trodden population of stateless people and racial tensions reaching a fever pitch, events quickly spiral out of control. Evan finds himself desperately attempting to stop an insidious conspiracy, prevent further bloodshed and give a voice to a voiceless people by the power of his pen.

Blood Upon the Sands -- A suspenseful thriller that will keep you nailed to the edge of your seats, Sheldon Charles weaves a masterful tale centered on real-world history and based on the current situation of Kuwait's Bedoon population.

In eBook, Paperback & Audiobook

Evan Davis is back in his most daring tale yet.

For decades, the United States and the Soviet Union trained thousands of nuclear weapons on each other—and those were just the weapons we knew about. Behind the military parades and bluster was a shadow war, and some of the deadliest weapons were kept far from the public eye.

From within the Firebird's Nest is a thrilling story about the resurgence of acrimony from the past. Years after the end of the Cold War, a former KGB agent plans to exact revenge on the United States by reactivating a horrifying bioweapon called the Crimson Firebird.

Our only hope of survival is an unlikely team of international spies and civilians, including a repentant former deputy of the Crimson Firebird Initiative, a former Stasi agent, and an American writer. Can these would-be heroes put aside their own complex feelings of the past long enough to avert an unthinkable catastrophe?

At your favorite Bookstore, in eBook, Paperback & Audiobook.

Coming Soon...

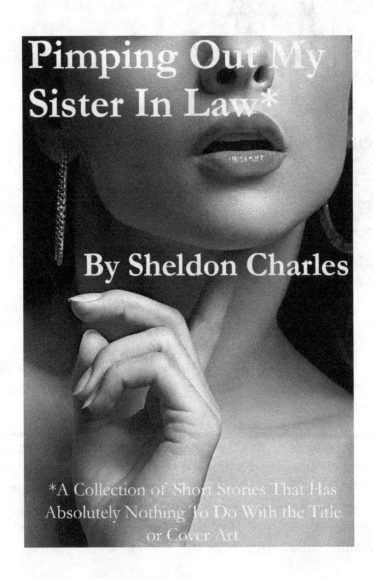

Pimping Out My Sister In Law*

By Sheldon Charles

*A Collection of Short Stories That Has Absolutely Nothing To Do With the Title or Cover Art

Critics & Readers on *Ferdinand's Gold*...

"★★★★★ A well-crafted thriller with perfect pacing! *Ferdinand's Gold* had every element a good story should have. An intriguing plot, attention to detail, but best of all fleshed out, well-written and well-rounded character development. There's an abundance of well-illustrated scenes that make you feel like you are right there in the story...It's one of those stories that come along once in a while that makes you want to read it non-stop until you get to the end." Piaras Cíonnaoíth, **Emerald Isle Reviews**

"★★★★ This novel is fascinating in its historical detail, but also woven together with fictional elements that make the story leap off the page. Charles is able to bring a barracks to life, even for someone who has never stepped foot in one, just as easily as he depicts a flurry of action or violence – confident, specific, and memorable. With increasingly high stakes and a powerful narrative voice that makes it hard to put down, *FERDINAND'S GOLD* is a tumultuous ride that is a perfect afternoon escape for fans of military thrillers and adventure fiction." **Self-Publishing Review**

"A riveting combination of fact and ingenious narrative ability that throws surprises at the reader on a regular basis *Ferdinand's Gold* proves a taut and exciting read with Charles leveraging his own experiences as a decorated Air Force veteran to good effect...**Sure to be met with approval by fans of the War and Military Action genre, *Ferdinand's Gold* is a must-read and is recommended without reservation!**" BookViral Reviews

"★★★★★ Sheldon's very brief synopsis offers the bait to seduce us into this terrific novel...once opened, the action and events and premises are so compelling that pausing the experience is not likely. Highly Recommended" Grady Harp, **San Francisco Review of Books**

"Air Force veteran Charles' novel feels entirely authentic, and his extensive knowledge of military aircraft and procedure lends weight to Dex's exploits, as when the character actually steals the gold from a C-141 aircraft. The author's prose style is largely crisp and direct…compelling, well-paced plot…every player proves memorable—especially for such a relatively compact narrative. A fast-paced adventure with some emotional weight." **Kirkus Reviews**

"As the plot thickens, these misfits struggle with heist logistics while trying to avoid Air Force authorities and, eventually, Madulás and his thugs…the characters are complex and intriguing, and the Filipinos present a palpable threat…heightened by brisk dialogue and Charles' admirable attention to detail. At its climax, the story offers gripping ultra-violence, offset by a surprisingly satisfying denouement. Overall, readers will find a tasty mix of criminal conspiracy set in unfamiliar territory, all spiked with political intrigue." **BlueInk Review and featured in *Booklist Magazine***

"★★★★★ I also appreciate (minor spoiler) that Angel was handled so wonderfully. I'm always apprehensive of queer and female characters in military stories because not a lot of people flesh them out more than stating their queerness, or womanhood. She was a great character; she went through some tough shit and came out on top and for that I've gotta give this writer props" Meranda, **Amazon**

"★★★★★ Each page keeps you gripped as you turn page after page, curious to know just what is going to happen next. The emotional grip of greed, mystery, and revenge all weave together wonderfully with the author's descriptive words" Jason Mann, **Amazon**

"The author of *Ferdinand's Gold*, Sheldon Charles, brought me into the story with his descriptive writing. Each character had ample time spent on them so that I could know and understand that character and get an idea of why they made the choices that they did throughout" Debbie F., **Amazon**

"★★★★★… a fun weekend read. It's got adventure, mystery, and is quite thrilling. The author, Charles, is a rather skilled story teller with his ability to use his descriptions to make the words come to life off the page, I ended up reading this in 1 sitting." Rory, **Amazon**